Praise for *I'm the Vampire, That's Why*

"From the first sentence, Michele grabbed me and didn't let me go! A vampire mom? PTA meetings? A sulky teenager? Throw in a gorgeous, ridiculously hot hero and you've got the paranormal romance of the year. Get this one *now*."   —MaryJanice Davidson

"Hot, hilarious, one helluva ride. . . . Michele Bardsley weaves a sexily delicious tale spun from the heart."
                    —L. A. Banks

"A fun, fun read!"   —Rosemary Laurey

"MaryJanice Davidson, look out! Michele Bardsley has penned the funniest, quirkiest, coolest vampire tale you'll ever read. It's hot and funny and sad and wonderful, the kind of story you can't put down and won't forget. Definitely one for the keeper shelf."   —Kate Douglas

I'm the Vampire, That's Why

Michele Bardsley

A SIGNET ECLIPSE BOOK

SIGNET ECLIPSE
Published by New American Library, a division of
Penguin Group (USA) Inc., 375 Hudson Street,
New York, New York 10014, USA
Penguin Group (Canada), 90 Eglinton Avenue East, Suite 700, Toronto,
Ontario M4P 2Y3, Canada (a division of Pearson Penguin Canada Inc.)
Penguin Books Ltd., 80 Strand, London WC2R 0RL, England
Penguin Ireland, 25 St. Stephen's Green, Dublin 2,
Ireland (a division of Penguin Books Ltd.)
Penguin Group (Australia), 250 Camberwell Road, Camberwell, Victoria 3124,
Australia (a division of Pearson Australia Group Pty. Ltd.)
Penguin Books India Pvt. Ltd., 11 Community Centre, Panchsheel Park,
New Delhi - 110 017, India
Penguin Group (NZ), cnr Airborne and Rosedale Roads, Albany,
Auckland 1310, New Zealand (a division of Pearson New Zealand Ltd.)
Penguin Books (South Africa) (Pty.) Ltd., 24 Sturdee Avenue,
Rosebank, Johannesburg 2196, South Africa

Penguin Books Ltd., Registered Offices:
80 Strand, London WC2R 0RL, England

First published by Signet Eclipse, an imprint of New American Library,
a division of Penguin Group (USA) Inc.

First Printing, September 2006
10   9   8   7   6   5   4   3   2   1

With lots o' love to my grandmother Virginia;
my mother, Brenda;
and my sisters Julii and Candy.
As always, to Dean and Katie and Reid. I love you forever.

ACKNOWLEDGMENTS

To all the vampires I've loved before . . . my eternal thanks to Evangeline Anderson, L. A. Banks, Mary-Janice Davidson, Christine Feehan, Charlaine Harris, Sherrilyn Kenyon, Rosemary Laurey, Katie MacAlister, and J. C. Wilder for creating worlds and characters that always bring me joy and always inspire me.

My husband, Dean, deserves a paid vacation to Tahiti. He took care of *everything* so I could finish this book. He brought me Starbucks peppermint mochas. He brought me chocolate. He brought me hugs. He listened to me whine and made me take much-needed breaks when my eyes glazed over and my fingers went numb. Every writer needs a Dean. (But you can't have mine. Go find your own.)

I owe a huge debt of gratitude to MaryJanice Davidson. The next time I see you, you get chocolate. We're talking Godiva, baby.

A big ol' thank-you to Jessica Growette, who let me steal her name and her attitude to create my heroine. She *rules.* (Literally. Don't mess with her. I'm serious.)

I'm very thankful to my agent, Stephanie Kip Rostan, who sold my weird-ass idea, and to my editor, Kara Cesare, who bought my weird-ass idea. You gotta love women who say, "PTA vampires? Cool!"

Jeana Paglialunga, Karen "MT" Williams, and Saira are goddesses! Not only do they have sharp eyes and kind words, they work for free. Ladies, your "I Proofed *I'm the Vampire, That's Why* and All I Got Was This Lousy

Acknowledgment" T-shirt is on the way. A high five to NAL's copy editors. Thank you for your diligent work on this novel.

I'm tremendously grateful to Evangeline Anderson, who always makes me laugh, who isn't afraid of anything, and who has the best stories. I'm so glad we're friends.

And finally, big sloppy smooches to Lady Carrassa, who keeps me supplied with food and drink and moral support. She makes the best damned cider in the world.

Finally, I'm very grateful for the abundant online information that helped me with so much of this book. Any mistakes made, by accident or on purpose, are mine. Just remember, I have a license . . . a creative license.

We desperately need a new and gentle light where the soul can shelter and reveal its ancient belonging.

—John O'Donohue, *Anam Cara: A Book of Celtic Wisdom*

Chapter 1

The night I died, I was wrestling a garbage can to the curb.

I had a perfectly healthy fourteen-year-old son who should have taken out the garbage after dinner, but he, and let me quote him directly here, "forgot."

Every Sunday and Wednesday night we had the same conversation, usually five minutes after he crawled into bed. Here's the script:

Enter the Mother into the Pit of Despair. I refuse to walk more than a foot into the Pit because I'm afraid a radiated tentacle might emerge from a gooey pile of papers and clothes and drag me, screaming and clutching at the faded carpet, into the smells-like-lima-beans clutter. I open the door, try not to inhale any noxious boy-room fumes, and delicately scoot one Keds-protected foot inside. *Cue dialogue.*

"G'night, honey. And Bry? Did you take out the garbage?"

"Oops."

"It's twice a week. It's your only chore. I pay you ten bucks every Friday morning to do it."

"It's a heinous chore."

"I know. That's why I pay *you* to do it."

"Sorry, Mom. I forgot."

At this point in the twice-weekly argument, variations occurred. Sometimes, Bryan faked snores until I went away, sometimes he actually fell asleep mid-lecture, and sometimes he whined about how his nine-year-old sister Jenny didn't do chores, and I still paid *her* five dollars every Friday morning.

So, yet again, just after ten P.M. on a Wednesday night, I found myself pulling first one, then the second thirty-gallon garbage can down the driveway, and trying to align the grimy plastic containers near, but not off, the curb. Do *not* get me started on sloppy, lid-flinging, half-trash-dumping garbage men who are extraordinarily picky about the definition of "curbside pickup."

When huge, hairy hands grabbed my shoulders and heaved me across the street and into Mrs. Ryerson's prized rose bushes, I didn't have time to scream, much less panic. The whatever-it-was leapt upon me and ripped open my neck, snuffling and snarling as it sucked at the bleeding wound.

Good God. What sort of man-creature could hold a grown woman down like a Great Dane and gnaw on her like a favorite chew toy? It slurped and slurped and slurped . . . until the excruciating pain (and honey, I've suffered through labor *twice*) faded into a feeling of weightlessness. I felt very floaty, like my body had turned into mist, or like that time in college when I took a hit of acid and had the "Tinkerbell" episode. I knew that if I just let go, I'd rise into the night sky and free myself from gravity . . . from responsibility . . . from Bryan and Jenny.

Just thinking about my kids slammed me down to earth. My husband had passed away a little more than a year ago in a car accident. Don't feel too sorry for me, though. I was in the middle of divorcing the son of a bitch.

I couldn't scream. I couldn't lift my arms. I couldn't open my eyes. But I felt my body again, every aching, pain-throbbing inch of it. The heavy, smelly thing pressing my limp body into thorny branches and noisily smacking against my throat grunted and rolled off. Dry grass crunched and leaves rattled as it moved, growling and groaning like a well-fed coyote. I didn't flicker an eyelid for fear it would try for a killing blow, though if the state of my neck wound was as bad as I thought, I was dead anyway. Then I heard the sounds of bare feet slapping against pavement and realized the thing was running away. Fast.

I don't remember how I disentangled my sorry self from the bushes. I have vague memories of the roses' too sweet scent as I crawled across the street and collapsed near my knocked-over garbage cans.

For those who know me, meeting my end amid muttered curses and spilled refuse was not a great shock. But, shock or not, it was still a crappy way to go.

Some people believe that dying ends all possibilities of humiliation.

Not so.

When I awoke, I wasn't standing at the pearly gates of heaven. Well, not unless the religious definition of "pearly gates" was way, *way* off base.

I was latched on to the velvety inside of a muscular male thigh, my teeth embedded in the flesh near his groin, my mouth soaked with warm, very tasty liquid.

No, the man was not wearing pants. Hell, he wasn't wearing underwear. Who am I kidding? The man didn't have on a stitch of clothing.

I wish I could say that the embarrassment of my cheek brushing against his testicles outweighed my need to suck his blood—and yeah, I know, *ew*—but it was like . . . it was like . . . a half-off sale at Pottery Barn. No, better. It was like eating, without gastrointestinal or caloric consequences, a two-pound box of Godiva's champagne truffles. No, no . . . like . . . oh God, like *finally* fitting into that pair of skinny jeans that taunts every woman from the back of her closet.

Uh-huh. *Now* you know the ecstasy I'm talking about.

After another minute or two of sucking on the stranger's thigh, I felt firm, long fingers under my chin.

"That's enough, love," said an Irish-tinted voice. "You're healed now."

With great reluctance, I allowed the fingers cupping my jaw to disengage me from the yummy thigh. I sat up, licking my lips to get every dribble of blood (*ew*, again) smeared on my mouth.

"Where am I? What happened? Where are my kids?"

"Ssshhh. Everything will be explained." He tilted

his head, looking me over in a way that caused heat to skitter in my stomach. "Your children are fine. Damian is watchin' them."

Damian? Who the fuck was Damian? Whoa, girl. Deep breath in. Deep breath out. Well, crud. The whole breath thing wasn't working. I didn't even want to think about my lack of heartbeat. I had to stay calm. I focused on the room and realized I could see everything clearly. What the hell? I had been relying on glasses to see past my nose for almost ten years. With this kind of vision, I probably could see all the way to Canada.

"So . . . with all the, uh, blood-sucking, I'm guessing I'm a vampire now." Just saying "I'm" and "vampire" together was so ridiculous, I wanted to giggle.

"Yes. We Irish vampires call ourselves *deamhan fhola.*" He grinned at me. "It means blood demon."

"Oh. Well, that's certainly . . . descriptive." In a bad, yucky, soulless way.

We were in a small white room. It had a long, uncomfortable steel slab sticking out from the wall and we were on it. About six feet from the steel slab on the left side of the room was a door without any visible knob or handle. I looked down at myself. I was in a white hospital gown and I smelled like antiseptic.

I was a vampire.

Jessica Anne Matthews. Vampire.

The stupid giggle erupted and I nearly snorted and snarfed myself into a seizure. "Me. A vampire."

"Yes." The guy who'd been my lifesaving snack was leaning against the wall, his knees drawn up slightly. Raven-black hair feathered away from his face, the ends of it curling on his shoulders. He watched me with the strangest eyes I'd ever seen. He looked like Pierce Brosnan in his *Remington Steele* days, except for the color of those eyes. "With eyes like the sea after a storm," I muttered, quoting one of my favorite lines from *The Princess Bride.* Those strange eyes were an ever-changing silver that seemed to eddy and swirl like a fast-rising river.

Given his size, my guess was that he was just about six feet tall. He was muscular and trim like an athlete, rather than bulky like a gym freak, with a light dusting of black hair on his chest and thighs.

I might've been delirious or crazy or dreaming, but I checked out his package. It was impressive, too. From a patch of black hair sprang a large erection. His testicles tightened underneath my blatant scrutiny and I remembered the soft feel of his balls against my cheek as I suckled his flesh just inches from his groin. His gaze dropped to his penis, his lips curving upward as his eyes met mine again. He seemed to ask, "Want a ride, little girl?"

And you know what? I did. *I wanted a ride.* I hadn't had sex in eighteen months. Sessions with the battery-operated boyfriend did not count. The last man I trusted to touch me, to bring me pleasure, had betrayed sixteen years of marriage by doing the same lovely, naughty things to another, younger woman. Then, before I could seek proper revenge, he had gotten killed in a car accident. I always thought it had been a mundane way to go for a man who had ripped out my heart and then stomped it to bloody bits with his cloven hooves.

But I digress.

"Do not have sex with Mr. O'Halloran." The command echoed around the room. Even with my new vision, I couldn't spot the speakers.

The Pierce Brosnan look-alike rolled his eyes. "She fed on me like I was the last Twinkie in the box. A little thanks might be in order."

"If you have sex with Mr. O'Halloran," said the voice, obviously unimpressed, "you will be mated to him for the next hundred years."

Chapter 2

"'Tis true," said the man . . . er, vampire. "But there are ways to find pleasure without making that mistake."

I asked, "There are?" when I meant to ask: *What's all this about vampire mating, buddy?*

My eyes were drawn to him again. I looked at his big feet, lingered on his calves and thighs, dipped to take another look at his . . . oh lord, had it gotten bigger? I dragged my gaze up to feast on those tight abs and pecs. Brown nipples poked through the curls of silky hair. By the time I got to the strong line of his jaw, the impudent curve of his lips, the aquiline nose, the silver eyes . . . I was on fire. I burned from the tip of my pinky toes to the tiniest hairs on my head.

"Aye," the vampire whispered, "there are."

"There are what?" I sounded hoarse and distant. I wanted to crawl into the Irishman's lap and kiss every beautiful inch of him.

"Stop that!" The fervent demand issued from the invisible speakers.

I blinked at the sharp tone. The hot, sweet tendrils of desire fell away, leaving me cold and vaguely creeped out. "Okay. What just happened?"

"It's a long story, Mrs. Matthews," said the exasperated voice.

I heard a steel scrape, and then *clang, clang, clang.* I looked at Mr. O'Halloran and nearly fell off the table. He'd put his hands on his knees and revealed that he was chained to the wall. I hadn't noticed because, well, I'd been looking at his genitals. That, and the fact he'd concealed his imprisonment by hiding his hands. The chains, maybe as thick as those that secured bicycles, looked too delicate to hold him. Swirls and weird words emblazoned the silver cuffs.

"You're a prisoner?" I sounded aghast. Given that I had been attacked by a snarling, hairy assailant, died viciously, and woke up munching on an Irish vampire, I had no right to be aghast. All the same, a thread of fear wound through me. "I thought vampires were super-duper strong."

He chuckled. "We are very strong. But these little beauties," he shook his arms, "have special charms on them. I cannot break them."

That Irish lilt was freaking deadly. Forget that whole "glamour" thing where vampires supposedly entranced their victims. Wait a minute. Earlier he'd mentioned magic, too, though I'd been distracted by the whole blood thing. "Special charms? As in . . ." I wiggled my fingers in a bad sorceress impression.

He nodded. "I had to be bound, love. Because of that ring you're wearin'."

On the ring finger of my right hand was the ring I always wore. My grandmother had given it to me just days before she passed on. I looked at it, as if doing so would make clear why the vampire needed chains to protect him from it. "My *Claddagh* ring?"

"It's a *fede*," said the man. "A faith ring. *Claddagh* rings have hands clasping a crowned heart and have only been around since the sixteenth century. Yours is only the heart. It's made from the purest silver and it's very old."

This was news to me. My family knew the legend of the ring—it was one of the stories always told at holiday gatherings. "My gran said it was crafted by a fairy and given to her true love. The ring granted protection to her lover, but only as long as he remained faithful. He met a beautiful mortal woman and made love to her. So, the ring's magic turned him into stone. The fairy reclaimed the ring and threw it into the ocean, swearing to never love again. A fish swallowed it and was caught by a poor man, who gifted his wife with it. The man was Sean Mc-Cree. And his wife was Mary McCree. She was my great-great-great-great grandmother."

"A descendent of Mary McCree," he said, shaking his head. "And you have the ring. My father was right. About everything." He nodded to my hand. "If it was a true *Claddagh* ring, do you know that wearing the heart turned inward means *your* heart is unoccupied?"

"Yes," I said softly. "Why do you think I wear it like this?" I looked at the silver ring, then back at the silver gaze of the vampire. "Why does it bother you?"

"It was mine." His eyes lost their devilish twinkle for a moment and the sorrow I saw in that blink started my heart tha-thumping wildly.

"It was . . . yours? You're kidding."

"Take it off and look at the inscription on the inside."

I realized that he had probably examined the ring while I was in la-la land. "Just because you know there's an inscription doesn't mean it's yours."

"Mo chroi," he whispered. "My heart. Believe me when I say that the ring belonged to me."

"So that makes you the unfaithful lover?"

"No," he said. "Your quaint family tale is not true."

"It's just a story. And it's just a ring," I said softly. I looked around the room. Chances were good that surveillance wasn't limited to audio so I bet there were cameras in here, too. I crawled between his legs, afraid and trembling, and leaned down to whisper, "Can I break the chains?"

"Aye," he said. "But if you do, I'll probably fall upon that lovely body of yours and fuck you until you scream with pleasure."

His blunt words startled me, but probably not in the way he intended. I liked the image created by his rough description and the evidence of how well I liked it trickled between my thighs. "What's the bad part again?"

His lips curled into a feral smile. "None. But I'm not of a mind to worry about things like accidental mating rituals. Are you?"

Well, yeah. I was horny, not stupid. I backed away, until I got to the end of the steel slab. I sat down with my legs hanging over it, and swung them like an antsy

kid at the doctor's office. I glanced at my fellow in-
mate, but his face was expressionless. He'd probably
had centuries to perfect the ultimate poker face. Hah.
Check me out. I'm sitting in a room with a chained
vampire that I would, even now, do the horizontal bop
with, and everything's so surreal and strange . . . I'm
dreaming or I'm in hell. Otherwise, I was handling this
freaky situation with considerable aplomb.

"My name is Patrick O'Halloran. But you, *a thaisce*,
can call me Patrick."

"Jessica Matthews," I said. "Um . . . thanks for . . .
you know."

"Saving your life with me own blood?"

"Yeah."

"Any time, love. Any time."

My gaze, unable to stop staring at his crotch for more
than a minute, delved between Patrick's thighs just in
time to see his penis jump, either involuntarily at the idea
of wild, sweaty sex or voluntarily to tease me.

I looked away, my cheeks feeling like I'd stuck my
head in the oven and set it on broil. I had a million
questions. What had attacked me? Why had these people saved my life? Was Patrick O'Halloran dangerous?
Why was he a prisoner? What did *a thaisce* mean?
And . . . oh yeah . . . "Why are you naked?"

"The better to feed you, m'dear." He pointed between his legs and my gaze roved along his cock. Then
I saw his forefinger tapping his inner thigh. "Femoral
artery."

"Riiight. And the major vein in your neck wasn't
good enough because . . . ?"

One black brow winged up and those delicious lips

curved into a naughty smile. "Ah. Because then I wouldn't have had an excuse to get naked."

"Or get chained to a wall."

"Hmmm."

"Why are you scared of my jewelry?"

"I'm not, love, but perhaps you should be. It is foretold that the one who wears the *sidhe fede* crafted by Brigid herself is my soul mate."

"What? No way."

His smile was feral. "Have you known any others in your family to wear it?"

Weirdly enough, no one in my family had worn the ring—not since Mary McCree. My grandmother had worn it on a chain around her neck, which was how all women before her had worn it. When Gran bestowed it on me, she slipped the *Claddagh* onto my finger and said, "Ah. At last." At the time, I thought she'd meant she was glad to pass along the heirloom to me. But what if she'd meant something else?

The door clicked open. Seconds later, the persnickety voice said, "Come along, Mrs. Matthews. We have a lot to discuss."

"Who is Damian?" I asked the fussy little man who sat on the other side of the steel table and stared at me through thick glasses. As soon as I'd slipped through the door, with one last wave to Patrick, I found myself in this room. The differences from the previous space was that it was bigger, it had another handleless door through which Dr. Michaels had entered, and it had a steel table with two steel chairs.

"Damian is Mr. O'Halloran's personal guard. He

insisted Damian be dispatched to watch over your home while we helped you. I assure you that your children are still in bed asleep."

"And I'm supposed to believe you because . . ."

He tapped on the little square object in his hand then faced its tiny screen toward me. I saw a split screen in full color—live camera feeds of Bryan and Jenny, both asleep in their beds. In the top frame, Jenny was splayed in her floppy doll fashion, her little chest rising and falling. Bry had burrowed under the covers, but I saw his usual squirming. The boy never stayed still, not even in sleep.

Somewhat mollified, I nodded and Dr. Michaels put the PDA on the table, tapping on it with the stylus.

"Gee, thanks for asking if you could install cameras in my house."

"It was necessary," said Dr. Michaels. "We are implementing measures for your protection."

"Really? I think we're a little late on the protection angle here, aren't we? I've already been attacked and killed."

"Unfortunately, Mrs. Matthews, there are other dangers to worry about."

"You're just full of good news," I said.

Dr. Michaels tapped on the electronic device. It looked like the iPod Bryan had been bugging me to get for his fifteenth birthday. Dr. Michaels used the stylus like a painter with his brush. *Tap. Tap. Tap. Ping. Tap. Tap. Tap.*

"Um . . . hel-*lo*?"

Dr. Michaels looked up. "Oh. Yes. Right. You must be very frightened."

"Or really annoyed."

"Indeed." He sighed, put down the toy, and folded his hands together. "The creature that attacked you escaped from our transport unit as we arrived in Broken Heart. I find it fascinating that there's a town called Broken Heart. Is it a Native American reference?"

"No. Much of Oklahoma was Indian Territory, but near the end of the nineteenth century, the government held land runs. Our little piece of sunshine started out as five farms staked by the Boomers."

At the doc's blank look, I rolled my eyes. "Boomers are the people who came from all over the place to participate in the land runs. Our area was staked out by five families during the first one held in 1889. One of the farming families was the McCrees. Legend has it that Mary McCree, the wife of Sean McCree, was a witch. When she found her husband cheating on her, it's said that she cursed this area so that all who entered suffered from broken hearts—then she threw herself into the creek and drowned."

"That's terrible."

"And true. At our peak, when we had almost two-thousand residents, we had the highest rate of divorce as well as the highest rate of single parents in the state of Oklahoma."

"Some legacy you have, Mrs. Matthews."

Ah. So the doc had been listening in on the conversation I had with Patrick. Well, I couldn't begrudge him too much. "Tell me what's going to happen now that I'm dead."

He looked at the PDA longingly, as if he'd take dealing with gadgets over humans any day. "Because of Mr. O'Halloran's blood donation, you should suffer no ill effects or reactions from the, uh, creature's attack."

I considered his words. "So what you're saying is that I shouldn't worry about turning into the thing that attacked me because Patrick's blood fixed me."

"Yes."

"Glad to know I won't morph into a raving, slobbering lunatic." But turning into a vampire might not be much better. "Did you catch the monster?"

"Not yet. But rest assured, we will find and contain him."

"You mean kill him."

"No, Mrs. Matthews. We were in a delicate experiment phase that required Lorćan to fast."

"You're experimenting on animals?" I asked, outraged.

"Of course not. We are trying to cure him of the Taint." Dr. Michaels obviously noted my blank expression. "It's a vampire disease. Please don't worry, Mrs. Matthews. You're in no danger." He blanched. "I . . . uh . . . well, Lorćan has never harmed anyone. He was very, very hungry when he . . ." He trailed off as he saw my expression.

Fury rolled through me, so fast and so hot I was fairly sure I could melt the good doctor's brain with one good stare. It took a second or two before I could formulate a sentence. *"Kill. It."*

He looked horrified. "No, no, no. That's not an option."

"It damn well is. That beast is not gonna run around my town and eat unsuspecting citizens." Oh no. No! I felt chilled to the marrow of my bones. "My son. Oh my God. If Bryan had been out there doing his chores, he would've . . ." I could not complete the sentence much less the thought. "You've got to kill that thing. Before it hurts another human."

Dr. Michaels' pasty skin turned a sickly gray. He was bald, short, and looked like an overfed weasel. His lab coat didn't do a lot to hide the basketball paunch of his stomach. "I'm sorry, Mrs. Matthews. Killing Lorćan is utterly out of the question."

We'll just see about that. What was a Lorćan anyway? If vampires existed, then what other kinds of weird critters lived in the world? I craved some reality, damn it. Then it occurred to me that this *was* reality. My new, awful reality.

"What time is it?" I asked, suddenly weary.

"Just past five A.M. We found you right after—uh, you know. We tried to save you, but I'm afraid you were well past the limits of human medicine. We had to clean you and dress your wounds and take some time to prepare Mr. O'Halloran before the transfusion could take place."

"Thank you." The words sounded insincere and damned if I could feel sorry about it. Should I be grateful that these assholes were trying to fix a problem they'd created? I noticed Dr. Michaels' puckered lips and narrowed eyes. Yeah, I guess so.

I looked down at my expression in the steel table and even though the image was fuzzy, I still could see that I looked . . . different. My hands and arms were paler than ever. I wasn't one to loll about in the sun. In the Oklahoma heat, I didn't leave the house without hat, sunscreen, and Off. Lots and lots of Off. I sighed. Mosquito bites were the least of my worries right now.

"Look, can we get on with the Vamp 101? My day starts in a few minutes. I have breakfast to cook, kids to take care of, a house to clean—*what*?"

Dr. Michaels was shaking his head. "You'll be, forgive me, dead to the world the very second the sun peeks over the horizon."

I absorbed this information. Remember all that considerable aplomb I had earlier? It fled like an exorcised ghost. Numb horror filtered through my bravado, which, up until now, had held out darn well. "I can't go out in the sunlight?"

"Well, it's more like your body will shut down until the sun sets. We've yet to figure out the biology of a vampire. Their bodies are complex and well, let's be honest, illogical."

"So, the sunlight thing?"

"Oh. Right. Some vampires who've been around a while, such as Mr. O'Halloran, can tolerate weak sunlight for limited periods of time, usually right before sunrise or sunset and sometimes during overcast or rainy days. Even though his blood and magic are powerful and you've consumed quite a bit of it, you, as a new vampire, wouldn't be able to stick your little finger into the daylight without frying." His hands formed a mushroom cloud and he made an explosion noise.

"Gee, thanks for the visual." Panic burbled through me, threatening to dismantle the calm I was clinging to with very fragile fingernails. Okay. *Okay*. The only thing worse than being undead was being dead. I couldn't help my kids if I was six feet under so that meant dealing with the present circumstances.

"Okay dokay, doc. Then pump me up with whatever's the equivalent of Jolt for vampires. I don't care what science thinks about vampire biology. I'm a mother, which means during the day, I'm busier than a one-legged man in an ass-kicking contest."

Dr. Michaels' mouth sorta crinkled. I assumed that was his version of a smile. "Mr. O'Halloran is aware of your predicament and has arranged for you to have help during the day."

Pride snapped my spine straight. "I will not have strangers in my home watching over my children. That's *my* job. I am their mother."

"You don't have a choice. You're dead. These are temporary measures until we figure out our next course of action." He reached over as if he meant to pat my hand, then he obviously thought better of it. "Please don't worry. Mr. O'Halloran will take care of you and your family from now on."

My mouth gaped at this news. "What the fu—"

Static issued into the room. "Dr. Michaels? This is Checkpoint Four. We have a visual on Lorćan. We are pursuing."

The doctor tapped his PDA and peered at its tiny screen. "He's returning to Sanderson Street?"

"Yes, sir. He appears to be following the first victim's scent back to her house."

"First victim?"

Dr. Michaels waved away my screech. "Capture and detain. Use only humane means."

"Yes, sir."

Sanderson Street. "That piece of shit is going back to my house? My children are there!"

"Please calm down, Mrs. Matthews. We have everything under con—"

Terror turned into unexpected action. I rose in the air like an avenging angel and, with one curled fist, punched through the metal ceiling. It was just like ripping through tinfoil. I sprang into the open air of predawn and realized immediately we had been ensconced in a high-tech RV that was, conveniently enough, located in my driveway. I heard yips and snarls behind my house so I pointed myself in that direction and hovered above the roof.

The Lorćan ran through my backyard, heading for the chain-link fence. It was bigger, hairier, and uglier than what I had remembered. Thanks to my new senses, I could smell its stench from fifty feet in the air. It nimbly jumped the fence and headed for the forest behind my house. Those woods were tangled knots of gnarled trees and overgrown bushes, dotted by a pond here and there.

Three men dressed head to toe in black chased after the monster. They carried wicked-looking guns that probably housed not bullets, but Dr. Michaels' humane means. My guess? Dart guns filled with knockout drugs.

I don't fucking think so.

My babies were asleep, unaware their mother had died, and in danger from the creature that had killed me and maybe others, too. Drug darts weren't comfort enough for me.

Before the last guy jumped over the fence, I winged

toward the beast. If I could fly, then I bet dollars to donuts I had the strength to wrench off its head. I landed in front of it and the thing skidded to a halt, breathing harshly, its muscles bunched and straining against the urge to run.

"Mrs. Matthews!" I heard Dr. Michaels yell. "Please, Mrs. Matthews! Don't hurt him!"

Weirdly enough, it didn't fight me as I placed my hands around its neck, with every intention of squeezing until it breathed no more. Silver eyes filled with tears peered at me through a dirty, furry face. I hesitated. *Silver eyes?* No. It couldn't be . . . *him.* Not Patrick. Had he escaped his chains after all?

"Sorry," the creature said. "Very sorry. Please . . ."

The Irish accent was unmistakable, even in those four softly growled words. My hands dropped from its neck as shock knocked the breath out of me. Or, the shock would have done so if I'd had breath. I stepped back, an invitation to the beast that had killed me . . . and saved me . . . to pass unharmed.

It nodded formally, a silent thank-you, and fled into the forest. The three men whipped past me, cursing and crashing into the brush. Dr. Michaels grabbed me and hustled me toward the house. "Thank you," he said, out of breath and in an apparent hurry. "You have no idea what it means for us to capture Lorćan alive."

"Why didn't you tell me that the Lorćan was . . . was . . ." The words slurred. My arms and legs felt heavy, like they were weighed down with anvils. My brain suddenly seemed filled with cotton. I wanted to lie down and sleep. *Tired. So tired.*

"Hurry, Mrs. Matthews. The sun is rising." He

pushed me over the fence. I felt a rip in both gown and skin, but there was no pain. There was no reason, really, to do anything else but lie down in the soft grass and sleep for a while.

I was vaguely aware of Dr. Michaels grabbing my arms and dragging me toward the house. My ass hit every rock and anthill in the yard, but I had no strength to help him. I just wanted to be left alone for a few minutes. Mothers never, ever get enough sleep. Was taking a nap so wrong?

"Look," I muttered. "Isn't the sunrise beautiful?"

The orange circle shimmered, its top curve rising above the treetops. The sun playfully chased away the last of the night, overtaking the sprinkling of stars still visible.

Then it was suddenly, incredibly, *painfully* hot.

"Shit!" yelled Dr. Michaels. "Shit!"

My skin rippled and split as it erupted into flames. The last thing I heard was the piercing wail of my own screams.

Chapter 3

When I woke up, I was in my own bed in a room I didn't recognize. Once again, I was sucking the thigh of Patrick O'Halloran. Sad to admit, but true nonetheless: I was a blood slut. I knew this guy was a hunky Irishman one minute and a rabid, killing creature the next. As I swallowed his rich, warm blood, I didn't give a flying flip. Drinking from him was like having champagne and strawberries after a lifetime of bread and water.

"Naked again?" I croaked, rising only after he pried me from his leg. "Is that really necessary?"

"No. But I like being naked around you," he teased.

Fortunately, I wasn't bare-assed, but it took one guess to discover who picked my outfit. I wore a shimmery pink teddy with matching, skimpy panties. "Been through my lingerie, have you?"

"Oh yes," he said. "It's a very interesting collection."

"Perv." I looked around, feeling well rested and well fed. I didn't want to consider what my sustenance would be once Patrick stopped offering his vintage self to me. After a moment, I realized this place *was* my bedroom. The furniture remained in the same locations, but the window was gone and the walls had been coated with some sort of metallic substance. My guess was that the new walls were the equivalent of sun protection with SPF 1,000,000.

Patrick stretched out, giving me a buffet-style view of his gorgeous body. Damnation. There was that delightful erection again. How easy it would be to just slide on over there and—*nope*. I scooted away from him, but he only grinned.

"Where are the chains?" I asked tartly.

"Now that you're Turned, it's easier to control my . . . urges."

"I don't know if I should feel delighted or insulted."

"You should feel blessed that the sunrise didn't turn you into ash."

"Good point." I felt properly chastised. "What happened?"

"Dr. Michaels—Stan—he pulled you onto the porch." For a nanosecond, his eyes went dark, but damned if I could decipher the emotion. "I arrived in time to put out the flames and get you to the bedroom. I forced my blood into you before you slept and it healed you."

"Thanks. Again."

I listened for the sounds of my children. With my new vampire senses, I tuned in to their slow, rhythmic breaths and the tandem beats of their hearts. They slept peacefully, thank goodness. Guilt dug into my conscience with poisonous claws. This was the first day in a very long time that I hadn't been there for my kids. I couldn't fathom not being the one to cook them breakfast or hurry them along for school. No more sunshine. Ever. I couldn't wrap my brain around that terrible fact.

Life's road often forked at unexpected moments.

Discovering my husband was not only cheating on me, but leaving our family for his secretary, the young, beautiful twenty-something Charlene, had been an unexpected twist in the path. Well, he didn't leave so much as I threw his ass out.

Six months after he packed his bags and moved in with her, Rich was dead. And sweet little ol' Charlene, who had no family and no fallback job, now worked night shifts at the Thrifty Sip. You see, she still had to care for the baby she'd delivered prematurely that awful night. Rich had been rushing to the hospital to be with her and his SUV skidded out of control on the highway, tumbling down a ravine, killing him despite seat belts and air bags.

"Are you thinking of your children?"

"Yes," I lied. I had been thinking of myself, of my pain, of my inability to let go of the past. Oh hell. I had thirty-six years of a past. I glanced at Patrick, who studied the teddy with an interest that sent daggers of heat shooting through me. He had a much longer past. How much did he remember? How much could he forget?

"How old are you?"

"I was born in the year 1869, in what archaeologists now refer to as B.C.E., which means 'Before Common Era.' "

"So . . . you're old."

"I was born almost two thousand years before Jesus Christ walked the earth." He grinned. "So, yes, I'm old."

I did the math and stared at him in shock. "You're telling me that you're almost four thousand years old."

He nodded.

"Wow. You look good for your age." Well, hell, I would never have to be worried about being the December to his May. He had a good four millennia on me, now, didn't he? I chuckled. Patrick looked at me oddly and I realized he didn't know the reason for my laughter. I shrugged, offering a smile instead of an explanation.

"Bryan and Jenny believe that you have a very contagious flu bug. We let them see you on the cameras and that seemed to satisfy them. They had a lot of questions about the RV, my men, and the sudden security system. For dinner, Stan found some frozen pizza in the freezer and made one cheese and one supreme. I read two chapters of *Harry Potter* to Jenny. And your *clann* were tucked into bed by ten P.M."

As Patrick reported on the day's activities, his gaze lingered too long on my breasts, which were barely covered by the teddy's flimsy lace.

"Clann?"

"Children." Patrick smiled.

"Huh. Well, sounds like you have everything under control." I sounded sullen even to my own ears.

"You don't sound pleased."

"That's because a mother wants to feel needed while invoking her right to bitch about how unappreciated she is."

"I see." His tone indicated his confusion. You would think that a man with centuries and centuries to study the human condition would figure out a few things about women. Just one or two really important ones. Hmph. Too much to ask from an immortal, was it?

I felt useless and helpless and very much alone. Last night, things happened so fast. The events had been so surreal that I hadn't really believed I'd been attacked and brought back from death. But here I was again, drinking blood, getting visited by Patrick, the hunky vamp, and contemplating a very long life that had no meaning. *A life where I would outlive my children.*

Pain riveted me to the bed and the sheets twisted in my agitated grip. *No, no, no.* Patrick and his crew had disturbed the natural order of the parent-child relationship by saving me. I hated the idea of Bryan and Jenny struggling in a world without their parents, but I couldn't fathom a world without them in it.

"Put it away, *a thaisce*," said Patrick. "If you try to figure out everything at once, you'll go mad."

I took his advice. I'd think about the vampire mom thing later. I would figure something out. I always did. Patrick rolled closer to me and stroked my hair. His kindness gave me the courage to finally ask the question I'd dreaded. "Why didn't you tell me you were the Lorćan?"

Patrick looked startled. He lifted up, leaned on one elbow, and frowned at me. "*The* Lorćan?"

"Isn't that the name of the creature that hurt me . . . and probably others, given that Dr. Michaels called me the first victim?"

"It's his name," he admitted softly, "but it's not a

variety of monster, love. Lorćan is a Gaelic name given to sons. It means 'little fierce one.' "

"Half of it is right." I glanced at Patrick. "He had eyes just like yours."

"He's me brother, darlin'." His silver eyes glinted. "Me twin brother."

Brother? *Brother!* I had almost wrenched off the neck of Patrick's twin. I didn't know how to feel about that. What if I had known without a doubt that the thing wasn't Patrick? Fear and repulsion skittered through me on tiny rat claws. I would've killed it. *Him.* I would've killed Lorćan to protect my children and myself. Was that the mother in me? Or the vampire?

Patrick seemed to be waiting for my reaction. I didn't know what to say or do so I went with, "That's why he had an Irish accent."

He was on me so fast I didn't see him move, not even with my improved vision. Before I knew it, I was underneath him, his hands clenching my shoulders, his face an inch from mine. "He spoke to you?"

Fear thumped inside my still heart. My stomach roiled at the fierceness of Patrick's gaze. His grip was painful. "I . . . he . . . damn, Patrick, you're scaring the crap out of me."

He closed his eyes, probably searching for patience, and after a moment or two, he opened his peepers. He looked less intense, thank God, and his grasp on my shoulders relaxed. He tucked me into a more comfortable position, which included fitting his semierect penis between my thighs. My breasts were flattened against his chest; my nipples, rasped by the teddy's shimmery material, peaked into hard buds. Patrick's growl let me know that he noticed the reaction. The cock between my thighs hardened, pushing against some really sensitive bits that hadn't been touched by male flesh in a while. I swallowed my moan.

"Tell me about Lorćan. What did he say to you?"

"He apologized," I whispered. His gaze reminded me of silver fire, leaping and crackling with restrained emotion. Was it anger? Did ol' Stan tell Patrick I almost beheaded the beast brother? Or was that desire sparking there? I relaxed against the bed, soaking in the feel of his skin against mine. I didn't care that he wasn't warm, that I couldn't feel his breath on my neck as he bent to nuzzle my collarbone.

There's something wonderful and safe about a strong man with his arms wrapped around a woman. And erotic. It had been a very long time since I'd felt a man above me, dominating my body in a gentle way, taking what I offered, asking for what I wanted.

Patrick lifted his head. "No," he muttered more to himself than to me. He pushed up on his forearms, his fists clenched near my shoulders. "Tell me the exact words."

"*Sorry. Very sorry. Please* . . . And he was crying when he said it."

Patrick rolled off me, the intimate mood vanishing under his sudden all-business movements. He muttered some words under his breath and to my astonishment, clothes appeared on his body. Wearing a black T-shirt, faded denim jeans, and a stylish pair of sneakers, he looked cuter than a vampire should.

"Holy shit. Can I do that?"

Patrick looked at me over his shoulder. "In time.

There's much for you to learn, love. Until then, you'll have to do things the old-fashioned way."

"Poop."

He smiled, revealing a glistening set of fangs. *Whoa.* "I must feed," he said. "I will meet you later."

"Hey!"

He was gone before I finished shouting the word. Who or what did he plan to nosh on? A horrifying thought struck. Were my kids in danger? I dismissed the thought almost as soon as it formed. I may have only been dead for two days and I may not know much about Patrick, but sipping from innocents didn't seem his style. Plus, he'd probably guessed that I'd stake his ass if he so much as wiggled a fang in their direction.

I got dressed in a crop top, jean shorts, and flip-flops, which was the necessary uniform of a woman battling Oklahoma summers. I brushed my hair and pulled it into a ponytail. The myth about vampires not seeing their own images in mirrors was a bunch of hooey. I could see my image just fine and, if I say so myself: *Wow oh wow!* My brunette hair sparkled like burnished copper; my dishwater-brown eyes seemed dark and mysterious; my lips looked as full as a ripe plum. My skin had cleared up of blotches, pimple scars, and sunspots. The laugh lines around my eyes and lips had disappeared, too. Forget cosmetics, honey. I no longer needed CoverGirl.

I pulled down my shorts and marveled at the lack of pooch. My stomach was as flat and smooth as a twenty-year-old's. I peeked inside my top. *Still a B cup, damn it.* The stretch marks on my abdomen and breasts—the badges of honor for any mother—were gone. Maybe I should feel a little sad about having those physical reminders erased. But, hell, I had a woman's vanity, too.

My butt felt higher, my breasts perkier, and merciful heaven, my thighs thinner. My body was now a pearlescent white, as fine as silk, and as taut as a supermodel's starved frame.

Huh. Guess being undead had a few perks.

I visited Jenny's room first. She slept deeply and I wondered if her unparalleled rest was due to vampire influence or drugs. Before I realized what I was doing, I was somehow in her mind, in her body, and knew, right away, she had not been tampered with. She shifted restlessly, and I soothed the ripples in her mind, crooning a silent, tender lullaby that she responded to with a sweet, girlish sigh. I knew, without a doubt, that Jenny was healthy. I smelled her, and noticed the baby powder and lavender scent she emitted.

"Mine," I whispered and placed my hand upon her bare neck. Something electric and powerful leapt from my palm to her skin and when I drew away my hand, I saw the faint impression of a honeysuckle flower on her nape. It faded quickly and made me wonder if I had imagined it.

In Bryan's room, I sat on the edge of his bed and lifted the blanket. He, too, slept deeply, wearing only a baggy pair of gym shorts. I checked him for vampire and narcotic influences, too. He smelled like German Chocolate Cake. I could almost taste the gooey caramel coconut frosting. I sensed nothing awry with my son and felt a surge of relief that he, too, was healthy. Being an immortal with powers had some advantages for a mother. I placed my hand on his shoulder and whispered, "Mine." The same jolt I had experienced with Jenny occurred again and when I lifted my hand, there was the fading impression of the honeysuckle blossom on my son's skin.

"Mom?" Bry blinked awake, staring at me through sleepy eyes. "You feeling better?"

My throat knotted. How would I ever explain to my babies that I was dead, but still walking around? I brushed a lock of hair from Bry's forehead and said, "Sleep." To my shock, he slumped against his pillow and started snoring.

Instant knowledge of health *and* the power to ensure obedience? Being a vamp mom might not be so bad. After kissing his brow, I shut the door to the Pit and headed downstairs.

July in Oklahoma sucked (har har). Walking into the summer night from an air-conditioned house was like walking into a tepid lake. The evening brought some relief from the aching heat, but the humidity was unrelenting.

The RV's middle door opened and Dr. Michaels, no, *Stan*, gestured me inside. I found myself in a room that had ceiling-to-floor consoles on either side. Two men manned the electronic doohickeys and neither gave me a glance. Well, so much for smooth skin and flat stomachs. Stan led me into the same room in which he'd interviewed me the night before. I looked up and saw that the hole I'd made had been patched.

"How are you feeling, Mrs. Matthews?"

Irritated. Scared. Dead. "Do you really want me to answer that?"

He looked at me, fiddling with the ever-present PDA in his hands, and shook his head.

"Thank you for keeping my kids safe and taking care of them."

"You're welcome." He seemed pleased by my gratitude. Hmmm. Maybe vampires didn't often express appreciation. "Patrick told me that Lorćan spoke to you."

"Yeah. You said something last night about the Taint. Did it make him into that slobbering beast?"

"No. The cure we attempted had an unexpected side effect."

"What was the cure?"

Stan considered me, as if trying to decide whether or not I deserved an answer. I resorted to crossing my arms and using the Look, which almost never failed to quell my children's pestering.

"The problem with the Taint is that once it's inside the bloodstream, it stays . . . latched. It doesn't matter if the diseased vampire drinks from clean sources after exposure, either," he said. "The Taint has been around for as long as there have been vampires, but it's recently become an epidemic."

"Nature's way of controlling the vampire population?" I asked.

"We think this strain was introduced on purpose."

"You mean like a biochemical attack? Who would do that? And why?"

He shrugged. Either he didn't know the answers to the questions or he didn't want to tell me.

"Lor fasted for a week—only a very old vampire can survive without sustenance for that long. We were trying to rid his system of the infected blood. Then we injected him with multiple rounds of lycanthrope—uh, werewolf—blood. We hoped that doing so would be able to kill off the Taint."

"Did it?"

"We're not sure. He awoke from his rest as you saw him, Mrs. Matthews. And he was starved. It seems the transfusion made him . . . well, ravenous, much more so than we expected. He also seems to have more strength, which is saying a lot since vampires are already ten times stronger than most humans."

"But why are you guys *here*? In Broken Heart?"

"Ah. That reminds me." He tapped on the PDA and frowned. "The meeting starts in fifteen minutes."

"What meeting?"

He pried his gaze away from the PDA. "Patrick didn't tell you?"

"He said that he needed to feed. Where does he get his blood?"

"From donors, of course."

Disgust roiled in my gut along with a very unfamiliar, weird desire. I felt my top gums split, then my incisors elongated. Holy crap. Had that happened before? Well, duh. I'd punctured and sucked on Patrick's thigh twice, but this was the first time I'd been aware of my fangs. "Please tell me," I said, talking carefully around my new incisors, "that by 'donors,' you mean there is a blood bank somewhere."

Stan stared at my teeth, and then his eyes lifted to mine. "Vampires need live, circulating blood. Humans are, for the most part, a vampire's main food source."

"You mean I have to kill others to survive?"

"No, no. Donors are not killed. It only takes a pint to satisfy most vampires."

Yet Lorćan had drained me and God knew who else to alleviate his thirst. Had he done so because he was starved or because he was a vampire-lycan? All this thinking and talking about blood was making me kinda hungry.

"You're human." I knew because Stan smelled like a ham-and-cheese sandwich slathered in mustard with a dill pickle on the side. I heard the blood frantically pumping through his heart as he picked up on my sudden interest in his neck.

"Didn't you feed?" His voice squeaked on the last word.

I nodded. "For some reason, though, I feel . . . peckish."

Stan flinched. He stood up and leapt for the door. Then he realized it had no handle and he yelled, "Ernie, open the damned door!"

"I'm not going to eat you," I said, even though I felt like gnawing, just a little, on his neck. I knew exactly where to place my new fangs, too, and how much pressure it would require to pierce his flesh and sip from him. "But, you know, if you're willing to donate a pint . . ."

"Ernie!"

Chapter 4

"**W**hy is Stan avoiding you?" asked Patrick, his hand slinking up my back to massage my neck. We were standing in the high school gym, near the end of the retractable seats on the left side. To my surprise, several townspeople and vampires milled around the basketball court, while others sat on the bleachers and chatted.

"I told him I was feeling peckish and he freaked out." Just thinking about drinking blood forced my creepy teeth to emerge.

Patrick stared at me. "You didn't take enough sustenance from me?"

I shrugged. I had felt replete this morning, er, evening until the incident with Stan. "Can't I have anything else?" I asked. "How am I going to live without chocolate?"

"Your body will reject regular food, including sweets," he said, dashing all my dreams of indulging in a champagne truffle. "You don't need them, love."

"Oh yeah? Well, here's some news, pal. Women cannot live without chocolate. Just try to get us through PMS without it."

A corner of his mouth quirked and he dipped his head near mine. "You don't have to worry about PMS. You will never have another period. Or menopause."

I had to admit, on some levels, this vampire thing was okay dokay. "I'll still miss chocolate."

"I will try to think of ways to keep your mind off it." Patrick nibbled my ear, his tongue darting out to caress the lobe. A different need shivered through me. I had no idea why we were so lovey-dovey after two days of knowing each other. I suspected my willingness to be fondled by Patrick had to do with drinking his blood. The man was almost 4,000 years old and I bet that meant his blood packed some wallop. And there was the mysterious *fede* ring to consider. Patrick seemed to believe that my ownership of it made me his soul mate.

"I'm not a sexual slave, am I?" I asked in half-jest.

Patrick pulled me into his embrace and placed a soft kiss on my lips. "Not yet."

Sure, I realized genuine desire threaded through the arrogant words, but just hearing the purr of possession in Patrick's voice was like getting a bucketful of cold water dumped on me. I wriggled out of his grip and stood back, crossing my arms and giving him the stink-eye. "I don't belong to you."

He seemed more amused than angered by my rebellion. One long, pale finger stroked my cheek. Then he whispered, "Not yet."

"Why, you son of a—"

"All right, everyone, please take a seat. We're about

to begin the meeting," yelled Stan, probably for the humans, because I could hear him like he was shouting in my ear. Patrick guided me to the front row and I sat down, still miffed at his high-handed behavior. Two rows of six metal foldout chairs were in front of the lectern where Stan stood, fiddling with his stupid electronic gadget. Behind him, there were eight chairs. Seven were occupied. One by Patrick and five by men who looked like they'd stepped out of the Mr. Romance issue of *Romantic Times BOOKClub*. All were tall and handsome with the same athletic grace I'd noticed about Patrick. All were dressed casually, but T-shirts and jeans couldn't hide the caged-panther energy they gave out. The seventh chair was filled by a tiny brunette who would make Kate Moss look fat. She looked drawn on paper she was so white, and impatient to boot, evidenced by the tapping of her itty bitty shoe on the floor.

Still in a snit, I looked at the person next to me and nearly swallowed my tongue. "Linda? Linda Beauchamp? What in the Sam Hill are you doing here?"

Her green eyes rolled up in her head in typical Linda fashion. "Last night when I was walking Buster, some ol' huge, smelly thing knocked me down and sucked me dry. Then, *apparently*, I died." Her red hair, worn big and fluffy, looked particularly big and fluffy. She noticed the direction of my gaze and snorted. "If I'd'a known this would be my last hairdo for eternity, I would'a splurged on a whole new look."

"I think it's you, hon," I said, and I meant it. "Let me guess the next part of your story. You woke up latched on to some handsome man's thigh?"

Linda snorted again. "I wish. I woke up sucking on a neck the size of the panhandle." She waved pale hands that showed off long, sparkly green acrylic nails. "That one on the end with the baby blues and dark hair? Ivan Taganov or some such. I just about ate him alive." She waggled her fingers at Ivan and he leered at her in a way that made her giggle.

"I tell you, I've been meaning to lose a few pounds and thanks to our new diet, that happened." Linda patted her waist. Yeah, she had lost a few pounds. She was still short and curvy, but the "chubs," as she'd called them, had disappeared. I watched as she gave me the once-over. "You're looking purty good, too, girl."

"Thanks."

"We aren't the only two, you know." She leaned back and I took a gander down the row.

Damnation! There was Patsy Donahue, the owner of Hair Today, Curl Tomorrow, the only beauty salon in Broken Heart. I saw Simone Sweet, who was the best mechanic at Joe's Garage; Louise LeRoy, who had just moved here to take her deceased grandmother's place as our librarian (the library was housed in the old LeRoy Mansion); Phoebe Tate, a waitress at Old Sass Café; and there were others. I counted nine women, including me, and one man, Ralph Genessa, recently widowed and trying to raise his twin toddler sons. He worked as a short order cook for Old Sass Café down on Main Street.

"Okay, toots," said Linda to Stan, which startled him so much he nearly dropped his favorite toy, "let's get a move on with these here proceedings. I'm hungry."

Stan turned the color of an unwashed gym sock.

Sweat poured off his brow and he wiped it away with his wrist, which he then rubbed on his khaki shorts. Sucking in a deep breath (lucky bastard), he placed the PDA onto the lectern then gripped its sides.

"We appreciate your cooperation—"

"As if we had a choice," interrupted Linda. "We all know that we're vampires. Hell, you're the only human here, shortcake."

I looked at Stan. Linda was right. The townspeople had been turned *into* vampires, probably the very same night I had. Lorćan had been a busy little freak, hadn't he? Foreboding crawled down my spine and lodged in my stomach. Maybe if I'd killed Lorćan when I had the chance . . . but no, by then the damage had been done. How could one man, *thing*, kill ten people by draining 'em dry? And why had Patrick and his grim-looking cohorts saved us all?

"Er, yes. Well." Stan cleared his throat. "I know you have questions. And we have a lot to cover before . . . um, you eat. If you'll look under your chairs, you'll find a personal digital assistant. It will be your way to contact us—"

"And when you say *us*," I said, "who are you talking about?"

"The Consortium," answered Patrick.

"Which is what?"

He lifted a shoulder, an elegant shrug that drew my attention to his broad shoulders.

"You'll find a fact sheet about The Consortium on your PDAs," said Stan.

Everyone retrieved their PDAs and turned them on. Some took out styluses and starting tapping and Stan droned on about how to operate the devices, where to find information, and how to contact the Consortium.

So, I turned on my electronic thingamajigger, too. On the left side was a row of icons. One looked like a little sheet of paper with "FAQ" typed underneath it. I tapped the symbol.

The Consortium FAQ

Question: *What is the Consortium?*
Answer: The Consortium is a five-hundred-year-old, not-for-profit organization created to facilitate relations between humans and non-humans. It is run by a council of duly elected officers who serve on the Board for hundred-year terms.

Question: *What is the Consortium's purpose?*
Answer: The Consortium's primary purpose is the betterment of all Earth's creatures through advances in science, technology, and medicine. Its secondary purpose is to build bridges between parakind and mankind so that one day, all sentient beings can live together in peace and prosperity. Our "bridge-building" is accomplished in many ways, and includes financing archaeological and historical research, creating safety zones for parakind, and donating funds to charitable causes.

Question: *Who can join the Consortium?*
Answer: Anyone interested in supporting the Consortium's goals and submitting a financial donation of $100,000 or more. Members must also take a blood oath to uphold the Consortium's Code.

I stopped reading. So this Consortium ran around and facilitated relations between boogeymen and humans? Hmmm. What did "creating safety zones for parakind" mean?

My gaze zeroed in on Patrick. "So . . . not all vampires are part of the Consortium?"

"No, but those who are must agree to follow our Code of Ethics."

"What happens if they don't?"

"Their membership is revoked."

"That's it?"

"It's a voluntary organization, love." He smiled. "We only want to help you."

"Yeah. By keeping us as hostages."

"As I promised, *a thaisce*, I will strive to keep your mind off such matters."

His voice was silky and his eyes, just moments before as cold as ice, now shimmered with heat. While Patrick tried to enthrall me, and I'll tell you it was working, I did a little vampire math and came up with an answer I didn't like.

"Who else shared your blood?" I asked.

The question surprised him. He settled into his chair, assuming his previous devil-may-care attitude. And he remained silent.

"Who else?" I waved at the Panel of Doom. "There are only seven of you. One of y'all did some overtime and you're probably the oldest, so it's only logical to think you'd offered your bloody charms to a couple more victims."

The other vampires shifted restlessly, their eyes slitted dangerously as they glared at me. I stuck out my tongue. That cracked up four of the men, who slouched in their seats and returned their gazes to the Vamp 101 participants. The rest, including Ivan Taganov and Miss Pixie With Fangs, kept their attention on me.

What's the matter, love? Are you jealous? Patrick's voice was inside my head. Inside my freaking head. Well, if he could be in my mind, that meant I could be in his. *No, I am not jealous!* I sent out a scorching wave of fury right into his brain. His head jerked as if he'd been slapped. I grinned in petty satisfaction.

His brows rose in either surprise or acquiescence. *Only one other*, he admitted, *but I do not claim her.* Before I could ask just what the hell that comment meant, the rear door to the gym squealed open and we all heard the slapping of flip-flops on the waxed floor. The hair on my nape electrified and I felt a snarl catch in my throat.

"Sorry I'm late," said the soft voice of a young woman. "My son wouldn't—"

Her voice choked off as I stood up and whirled around. The fury I'd just directed at Patrick was nothing compared to the rage burning inside me now.

One more new vampire had joined our ranks. And it was the only person in town I'd want to see dead . . . the conniving bitch who'd stolen my husband with her youth and her charm and her goddamned big breasts.

Charlene Mason.

Chapter 5

I had Charlene flat on her back, my fangs at her throat, before that bitch could blink. I was hungry, too, and the idea of slurping the blood of a betrayer made me salivate.

Then Patrick was there, hauling me off and dragging me out of the gymnasium. The last thing I saw was Stan helping Charlene stand and the smirk on Linda's face as she gave me a thumbs-up.

"What the hell is going on?" asked Patrick. He pinned me against the wall and I knew that even with my newly acquired strength, I wouldn't be able to budge him.

"I'm hungry," I said.

"Hunger isn't the reason you attacked Charlene. You intended to kill her."

I processed his accusation and felt a teeny tiny stab of guilt. So, okay, maybe I didn't want Charlene dead. Well, *more* dead. "I bet her blood tastes like a septic tank anyway."

"Why do you hate her?"

"It's a long story."

"We have time."

"No kidding."

He sighed and his grip lessened. "If you don't want to tell me, *a thaisce,* I can always ask Charlene. She is under my protection."

"Yeah, yeah. The Consortium. Blah, blah, blah."

"No, Jessica. My personal protection. When a human goes through the Turn, the Master is bound by tradition and by blood to protect those he brings into our world."

Cold horror filtered through the burning embers of my anger. "No. Goddamn it, no! Please tell me you didn't let Charlene suck your thigh."

"Of course not," he said, "she took her salvation from my neck."

Well, what was the damn difference? I leaned against the wall and shrugged off his grasp. His hands slid down my shoulders, his fingers grazing my bare arms before he stepped back. The kernel of guilt wedged in my gut blossomed into a painful, pulsating ache. A light wind brought the scent of honeysuckle. My gaze lifted to the sliver of pale moon that hung in the black sky.

"I'm being a royal bitch," I said. "I'm sorry."

"Forgiven." He smiled, looking as if he wanted to kiss me, but thought better of it. "And Charlene?"

I looked at my feet. "She fucked my husband, okay? Then she had his kid. Rich and I were in the middle of a messy divorce when he got into a fatal car accident a year ago."

"I see."

"I'm glad someone does because I can't see clearly at all. Rich is dead and Charlene is an outcast and I *still* feel hurt and angry and mean-hearted. And now I'm a vampire and I don't even get the satisfaction of outliving Charlene. I don't get to watch her get old and fat and gray. And she will always be younger than me. Forever." Oh, I was pitiful. Pathetic. I felt Patrick's thumb slide under my chin. He pushed gently until I looked at him. "What?"

"Would you like to get out of here?"

"Desperately."

He grabbed my hands and we rose into the air. My stomach dipped and twisted. Last night, I'd flown over my house without a thought about how I was doing it. This time, with Patrick, I suddenly realized I was hovering above the ground with nothing to hang on to if I fell.

"You can't die, love," said Patrick.

"Stop reading my mind."

"I'm reading your expression."

We rose higher and higher until we floated above the gymnasium. The air was thick with humidity and even though I no longer breathed, the wetness seemed to fill my lungs. Patrick guided us upward until the high school looked like a big stack of yellow LEGOs.

"Where are we going?" I asked.

"Where do you want to go?"

Loaded question, buddy. Where did the undead go, anyway? I wanted to go somewhere where I felt alive, where I felt human, where I felt *normal*. Unfortunately, I didn't get a chance to decide. One second, I was flying along like a wingless bat, and then the next, whoosh . . . down I went, like a freaking lead balloon. Luckily, Patrick grabbed me and lowered me to the ground.

When I was done cursing and shaking, I broke away from his very yummy arms and looked around. We had landed at Putt 'Er There, a mini-golf course that had gone out of business last winter. Broken Heart, Oklahoma, might be a haven for women and men suffering from lost love and bad relationships, but the town itself was suffering, too.

Like most small towns, we relied on agriculture and tourist trade to keep us going. But the farms in the area were struggling badly and had been for a while, thanks to drought and low market prices caused by heinous factory farming. Tourists didn't stop here anymore to do antiquing or have lunch at quaint tea shops. Those places had closed up. Many people had sold their homes or their businesses and left.

Somewhere along the way, we'd lost the desire and drive to save Broken Heart. We had no hope, but you know, we also seemed to relish the despair. Souls trapped in a purgatory of our own making. Sheesh. Was being a vampire making me über morbid or what?

I watched Patrick check out the place. His gaze took in the dilapidated buildings and knee-high grass. He rounded the small but deep pond and walked to the windmill, which had toppled over after Wilson Jones rammed his truck into it. Willie lived a mile away, but after one too many whiskeys at the Barley & Boob Barn, he missed the dirt-road entrance to his place and plowed into Putt 'Er There.

"Barley and Boob Barn?" asked Patrick.

"You are really creeping me out with the mind-reading thing." I gestured toward the west, where the only viable business near Broken Heart still existed. "Old Farmer Smythe sold his farm to some guy from Las Vegas. He razed all the buildings except the barn. That he converted into a strip club. We think hanky panky goes on out there, too, but no one really bothers to check."

"Why?"

"For one thing, it's the only place bringing in people. They gas up at the Thrifty Sip and buy dinner at the Old Sass Café. The girls at the Barn get their hair and nails done at Patsy's place." I poked at a tuft of grass with my shoe. "For another, the county sheriff gets paid to look the other way. Truthfully, the activities at the B and B are the least of our worries."

"Yes," said Patrick, nodding. "It does seem that your town is in a lot of trouble."

"Broken Heart barely exists anymore. We have two bona fide police officers and a voluntary fire department. The elementary school burned down a while back, which means all the kids go to the high school. Businesses are failing and citizens like me, who can trace their roots all the way back to the founders, are leaving. We have, maybe, three hundred people living here now. It's like the place really is cursed."

"Why haven't you left?"

"That very question has been on my mind," I admitted. "We have enough money from Rich's life insurance and the sale of his business to live on for a good long while. But, it's a moot point now. The choice has been taken from me."

"Temporarily." In the blink of an eye he moved from his position near the broken windmill to two inches away from my face. My mouth went slack with shock.

"What other secrets do you hide, Jessica?" He leaned in, his lips very close to mine. My gaze was drawn to his mouth—his plump, red, juicy, kissable mouth. *Yum.*

"Well, if I told you, they wouldn't be secrets." I tried to back away, to get some breathable (figuratively, of course) space between me and the cute dead guy, but he tracked me until my back hit the wall of the shed that used to store the supplies for Putt 'Er There.

I felt a flicker in my mind and realized Patrick was poking around in my thoughts again. "Will you stop that? I'm boring! Reading my mind is a big snore-fest, okay? It would severely damage my self-esteem to see you fall asleep in mid-mind read. So, really, stay out of my head."

"No." He flattened his palms on the wall just above my shoulders. His hair tickled my cheek as he leaned close to my ear. "I like being inside you."

Oh. My. God. An erotic image flashed: Me and Patrick naked and sweaty, moans echoing as his cock thrust . . . oh shit. Desire beat a tempo in my veins; hell, it mamboed all the way down to my nether regions. My poor, sexually deprived womanhood almost went into nuclear meltdown.

"You did that on purpose," I accused, my voice barely a whisper.

"Did what?" he asked, all sweet innocence. The look in his eyes was another story, though. I've seen lust in a man's gaze, but the emotion lurking in

Patrick's eyes was a deep, dark, very dangerous version of sexual attraction. What I saw there, glittering in those silver orbs, sent skitters of fear—and terrible desire—up my spine.

"Quit putting those . . . those suggestions into my brain."

"Whatever you imagined, *céadsearc*, is of your own making."

"What does that mean?"

"It means you probably want to do naughty things with me." He grinned and I saw his fangs. You would think that someone with limited vamp experience and a not-so-great reaction to piercing, pain, or blood would run screaming away from a man with teeth like that. But I didn't. I kinda sorta maybe wanted him to use those fangs on me.

"I meant, smart ass, what do those weird words mean. Hey! Are you insulting me in Irish?"

"Gaelic. *A thaisce* and *céadsearc* are not insults."

I waited for him to define the terms, but he did not explain. Instead, he chose to explore my neck. *With his lips.* Pure lust shuddered through me as his mouth scraped my collarbone, his tongue tracing an intricate pattern to a sensitive spot behind my ear. My hands crept into his soft, thick hair, raking through the strands because the alternative was to put my hands elsewhere on his gorgeous, muscled frame . . . and . . . and . . . what was my objection again?

"I feel your hunger," he said. "Would you like to feed?"

"On you?"

"If you like." The whispered invitation promised ecstasy. If I still had a heartbeat, it would've gone into convulsions. Dare I convey my earlier desire for Patrick to nibble on me? Just a little bite? Hmmm?

"No," he said, answering the question I hadn't voiced. "I cannot."

"Why not? I've feasted on you like you're a two-dollar buffet."

He lifted his head and my fingers sifted out of his hair, fell to his shoulders, and, of their own accord and without express permission, stroked down his pectorals. Mmmm. Abs of steel. I sighed (okay, I *tried* to sigh) in delight.

"I do not think being compared to a cheap meal is a compliment," he said, though his lips quirked in suppressed laughter. "You don't know what you are asking." *Or realize what I've allowed.*

"Allowed? What did you allow?"

"Damn." He stepped back and the torturous ache of need building between us fizzled away. Poof. Gone. I lamented the loss of feeling wanted—and of wanting. "I begin to see your reasons for wishing I would not poke around in your mind. I will explain everything, Jessica. But please understand that what exists between you and me is . . ." He struggled, apparently trying to find the right word. "Rare."

"Because I'm wearing your lost ring?"

"Do you really think it's only about the *fede*?"

"I don't know what to think. It's really weird that a bunch of vampires and werewolves caravanning in expensive RVs ended up here. And I just happen to be wearing a ring that once belonged to you?"

Patrick nodded. "We meant to come here. Our other

facility was destroyed and my father suggested the Consortium would find the town suitable for its needs. I didn't realize he also meant for me to find the descendent of Mary McCree."

Questions crowded my mind. "Your father? Well, if you're still having conversations with him, he's gotta be a vampire, too. Why would you need to find someone descended from my grandmother?"

He put a finger to my lips. "There's a lot to tell you—and you're still getting used to being a vampire."

"That's an understatement." My hands had drifted to Patrick's waist. As my fingertips brushed his left hip, I felt a vibration. *What the*— I uttered a sound of surprise.

Patrick lifted his shirt and pulled free a tiny cell phone from its clip. "Yes?"

Foreboding rippled through me. I saw Patrick's expression go flat; his eyes turned the color of a rain cloud.

"Don't do anything until I get there." He flipped shut the phone and reattached it to the clip. "We must go."

The foreboding turned hard and cold in my gut. I swallowed the knot of fear clogging my throat. I knew my kids were not the ones in danger. It wasn't parental confidence, either. It was the real and true knowledge they were safe and sleeping soundly in their beds.

He took my hands and we lifted into the air. We sped back to the high school and before I knew it, we had landed in the same spot we'd launched from.

"What's happening?" I asked.

His only response was a grimace as we went

through the doors. The meeting was apparently over, though it seemed everyone was still in the gym socializing. Charlene sat apart from the other townspeople, who had, as always, shunned her. She messed around with her PDA and pretended not to be bothered by how everyone ignored her. Not even being one of eleven people Turned was enough to merit a little acceptance. I had never understood why Charlene hadn't packed up her kid and her possessions and just hit the road. With Rich dead, she had nothing and no one. An itty bitty iota of sympathy welled, but I quickly stomped on it. *I did not feel sorry for Charlene.*

"Stay here." Patrick let go of my hand and strode like some bossy general toward Stan, Miss Tiny-Ass, and two men I hadn't seen sitting on the Panel of Doom. Hmmm. Why were they having a private pow-wow?

"Hey, girl, where'd you go to?" Linda asked, smiling. "Some show you put on there with ol' Charlene. And there wasn't even a two-drink minimum."

"Har-de-har." But I grinned. "What happened at the meeting?"

"Well, Stan blathered on about the Consortium, then one of the other guys . . . that one . . . he looks like melted chocolate, don't he? Anyhoodles, he got up and blathered on about some dig in Egypt. And then Ivan got up and talked about how he's been newly elected to the council and how the Consortium is here to protect us." Linda's eyes rolled. "Bored me outta my fucking gourd." Her gaze wandered to Patrick. "Who's that bit of fluff next to Patty O' Hunk?"

Well, now. Wasn't that a sight? Miss Skinny Fangs

was sidling next to Patrick. I nodded to Linda. "I'll talk to you later."

"Yeah. You do that." She chuckled.

I marched right up and insinuated myself into the little group. It gave me no small amount of pleasure to elbow aside the pixie so I could stand next to Patrick. She bared her teeth at me, her eyes narrowed into slits. *Oh screw you, honey.*

"Go dtachta an diabhal thú!" she spat.

Oopsie. I must've sent my little insult into her teeny brain. Heh. Heh. *Cut it out, love. You're too open with your thoughts.* I smiled at Patrick with a "who me" expression.

"Nara!" he said, his voice low and dangerous. "Do not curse *a ghrá mo chroí.*"

I didn't think it would be possible for a vampire to pale, but Nara did. She went white as Wonder Bread, her lips rounded in soundless denial. Ooookay. I was so Googling Gaelic terms when I got home.

What did you tell her? I aimed the question right at Patrick.

I merely told her the truth about you.

And that was . . .

Ssshhh.

I gritted my teeth. Patrick was the most gorgeous man I'd ever had the pleasure of lusting after, but he was also the most stubborn, secretive, insensitive . . . um . . . er . . . did I say stubborn?

Yes. Now be quiet.

"Where is she?" asked Patrick.

"A donor found the body near the communications RV," said Stan. "We were too late to save her."

Patrick's expression held no emotion, but I felt his anguish. It slithered through me, clawing at my guts. I put a reassuring hand on his shoulder and squeezed.

"Did Lor . . . was he responsible?" he asked quietly.

Stan couldn't meet Patrick's gaze. "I don't know."

"If the human is dead, there's nothing we can do. Give it to the mortals for disposal and let's be done with it." Nara sounded bored and petulant. Her gaze raked me. Anger boiled through me. Someone had died . . . and Nara didn't give a shit.

"Who is it? Someone in your crew?" I asked.

"No," said Stan. "We do not know the identity of the woman."

Nara studied her nails and sighed as only a heartless bitch could sigh. Damn her. How *did* she do that fake-breath thing? "Let Patrick's new play toy deal with it," she said. "She is the leader of this pitiable band of fools."

Oh no she didn't. "Listen, sister, I'm not a play toy and I'm not leader of anything unless it's the Smack Nara Squad."

"Why you insolent little Turn-blood! How dare you speak to your betters that way!" She looked as if she were contemplating the removal of my head.

Okay, I had no idea why I didn't like this chickie-poo. Oh wait. She insulted me and she thought she was my better. Hah. And HAH again. Something else about her raised my hackles, too. I had an icky feeling in my stomach. Some people might point out I didn't like Nara because she was beauty personified and really, horribly thin and she had, if I wasn't mistaken, a thing for Patrick. Not that Patrick and I had done much more than share some blood and argue, but I still felt like he was mine. However, I didn't hate Nara because she was pretty, skinny, and hungry for Patrick.

I didn't.

Much.

I looked at Nara, who was staring at Patrick. I resisted, *barely,* the urge to gouge out her eyes.

You have no worries about Nara, a thaisce. *I may need you to identify the woman who was killed. Are you able to do so?*

I'll try.

Finally it sunk in. A woman was dead. Had Lor started feeding again? Surely he wouldn't be hungry so soon after practically devouring eleven people. *Patrick, does anyone else know about the . . . uh, dead woman?*

None of the townspeople know, love.

Nara wrapped her pretty little fingers around Patrick's muscled bicep. "You do not need to go with her. Send your drone. Go on with her, Stan. Your Master and I have business to discuss." Her gaze glittered as she smirked at me; her eyes suggested the kind of business she wanted to discuss involved beds and nakedness.

"Stan isn't my drone. The Consortium does not condone the use of mortals as drones—you know that." He glared at her. "There is only one thing I want from you, Nara."

"Hmmm . . . and there is only one thing I will trade for the object you desire." Nara clutched at him, desperation overcoming her arrogance. "We were good together once. We can be again."

Again? As in . . . she and Patrick had a thing? Her gaze slid toward me, her eyes glowing with triumph. I have faced down bitchy PTA presidents, power-hungry principals, and Girl Scout leaders with cookie-sale complexes. Nara had no idea who she was dealing with.

I slid my hand under hers and pried her fingers off Patrick's arm. I bent the digits back until they snapped. Shocked, she glared down at her crooked fingers, and then at me.

"That hurt!" She looked at Patrick, her face a mask of suffering. "You see what cruelty lies in this one's heart?"

"I believe cruelty is your forte," he said softly, his expression blank. "You know who she is and yet you taunt her with innuendos."

Nara licked her lips; her eyes filled with longing. *"Padriag . . ."*

"I have had enough of weird languages and melodramatic vampires," I said. "Keep your mitts off him, Nara, or I'll break more than your hand."

In an instant, the emotion clouding her face dissipated. She hissed, baring her teeth to show off her fangs. Her eyes glowed with hatred. "You're such a *bitch.*"

"No, honey. I'm not *a* bitch. I'm THE bitch." Just to piss her off, I put my hand on Patrick's neck and said, "Mine."

"A thaisce!" yelled Patrick.

"Mrs. Matthews!" squeaked Stan.

"No!" raged Nara.

I yanked away my hand. The imprint of a honeysuckle faded into Patrick's skin. I remembered seeing the same pattern on my children when I claimed them. Wait. Claimed them? How did I know what it meant? Oh shit! Did that mean I had claimed Patrick, too? "Did I break some sort of vampire policy? Someone needs to tell me the rules, damn it."

Nara's fury rolled off her in big, black waves. If she'd held a stake, she would've gladly plunged it into my heart. Cradling her injured hand, she whirled and stalked off, muttering and cursing.

"She's really nice," I said in a saccharine voice. "We should have her over for dinner some time."

"Patrick," said Stan, his eyes round with worry. "Did you tell her—"

"In time," said Patrick, his enigmatic gaze on mine. "Do you not find it interesting she performs the steps on pure instinct?"

"Hmph," Stan huffed. "I'll meet you by the RV." He walked away, PDA in hand, the *tap-ping* of the stylus meeting screen beating a nervous tattoo.

"I like her," said one of the tall males who remained in our circle. He had a Slavic accent . . . German, maybe. I gazed up at him and blinked. There were *two* of him.

The men looked exactly the same—from the black leather vests and matching pants to their inky-black hair tied back with black leather thongs. They wore biker boots, too. In the belts around their waists were an assortment of lethal weapons, most of which were strange-looking blades and knives. They had the same yummy build as Patrick. I looked at their faces: chiseled jaws, eyes as green as jade, and necks the size of Greek columns.

"Twins?" I asked.

"Darrius and Drake at your service, *liebling*."

"Really?" I asked. "Because I could think of all kinds of ways for you to serve me."

"Jessica," said Patrick. "Do not say things like that to those two."

"Do not worry, *mein freund*. We will not bite her. Too hard," said Darrius . . . or Drake. They grinned at each other, and then at me.

There was something very different about them. Something strange. "You're not vampires."

The twins grinned again, their lips curling with a touch of wickedness. "We are lycanthropes," said the one on the left. "We're shape-shifters, *liebling*. We are the wolf guardians for our vampire friends."

"Vampires have used lycans to guard their crypts for centuries," said Patrick. "They're not immortal, but they live a long time."

"The oldest recorded lycanthrope was one thousand and eighty-two," said the one on the right. "But most of us only live to our eight-hundreds."

"Tough break," I said drolly. "So you're the muscle, eh?"

"We compensate our lycans for their security expertise. The Consortium doesn't keep drones or guardians."

"Yeah, I get it. The whole live-in-harmony thing." I looked at my Irish vamp and tried to do the sigh thing. It didn't work. "Okay. Gimme the bad news. What did I do to your neck?"

"Later, love." A shadow flitted in his gaze then disappeared into the beguiling silver. Surely I imagined the combination of fear and of need. What could Patrick fear? And what could he want from me that caused such yearning?

Truthfully, I'd been trying to avoid the gruesome task of IDing a dead girl. If she was a resident of Broken Heart, then chances were good I knew her. A year ago, we'd been a quaint, old-fashioned town of seven hundred and three residents. Nowadays, we had fewer than three hundred people who called Broken Heart home. My guts clenched.

"Let's get this over with," I said, grabbing Patrick's hand. "Are the Bobbsey Twins coming, too?"

"Bobbsey Twins?" they said together in a tone that suggested death and dismemberment.

I laughed. Then, because I had a survival instinct, I broke into a run and took Patrick with me.

Levity faded as we exited the gymnasium and walked across the parking lot to a very large white, windowless RV. On the far side, I saw Stan and several others waiting for us. Slowing my steps, I readied myself to see a dead body. Technically, *I* was dead but I was still walking and talking. My stomach roiled at the thought of seeing some poor lifeless girl.

Patrick squeezed my hand, a silent show of tenderness, and nodded at Stan. He bent down and removed the white sheet that had been draped over the body.

"Oh my God." I clapped a hand over my mouth as I looked, horrified, upon the ravaged remains of a young woman with red hair. Her body looked as if it had been mauled. Her yellow summer dress was shredded; she wore only one yellow flip-flop on a manicured foot. The despoiled state of her body contrasted with the pale serene quality of her untouched face. Her lips were blue; her eyes a faded unseeing green.

"Jessica, do you know her?"

"Yes," I said. I stumbled back and swallowed my wail of despair. "Is there any way to save her?"

"Non, ma chère," said a handsome man with short black hair and sky-blue eyes. I remembered him from the Panel of Doom. What was his name? François something-or-other. He knelt at the woman's side, his fingers brushing away stray red strands from her face. "This one cannot be saved."

"Who is she?" Patrick asked.

"Emily," I whispered. "Emily Beauchamp."

Patrick frowned, obviously trying to place the last name. I laid a hand on his arm. "Emily is Linda's sister."

Chapter 6

"What happened to her?" Linda cried, which was a hard thing to do when you couldn't shed tears.

"We don't know," said Stan, patting Linda's hand. "But I promise you, we will find out."

After we told Linda the bad news, she demanded to see her sister. By the time she'd gotten a glimpse of Emily, the girl had been redressed and laid out on a metal slab in a refrigerated truck. (No, I didn't ask why the Consortium had a refrigerated truck with metal slabs big enough for bodies.)

Watching Linda's face as she recognized her sister was hell. She fell to her knees and pounded the truck metal flooring. Despite her vamp strength and tremendous grief, she didn't dent the floor. The Consortium knew how to construct things that wouldn't crush under a vamp's strength.

Emily was Linda's only sister and the only family, other than her own daughter, she had left. She held

Emily's small, cold hand and wailed. It was a good, long time before I was able to draw her away.

Patrick, Stan, Linda, and I assembled in my living room and tried to make sense of why Emily was dead. Linda sat between Stan and me on the tan couch; Patrick stood near the fireplace with crossed arms and a closed expression.

"Emily was a surprise baby," said Linda. "Mama nearly died when she found out she was pregnant at forty-six. Shoot, I was twenty years old, already married to that shit-eating prick Earl."

Stan handed her a tissue from the box I kept on the coffee table. He realized right away it was a stupid move, but Linda seemed to appreciate the gesture. She plucked the tissue from his hand and held on to it.

"My Marybeth was born when Emily was two. They grew up together, closer than sisters. Marybeth's birthday is next month. She's gonna be eighteen." Her lips lifted into a slight smile. "Emily is only twenty. Oh my God. Was. Emily *was* twenty." Linda lost it. She sobbed without the wet satisfaction of tears until her entire body shook. I wrapped my arm around her shoulders and squeezed, heartbroken for her.

After several agonizing moments, Linda lifted her head. The tissue had turned into paper snow, fluttering to the floor as she twisted and ripped it. "Marybeth is all I got left. Mama's gone and now Emily, too. And I ain't even human anymore. What's gonna happen, Jessie, when I outlive my own child? And her children? And their children? It ain't right to be this way. It's unnatural. It's *wrong*."

Her words were arrows of pain into my heart. I

faced the same anguish with my own kids. With the rest of my family. All of us bitten by Lorćan and saved by the Consortium had the same problems. How could you be an immortal parent with mortal children? How did you cope with outliving those you loved?

My gaze sought Patrick's, but emptiness glittered in his eyes. I wanted to ask him so many questions, but I doubted he'd give me the answers I wanted to hear. I wondered who he'd lost when he was Turned. Had he been a father? He'd certainly been a son. Maybe a brother. A husband. A friend. What happened to your heart when it had to bear witness to the deaths of mortals, especially those who loved you and whom you loved?

Linda's gaze followed mine. In that instant, her grief hit a flash point. Her distress melted to rage. She rose on shaky legs and pointed an accusing finger at Patrick. "This is your fault. You and your soulless vampires have damned all of us."

"Would you rather be dead?" asked Patrick coldly. "Would you rather your darlin' Marybeth speak prayers over your grave? If she didn't have you, she would have no one."

"If you had kept control of that creature, we'd all still be breathing. Don't you think for a second I'm gonna be grateful you saved my life when you and the Consortium are the reason I lost it. And now that *thing* has killed my baby sister!"

"Lorćan did not do this," said Patrick. "He would never murder an innocent."

"Bullshit!" screamed Linda.

Patrick looked as if he'd been slapped.

I nibbled on my lower lip. "You don't know that it wasn't Lorćan."

Stan and Patrick exchanged a look. Goddamn it. I hated when men did that wink-wink, nudge-nudge crap.

"Mrs. Matthews, I explained to you earlier that Lor changed into something unexpected. He escaped because he was hungry. And he fed until he was full."

"Eleven fucking people! And he did kill us!"

"*Drained* you because he hadn't eaten in weeks. It wasn't his intention to kill any of you," said Patrick, his eyes blazing with fury. "Lor is a man of faith. A man of God. He has carried that devotion to the Almighty in his heart for centuries, even after—" Patrick's nostrils flared as he regained control of his emotions. "I tell you, Jessica, that he did not murder an innocent young woman!"

I think Patrick loved his brother, but was too blind to see the truth about Lorćan. He wasn't a human. He wasn't a vampire. He was a beast. Whatever humanity he might've retained was surely gone.

Besides, what else was running around Broken Heart that had the ability and the power to do what was done to Emily?

It was a short list with only one name.

Chapter 7

I knew dawn was approaching because I felt weighed down. My body was shutting itself off without my permission. It sucked to feel this way. And it really sucked that I was going to spend another day without seeing or taking care of my children.

I crawled onto the bed and debated whether or not I should use the last vestiges of willpower to undress. Nope. Not gonna happen. If I was lucky, Patrick would join me, de-clothe me, and . . . well . . . keep his mitts off me. I didn't need to have sex with him.

But I wanted to.

That night, I called a meeting. All the new vampire citizens of Broken Heart gathered in my living room. I tried to keep the meeting a secret from Stan and the vamps, but Patrick poked around in my head and found out. Having my friends milling around in my home reminded me of other social gatherings. Barbecues, Christmas parties, Easter egg hunts. We ate desserts and drank wine and laughed. Rich had been by my side, the perfect host, the perfect husband. I had been so happy being his wife. Maybe that's why his betrayal pierced me so deeply. I couldn't understand how or why he fell in love with another woman.

After I caught Rich and Charlene banging each other stupid, Rich had pulled up his pants and admitted he was going to leave me. Right there. In the Motel 6. With his mistress splayed on the cheap comforter, still sweaty and half clothed and postorgasmic.

He moved out that night. The next day, I drove to Tulsa crying and bitching and listening to sad love songs so I could buy myself new bedroom furniture.

The wood was burnished cherrywood. I bought the king-sized four-poster bed, the dresser with its ornate mirror, two nightstands, and a rocking chair. Later, I added a red wingback—a garage sale find.

It was necessary to recreate the space. To wipe out the memories that lingered. To know that Rich's clothes had never occupied space in that dresser. To know he had never slept in that bed or turned to me in the morning, his hands palming my breasts as he leaned down to kiss me. To know that I had changed what had been "ours" to what was now only "mine."

The bitterness had faded. The pain had healed. Yet, my hatred for Charlene had always been too pure, too focused to free myself from it. I don't think I could forgive her for being the reason Rich left me. And the reason he died.

I admit it. I debated for a full hour about whether or not to invite Charlene, but finally made the call. In typical fashion, she was alone, at the back of the room, observing. No matter where she went, it was like she had an invisible force field. Everyone gave her at least three feet of space. I felt a twang of conscience. And a sliver of respect. Charlene always held up her head, always smiled, always pretended like she didn't see the way people treated her like the town whore. Maybe falling in love with a married man was her only mistake, but she paid penance for it daily. I'll tell you, that stuck in my craw.

But because I couldn't offer friendship to my husband's mistress, I turned to Patrick. "What are the Consortium's plans for us?"

The buzz of conversation ceased and all eyes turned to him.

"We have made financial arrangements for everyone," he said. "Notices have been given at jobs. The children are cared for during the day."

"How am I supposed to raise my sons if I never see them?" asked Ralph. "And I worry about . . . about the need for blood. If that desire will make me . . ." His face grayed.

"You are incapable of hurting your children," said Patrick. "It's physically impossible for a vampire to do harm to anyone he loves."

I perked up at this news. I was incredibly relieved to know that my children were safe from my undead thirst. Now, Patrick, on the other hand . . . yum. Except he hadn't given me any *yum* tonight, the wanker.

I asked, "What if the vampire doesn't love anyone?"

"If he goes too long without companionship or friendship, without feeling compassion or love . . . a vampire loses his connection to his own humanity. When that happens, he becomes a *droch fhola*."

"Dracula?"

"*Droch fhola* is Gaelic for 'bad or evil blood.' A *droch fhola* serves his own needs and doesn't care who he hurts to fulfill those desires. Once a vampire becomes a *droch fhola*, the only kind thing to do is kill him." His eyes sparked for a second, a flicker of that mysterious emotion I'd seen in his gaze before. Then he turned to face the others.

"What about sex?" asked Patsy Donahue. "I hear tell if we have sex with another vampire, we have to bind with 'em. And let me tell you, I ain't getting hitched to someone just 'cause I like his penis. So there better be a loophole because if I'm going live forever, it ain't gonna be without sex."

"The binding ritual was created by the ancients for two reasons. One was to prevent a vampire from turning *droch fhola* and the second was to prevent a vampire from sexual misconduct during blood-taking. When the ancients created the binding," explained Patrick, "they used powerful magic and prayers to craft its ritual. It cannot be changed or broken. Three steps must be taken to make the binding a recognized union, which affords mates with certain protections. But . . . the sex act is the true binding and the other two steps aren't needed for it to work."

Patsy looked at him, her eyes twinkling. "So, Einstein, what are the steps?"

"First, the Claiming. Second, the Word-giving. Finally, the Mating."

"Whoa," I said. "So the ancients were thinking it

was better to bind a vampire for a hundred years, whether or not they wanted to, than to have 'em turn into a *droch fhola*?"

"Are they all men?" interjected Linda. "Because this sounds like some guy's bright idea to make sure he'll get laid for a hundred years in a row."

"Three of the seven ancients are women," said Patrick.

"What about oral sex?" asked Patsy. Bless her heart. Her mouth just didn't have an off switch. "Or using things other than the regular working parts?"

"Actual intercourse is required. The typical penetration with the . . . regular working parts," said Patrick. He didn't sound embarrassed. He sounded amused. I guess four thousand years of hearing every dirty joke in the world might inure a person to getting red-faced about a sex discussion. "The binding has other purposes, too. It's a protection for nonvampires, especially humans. Since the vampire will bind with his object of affection, no matter what species, he is less likely to attempt intercourse. Indeed, once he binds, he cannot have sex with anyone else—not for the next century."

"You mean if a vampire has sex with a human, he's chained to her for hundred years?" asked Linda. She sounded as horrified as I felt. "No matter what?"

"Unfortunately, many vampires have attempted such bindings and found themselves the caretakers of decomposing bodies and crumbling bones for the requisite number of years."

"But there's no way for them to . . . uh, penetrate," I said. "Right?"

"Once the binding sex has been completed, there are no other requisite sex acts between the bound couple."

"I sure don't want to hear no stories about what else a vampire has hitched hisself to," said Patsy. Her eyes narrowed at Patrick. "Especially sheep. Don't want to hear about how some stupid dickhead got married to a farm animal. Sure as shit happened, though, I know it."

"There was Claudius," said Patrick. "He was a Roman—"

"Patrick," I screeched, "spare us the details."

"Anything for you, love." Patrick leaned next to the brick fireplace and surveyed the room. "I know it's been difficult for everyone to deal with the new circumstances. The Consortium is moving its facilities to Broken Heart. We've already purchased land and will break ground tomorrow to begin building a compound to house our laboratories and offices."

"Like a prison," said Linda.

"You don't have to live in the compound that we're building, but we are going to insist that you remain in Broken Heart under our protection." Patrick met the gaze of each person sitting in the room, then he looked at me. "Give us time to show you how to protect yourselves, how to feed, how to set up your lives so that humans do not recognize you for who you are. Then you will be able to go anywhere."

"How did you do that so fast?" I asked. "Usually it takes at least a month to close a sale for a residential property. Commercial properties take at least sixty days."

Patrick's eyebrows winged upward. I shrugged. "I took a real estate course once."

"We bought private land. With cash. The owner was thrilled. I believe you're familiar with the Barley and Boob Barn?"

"You're shitting me!"

"Certainly not."

"What about the strippers?"

"I brought them into my harem."

My mouth went slack. "You *what*?"

Patrick rolled his eyes. "We paid them, love. A great deal, in fact, to pack up and go elsewhere." *No*, he shot into my mind, *I don't really have a harem.*

Good. Then I won't have to stake you. "Sounds like you know what you're doing," I said begrudgingly.

"We've also been buying out the businesses and residences of the other townspeople."

My nape tingled. "Why?"

"The town is small and it's isolated enough that the Consortium will be able to finally implement our long-term goal for a parakind safety zone. A permanent community, rather than pockets created within human cities."

The tingling traveled down my spine and spun a cold circle in my stomach. "You're getting rid of the humans so you can invite other vampires to live here."

Patrick nodded. "Not just vampires, but other non-humans who want to settle down in a community where they don't have to hide their true natures."

"You can't just run our citizens out of their own town," said Linda, outrage vibrating in her voice.

"No one has turned down our offers, which are more than generous compensation." Patrick's gaze softened with empathy. "I know you've been struggling to keep

Broken Heart alive. But it's a dying town. At least with the Consortium's plan, it will thrive again . . . just in a different way."

It was hard to believe that a few days ago my biggest concern was balancing my checkbook and counting the carbs in a Ben & Jerry's pint. Now, I was not only one of the eternal undead, I was just one kind of creature that most people believed were Hollywood creations.

"Has everyone in town sold out to the Consortium?" asked Ralph.

"Yes."

"You're kidding me," I said. "You got to everyone in a day?"

Patrick looked at me strangely. I couldn't interpret that glance, but it made my stomach dip.

"We've been buying out the businesses and houses in town for the last six months," he confessed.

Stunned silence followed his announcement. Then voices started up all at once. After getting my own emotions in order, not an easy thing to do in the middle of a crowded, noisy room, I whistled shrilly and everyone shut up again. It occurred to me that Patrick might be pulling our chains. Maybe we were getting hazed—you know, teased and tormented before being allowed to join the vampire fraternity.

"As I said, we've been looking for a place to create a community for non-humans. We realized that a small town in Oklahoma would be perfect. No one would think of looking for our citizens in the Midwest."

Guess I hadn't done too good a job getting my emotions packed up. Shock had me sinking to the floor. I thumped down on my ass like a drunk who'd lost his balance and tried to comprehend that Patrick and his Consortium had been on the way here from where-the-hell-ever with every intention of taking over Broken Heart.

"We were forced to vacate our previous location," said Patrick. "Unfortunately, not all parakind are interested in a kinder, gentler future. We've had problems with a group of vampires who call themselves Wraiths. They destroyed our other facility and forced us to accelerate the timetable for our Broken Heart venture."

"Wow. You're just full of good news," I muttered.

"It doesn't seem real," said Linda. "None of this. It's like we're all dreaming or something. Or maybe we really are dead."

"Nah," said Patsy, fluffing her bleach-blond curls. "If this was heaven there'd be more naked men."

"Stop glaring at me," said Patrick.

Since I had refused to hold his hand, to accept his kiss, and to take his suggestion that we fly to the gymnasium, he was in a snit. Maybe he didn't like walking. It's not like he needed the exercise.

I, however, had gone way past "snit." I was monumentally pissed off.

"You've been buying out the town for months. When you said you meant to come to Broken Heart, you failed to mention that you had your minions already here, buying up property."

"I don't have minions." He looked at me. "How long are you going to stay angry?"

"Years." I pursed my lips. "Maybe a century."

His mouth twitched, but he apparently managed to quell the laugh that threatened. Instead he said, "Fine."

And I said, "Fine."

Then we both shut up and let our silence chill the air to below zero.

After the meeting at my house had ended, I checked on my babies. Stan told me they weren't buying the flu story anymore. Three days was too long to go without seeing their mother, even with all the cool new distractions provided by Stan. If he kept up his gift giving, Santa Claus was gonna have a tough time coming up with appropriate gifts in December.

"If you hadn't called that ridiculous meeting to plan a mutiny—"

"It wasn't a mutiny," I interrupted. "I didn't get to plan anything with all those information bombs you dropped on us. Jerk."

"This is a strange situation for everyone. Vampires cannot have children and it's been centuries since a parent has been Turned."

"Let me guess. Part of the Consortium Code?"

He nodded.

"Lorćan totally blew that rule."

"He's not in his right mind. When he's cured, I guarantee you he'll say penance for centuries. He abhors the idea of hurting innocents."

I stopped walking. "He's changed, Patrick. Maybe the werewolf blood cured the Taint, but he won't ever be the same."

Patrick stopped, too. Then he turned around slowly to face me. We were standing on the soccer field on the left side of the high school. The rich scents of earth and fresh-cut grass weaved through night air. Summertime in Oklahoma. I felt a pang of loss . . . of unbearable sadness. I was never going to see the sun again. Ever.

"No one knows better than I what my brother has suffered," he said. "You're hungry and you need to feed."

I was hungry. Since Patrick hadn't offered me a thigh, I was worried about where I was supposed to get my new icky sustenance. I didn't want to think about a "donor." I crossed my arms and gave Patrick the Look.

"You're being stubborn, Jessica." He scooped me into his arms and rose into the air, the show-off, and we flew over the roof of the gymnasium. He set us down in the back parking lot. I glanced at the area where Emily had been found. Poor sweet thing. Linda was planning a special night memorial for her little sis.

Patrick led me around the huge, white RV. We crossed the lot to a pink camper parked near a copse of pine trees.

"It looks like a big pink Twinkie," I said as Patrick knocked on the metal door.

The door opened and a brassy red head poked out. "It's a 1956 Safari Airstream, honey," said the woman in a sultry Southern twang. "It's been refurbished and customized to my specifications. Hello, Paddy. Here for a nibble?"

Patrick drew me forward and ushered me up the two metal stairs. The lady moved back into the Airstream and sat on a long couch that was made out of pink fuzzy material. A flatscreen TV was suspended on the opposite side. It looked like it could be raised or lowered into the ceiling.

"It's like walking into a room made of cotton candy," I said. Everything was pink. What wasn't pink was . . . well, no, everything was pink. Except me. Patrick. And the lady. But she *was* dressed in a pink muumuu.

"I like pink," said Red. She plucked a chocolate from a ceramic pink bowl and plopped it into her mouth.

"This is Sharon," said Patrick. "She's a donor."

"A donor." I smiled wanly. Then I turned around and headed for the door.

"Love," said Patrick gently, his arm shooting out to stop me. "You must learn to take blood from donors."

"Why do I need a donor?" I asked, knowing I sounded petulant. "I have you."

"I won't always be around."

What? Why the hell not? The very idea that Patrick wouldn't be my . . . uh, whatever-he-was made anguish wrap around me.

He rolled his eyes. "I meant that I will sometimes be temporarily unavailable to you—not that I will leave you to pine for me forever."

"Your ego is the size of Montana," I said. "Pine for you? Not likely."

"She's just nervous, Paddy. Don't worry, hon," said Sharon, her lips pulled into a generous smile. Her eyes sparkled with warmth and sincerity. "I'm used to these neck nibblers."

"No offense, Sharon. But I'd rather have the chocolate," I said.

She laughed and slapped her thigh. "Hell's bells, Patrick! She's the reason you've had me eating these Godiva truffles all day?"

I looked at Patrick. "You're mean."

His black brows formed question marks. Then his lips curled into a smile.

"No, not just mean. Cruel."

"I had her eat truffles for you," he said.

"Are you insane? How is her eating *my* chocolate in any way helpful?"

Sharon chortled. "You might not be able to eat the truffle, sweetie, but you'll taste it. Prob'ly be the best chocolate you ever eat, too."

I looked at Sharon, then at Patrick. "Are you telling me that she's gonna taste like chocolate?"

"Yes."

I crossed my arms. "Puh-lease. You liar. You're just trying to make me bite her and suck her blood."

"Jessica." Patrick managed to infuse my name with affection and impatience. "I'm not lying to you. But even if I was, if you want to continue to live, such as it is, you must learn to drink blood."

"She's been a vamp three days and hasn't had a donor yet?" Sharon studied me with narrowed eyes. "She doesn't look starved."

"I've been sucking Patrick's thigh," I said. "And while you certainly look . . . uh, tasty, I *prefer* his thigh."

"Oh honey, I would, too," said Sharon, laughing. "But as far as I know, Patrick hasn't allowed any thigh sucking since—"

"Sharon." Patrick's expression was shuttered, but a muscle in his jaw ticked. Oh-ho. He was annoyed that Sharon had revealed this tidbit.

"Usually only mates take blood from the femoral artery," supplied the ever-helpful Sharon. "So, kiddies, when's the ceremony?"

Patrick groaned and rubbed his face.

I sat down next to Sharon, o-fount-of-information, and watched her chew on another truffle. "Ceremony?"

She licked chocolate off her plump lips (bitch). "I guess the ceremony part isn't as important as the mating. You guys skipping it? Too bad. I love a good wedding."

Chapter 8

"Wedding!" I jolted to my feet and poked Patrick in the chest. "What the holy hell is going on? We haven't even had *sex* yet and we're getting married?"

"Stan told me that you claimed Patrick," said Sharon.

I watched Patrick send another shut-up look to the redhead. She shrugged and ate another truffle.

The honeysuckle thing? Well, shit-a-brick. How was claiming Patrick different from claiming my kids? I swear to heaven, if somebody didn't give me Vampire 101 right now, I was going to remove dangly bits. Starting with Patrick's. I crossed my arms and glared at him.

"Remember that I explained the three steps of a binding? Word-giving could be construed as . . . well, a wedding," said Patrick.

"Hmph," said Sharon. "Did you know that the numbers three and seven are sacred to vampires? There are seven vampire sects."

"Seven sacred sects," I repeated. "Say that three times fast."

"How about I spank you instead?" asked Patrick in a benign tone that belied the flare of irritation in his gaze.

"Only if you tie me to a bed and use a paddle."

His silver eyes went molten. Uh-oh. Me and my big smart-aleck mouth. "I . . . uh, sorry. I didn't mean that. I saw *Secretary* a few too many times. I'm impressionable."

He stared at me with that inscrutable gaze until heat swept my cheeks and my heart hammered. God knew what Patrick had experimented with during his really, really long life. I would've never thought it possible, but had sex gotten boring for him? What had he done to liven things up in the ol' bedroom? Did I want to know?

Yes. Yes, I did.

Erotic tension weaved around us. Patrick's eyes were beautiful. I wanted to know what secrets lay in the silver depths, what sorrows he'd suffered, what joys he'd known. It was as if *he* were the chocolate I couldn't taste, the one thing on the whole planet I couldn't have . . . and had always craved. What the hell was wrong with me? I was mentally waxing poetic and I was getting really hungry. And not for Sharon.

"Y'know," said Sharon. "I really don't want to witness step three. If y'all wanna come back later . . ."

"Please, Jessica. Take sustenance."

"I don't know how to do it," I whined.

He slipped past me and seated himself next to Sharon. She looked from him to me then sighed. "Y'all got it bad, don't you?"

"Got *what*?" I challenged.

"Not my business now, is it?" Sharon closed her eyes then dropped her head back. "Hell's bells. Let's get this show on the road." Her red hair slid away, revealing a throat as pale as cream. Well, okay. I admit it: She had a nice neck. Her scent wafted to me. Cotton candy. Yeah, it figured she'd smell that way. Seemed like every person I scented reminded me of food I could never eat again.

"It's instinctual, love. Every animal knows how to hunt, how to feed. You do, too. With donors, the best way to drink is when they're sitting, that way they're supported. If you have to do it standing, you hold tight to their shoulders, but not too tight. You can hurt them without meaning to because you're very strong. Every human reacts differently to blood-taking, but for the most part, they get woozy."

"Like when you go to the Red Cross to donate blood."

"Exactly."

"So after I drink my fill, do I offer Sharon some Kool-Aid and a chocolate-chip cookie?"

Patrick laughed and his lips quirked into a sexy smile. "Donors know how to recover. If you have to take from a non-donor, make sure you take only what you need, that your victim is in a safe place, and that you do a memory-wipe."

"How do you do a memory-wipe?"

"You look into the human's eyes. Once you have his attention, you tell him that he won't remember you. That he wasn't feeling well and decided to sit down. It's sorta like instant hypnotism."

I considered his words. "Huh. I guess I'll have to practice."

"You'll do fine, love." He opened his mouth and I watched, fascinated, as his fangs emerged. My own fangs extended as a rush of . . . I could only call it lust . . . washed over me.

Then he dipped toward Sharon.

"Wait! Aren't you supposed to put her under a spell or something?"

"With donors, we don't have to use trickery. Our fangs inject what amounts to anesthesia into the skin, numbing the area pierced."

He bent to Sharon's throat.

"Wait! Aren't you gonna make her all bloody and yucky?"

Patrick shot me a look of disbelief.

"Hel-*lo*. I'm a mother. Cleaning up blood is the worst."

"Our saliva contains an enzyme that helps the wound heal almost instantly. I promise you that Sharon will not be all bloody and yucky."

He gazed at me and waited. I gazed back at him and smiled. After a few seconds, he once again leaned down and, with open mouth, grazed Sharon's flesh.

"Wait!"

He let Sharon flop out of his embrace and roared, *"WHAT?"*

"I don't like you biting other people."

His annoyed expression melted into confusion. Then he grinned. "It makes you jealous?"

"No." *Yes.* I wiggled a get-over-here finger at him. "I'll stick my fangs into her neck, okay?"

"I thought you wanted me to show you."

"I can figure it out."

"I don't mind. I've nibbled on Sharon before."

"Patrick, get your lips away from her."

Sharon's head snapped up. "That's enough! I don't mind being a donor, but I'm not a booby prize. Now, either someone feed on me or get your asses out of here. *Survivor* comes on in ten minutes and I ain't missing the tribe merge because you two can't decide who's gonna eat."

"I don't think *food* should *talk,*" I snarked.

"If you don't want a truffle stuffed into your eye socket," Sharon retorted, "you'll mind that sassy tone."

My ire faded. *The Royal Bitch rides again.* Sheesh. Who said vampires didn't get PMS? "Sorry, Sharon," I said meekly.

"It's all right. Now sit down and drink a pint."

Patrick switched places with me. I settled close to Sharon and watched as she once again bared her neck. Was I really going to slobber on her delectable throat?

Patrick kneeled at my feet. "Go on, love."

I wrapped one arm around Sharon's shoulder and bent over her. It was damned unnerving to lean forward with giddy anticipation . . . to instinctively know where to put my fangs . . . to sink my teeth into the pale skin of this stranger.

But I did it.

Her blood flowed into my mouth. I swallowed convulsively, but truthfully, I didn't want to taste it. It was warm and thick, the consistency of tepid soup. After a moment or two, I allowed myself to think about the taste. And y'know, it was good. Different from

Patrick's, but good. Delicious and sweet. I sucked and gulped and delighted. Chocolate-flavored blood. Not just chocolate, but champagne truffles. *Oh God.* Willy Wonka's most clever creations had nothing on this babe. I moaned and held her tighter and sucked on her neck some more.

"That's enough," said Patrick.

No. It wasn't enough. It would never be enough. I drank more. I felt powerful and happy and sated.

"Jessica!"

I was yanked backward by my ponytail. My fangs popped free. "Hey! I'm not done!"

"You only take what you need. *Chocolate addict,*" he accused.

Since he still held my hair in an iron grip, I could only look longingly at Sharon's beautiful neck. The two bloody points closed in seconds, leaving twin trails of crimson on her throat. I wanted to lick 'em away, but she swiped a hand over the closed wound.

She looked at me in disgust. "First timers," she slurred. Then her eyes rolled back into her head. She slumped sideways onto the couch, tipping over the bowl of truffles. Little chocolate balls rolled onto the pink fuzzy carpet. But I no longer cared about the treats. I had Sharon! Yummy, yummy Sharon. I reached for her arm, but Patrick pulled me to my feet.

"You've had enough." He took me out of the Airstream. He wrapped his arms around my waist and we flew upward.

"But you didn't taste her. She's . . . she's . . . scrumptious."

"As are you."

We landed on the gymnasium's roof. I traipsed in the direction of Sharon's abode, but Patrick grabbed my wrist and spun me around. "You've got blood on your face," he said.

He dragged me into his arms and licked my mouth. Yeah. *Licked. My. Mouth.* He nibbled on the corners and suckled here and there. *Hoo-wee.* And I thought sucking on Sharon's neck had been fun.

"Fun," Patrick said as he wrenched his lips from mine. *"Fun?"*

"Quit bitching about my adjectives. And stay out of my head." I grabbed him by the shoulders and pulled him close. He gathered me into his embrace with what I thought was a tad too much reluctance.

"Jessica, you are the most exasperating woman I've ever had the misfortune to meet."

"Bite me."

"See what I mean?"

"I really mean it. Bite me." I felt an overwhelming need to be bitten. I wanted to feel his teeth pierce my flesh and drink from me. It was an inclination I couldn't explain. It was just there—pulsing and greedy and urgent.

He shuddered. Then his arms tightened around me and his head fell to my shoulder. "No, love."

Lifting his head slowly, as if it were an anvil instead of his thick-headed skull, he released me and backed up a couple of steps. "We have a lot to discuss."

"Yeah. You keep saying that." I plopped onto the tar-and-gravel roof and wrapped my arms around my knees. My butt protested the uncomfortable spot, but I was staying put. "Give me the four-one-one."

He stared blankly down at me.

"Information," I clarified. "Tell me what the hell is going on."

"Ah." He sat down cross-legged, facing me. Our knees were inches apart. "Most of those who are Turned get what Stan calls the Basic Package. Strength, speed, psychic abilities, hunting, and feeding instincts. The full body makeover." He grinned at me. "Not that you needed any improvement, *a thaisce.*"

"Ooooh. You get points for that one."

His grin widened. His gaze meandered around my chest for a while until I cleared my throat. He lifted his eyes to mine, his playful smile gone. Heat smoldered in that gorgeous silver gaze. My skin prickled in sudden awareness as lust skittered into my belly. "Now . . . every vampire can trace his or her lineage to one of seven original families. When a human is Turned, they gain the blood of the Sect—depending on which Family the vampire belongs to.

"A binding can be performed between vampires of any Family. Believe it or not, Jessica, there is still a class system within the vampire community. The older your blood, the older your connection to a Family, the more power and status and wealth you have. Status matters within the Families. A Turn-blood who is created by an ancient has more status than a Turn-blood created by a new Master."

So this was Patrick's nice way of saying new Turn-bloods like me were considered mere peasants. Generational wealth vs. nouveau riche. No wonder Nasty Nara looked at me like I was gum stuck to her Jimmy Choos. I rolled my eyes. "Yeah. Like I care about that crap."

"You should also know that not every human makes the transition." He looked at me, his gaze unrelenting and sharp, so that I would understand the importance of what he was telling me.

"What happens to those who don't Turn?"

"Most die. Some . . . don't. The closest approxima- tion to what they become is a zombie. They are eating machines. They have no intelligence, no conscience, no emotions."

"You're kidding." I knew he wasn't, but I just didn't know how much more I wanted to learn about this new world I lived in. "But most humans make the Turn, right?"

He shook his head. "No. Maybe one in ten makes it."

"There were eleven," I said faintly. "You thought only one or two of us would Turn."

Despite the odds, the Consortium had tried to save us all. They could've buried us, maybe taken care of our families in some way, good or bad, and gone on with their plans to convert Broken Heart to Weirdsville. I figured Patrick had something to do with that decision. I was grateful I was still walking around and I reckon I had him to thank. "You think we all Turned because of who bit us."

Patrick nodded. "The lycanthrope blood has obvi- ously changed Lor in some indefinable way. I'm wor- ried about him. I don't know why he's hiding from us." He looked at me. "He didn't kill Emily."

I said nothing, but I figured Lorćan hadn't turned himself in because he wasn't in any condition to do so. If he was a beast still in killing mode . . . well, no one was safe in Broken Heart.

"He's not the only danger," Patrick admitted. "We have to worry about the Wraiths, too. Chances are good that they know we're here. They may be plotting against us . . . and I have to tell you, a second strike could cripple us seriously enough that our plans for Broken Heart will be abandoned." He rose to his feet and helped me to mine. "I need to teach you to fight."

"Fight?" I blinked at him, confused. "You want to fight?"

Patrick stretched out his arms, his hands half-fisted. I watched as two small swords materialized.

"Are they made of gold?" I asked in awe.

"Yes. They're made of the purest gold and were crafted by my grandmother with *sidhe* magic," said Patrick. "They're called Ruadan swords. They are very powerful, very dangerous. And they are yours."

"Patrick . . . no." It was a weak protest. I wanted the swords. They were beautiful, and I felt drawn to them. Still . . . "I don't know what to do with those things. The most dangerous blade I've ever wielded was a butter knife. I'm guessing these aren't used for cutting ham sandwiches or weeding my garden."

He laughed. "Well . . . you could do weeks of training with these, practice lopping off fake heads for hours and hours, or. . . ."

"Or what?"

"Ever seen *The Matrix*?"

"Duh. I'm a lifetime member of the Keanu Reeves fan club."

Patrick rolled his eyes. "I was thinking about how information got downloaded into Neo's brain."

"You mean you can just . . . zap! And I'll know how to use these?"

He nodded. "You have strength, speed, and flight. Once you know how to use the swords, you'll kick serious ass."

"What are you waiting for? Get on with it."

Patrick handed me the swords. Then he touched my temples with his forefingers and stared deeply into my eyes. When he said "download" he wasn't kidding. Everything I needed to know was shot into my mind like a movie playing in extreme fast-forward. When he was finished, he looked at me. "Just promise you'll practice every day."

"Yes, Mom," I said. I felt the energy that pulsed between my palms and the metal. Even with the knowledge of how to use them, did I have the gumption?

"Go on. Give 'em a whirl."

I did. I whirled them like I was Buffy the vampire slayer. I slashed and lunged, amazed that I knew the moves, much less that I could use them. "This is killer kewl," I said, borrowing a phrase from Bryan. "Look at me go!"

He laughed. "Yeah. But you still have to practice. Every day."

"Why can't you just download again?"

"I can. But knowledge is more valuable with experience."

I spent a few moments practicing—kicks, leaps, twirls. I couldn't believe how easy it was for me to execute moves I'd only seen in action-adventure flicks. I felt like a Rambo ballerina. ARamballerina. I grinned.

"Jessica."

I stopped messing around and looked at Patrick. His expression was serious and I knew we had more to talk about. Well, shit. "I need a cool belt or something for the swords to fit into."

"I'll see to it."

"Thanks. Okay, Patrick. You're getting ready to tell me something else I don't want to hear," I predicted. "Just spit it out already."

"Your ring . . . the one passed down from Mary Mc-Cree . . . it was my wedding band. My grandmother made two . . . one for me and one for my wife. Two *fede* rings gifted to us on our wedding day."

"I'm still amazed your granny knows how to do metal work. That's not a skill most grandmothers have." My voice shook and I couldn't stop its betraying tremble. Why did it bother me to know that Patrick had been married? The man had lived for four thousand years; he was bound to have some prior relationships.

"My grandmother, Brigid, is very . . . unorthodox." He grinned then the smile slipped away. "Remember when I told you that it was foretold that the one who wore my ring was my soul mate?"

"Yeah?" If my heart could go thuddy-thud, it would've been trying to leap out of my chest right about now.

"I was once a mortal. A simple farmer in Ireland. Well, I was part *sidhe,* so I had some magical skills. But Lor was really the one who had talent as a sorcerer." He shook his head as if doing so would dissipate the memories. "My wife, Dairine, was killed and I was Turned. After a few decades had passed, my father predicted that only my soul mate would be able to wear the rings. Up until then, I had worn them on a chain around my neck. I couldn't bear the thought of anyone else wearing Dairine's *fede* . . . so I asked Brigid to melt it and re-craft it as a coin. The other, mine . . . I threw it into the ocean."

"How did Mary McCree end up with it, then?"

He shook his head. "I don't know. I only know . . . when I drained you for the Turning, that you were meant for me."

"You're a piece of work, you know that? I can't respond to that assumption. Bryan and Jenny don't even know that I'm . . . I'm . . . life challenged!" Fury whirled through me, a tornado of fear and anxiety. "Oh gawd. What about the honeysuckle thing?"

"You've claimed me." He shrugged. "It's a mark of possession. Any vampire who knows where to look will see the mark. If we don't bind, the mark will fade."

"My kids. The same thing happened."

"That is different," said Patrick. "They're mortals. You've marked them and they will remain under your protection for as long as they live."

God, that cut at me in a way nothing else could. My babies. My sweet mortal babies. I chewed on my lip and tried to settle my thoughts. I really should've studied the files about vampires and the Consortium that were in my PDA. I knew how to turn on the little machine and tap buttons with the stylus. But I hadn't used it for much other than a paperweight.

"What you want to know is not in there," said Mr. Mind Reader.

"I would like to kill you," I said cheerfully. "You brought a creature into our town that sucked the blood out of eleven people and brutally killed Emily. *Shut up.* I'm not in the mood to debate Lorćan's mental state." I paced. My flip-flops crunched on the gravel-strewn rooftop. "Then you inform us that you and your pals have been planning to take over Broken Heart for a while. And now you're telling me that I'm your mate."

"All that is true." He looked at me. Do you know he had the *cajones* to look all cute and vulnerable and sorry? Goddamn it. I wanted to kick his ass.

"I can't deal with this," I said, my voice tight. I felt the press of tears behind my eyes, which was weird because I couldn't freaking cry, and a riot of emotions squeezed my insides. "It's just too much. Limit reached. Got it?"

"Yes." He looked as if he wanted to touch me, to comfort me.

I couldn't bear that restrained tenderness . . . so I rose into the air and flew away.

Chapter 9

I landed on my driveway next to the RV that still housed Damian and crew. I had yet to actually meet Damian, but maybe his ability to remain out of sight was part of his talents as a security specialist.

I trudged up the driveway, my thoughts weighing heavy. I was tired of thinking and of worrying. That's what I did all the time as a mother and I just wanted to cave in on myself. Sometimes, when I was alone, that's exactly what I did.

With the night stretching ahead of me and no other distractions, I thought I might clean out the basement. It was filled with leftovers from life with Richard. After he moved out, I had vacillated between angry bursts of energetic cleaning and packing his shit and long sad bouts of curling up in bed and weeping. I managed okay with the kids. At least, I thought I had. It was hard on them to lose their full-time father. They watched a man they once believed was devoted to his family turn his love and attention to a woman who was not their mother.

I had to give Rich some credit. He tried to maintain his relationship with Jenny and Bryan. And if I was honest, he tried to be more than civil with me. But how did a dad who used to come home every night and spend every weekend with them keep connected with children on a two day a week schedule?

They knew that Charlene's baby was their half brother. Richard and I argued a lot about that connection. I still resented that he'd made a baby with Charlene. A baby who would never know his father. That thought stopped me cold. I stood at the concrete path that ribboned to the front porch, staring blindly at the recently trimmed hedges. Rich Junior would never know his daddy. Not ever. At least Jenny and Bryan had memories and pictures and keepsakes. How cruel and petty of me was it to deny that little boy the only other link he might have to his dead father?

Wasn't this a night for crappy revelations? I had to think about the situation. I caused the people in my life no amount of frustration because I was, as my mother said, "one who mulled too much." I liked to roll things around in my head before I made a decision.

I walked up the concrete path. My gaze traced the fancy scrollwork that looped the eaves. That porch, with its flower boxes and big white swing, was the reason I fell in love with the house. It was a Victorian two-story, one that had been lovingly cared for by the previous owner. Like most houses in the neighborhood, it was almost 100 years old. Most of the residents were from generations of people who lived and died in these homes. Most of us could trace back our roots to the town's beginnings. My ancestor Sean

McCree had been one of the first farmers to sow wheat and slop hogs and eke out a living from the Oklahoma soil.

Now, these houses were all sold to the Consortium and would soon be home to the first generations of who-knew-what.

I wasn't sure how I felt about that. Or about being one of the who-knew-what things that now resided in Broken Heart.

Lingering on the steps, my hands still clutching the gorgeous, deadly swords, I thought about being a vampire. I didn't know a whole lot about my "condition." I hadn't really had time to figure out what I could or couldn't do. Hmm. The teeth thing . . . could I make that happen without being hungry? Yeah. Figuring out how to extend those fangs would be an excellent way to scare mortals into doing my bidding. I chuckled at the idea of forcing some schmuck to do dishes and mop floors.

"Okay, fangs . . . activate!" I ran my tongue over my teeth. No go. "Uh . . . extendeth thy fangs noweth?"

Still fangless. I thought about what it was like to chomp on Sharon's neck, the way her warm blood tasted of chocolate. *Oh . . . ecstasy, your name is Sharon.*

I felt a rush of heat through me. I felt the slight splitting of my gums, the extension of the sharp incisors. I poked at the fangs with my tongue. Ouch. Those babies were sharp.

A gasp interrupted my experiment. I met the horrified gaze of my daughter, Jenny. Framed in the front door, her face pale and her eyes wide, she held Mr.

Fluffykins in a tight grip. The tattered bunny only made the journey from her dresser to bed when she was having nightmares.

"Jenny," I said. "Are you okay, honey?"

She whirled around. The door thudded shut behind her.

Crap. Crap. *Crap.* I entered the house and hurried up the stairs. This isn't how I wanted to break the news to my children that I was not only dead, but that I was on a blood-only diet.

Jenny wasn't in her room. I didn't think she'd be in mine, either, but I checked. Nope. That left the Pit. I tossed the swords onto my bed and hurried out. As I approached Bryan's closed bedroom door, I heard my daughter crying. It sounded like she stood next to me sobbing rather than ten feet away in a room with a closed door. It was easy to eavesdrop on their conversation.

"Mom's not a monster," I heard Bryan say. "She's grumpy sometimes—"

"Not like that!" cried Jenny. "She's a real monster. That's why we never get to see her. Those people have us locked up and will never let us go and will use our brains for experimentation and . . . and . . . they killed her and put a robot in her place."

I heard Bryan sigh. "I thought you said she was a monster."

"She's a robot monster."

Okay, seriously. Jenny was not watching the Sci Fi Channel anymore. I paused. Then again, I was getting ready to admit that I was something far more frightening than a robot or the boogeyman.

I knocked on the door and opened it.

Jenny was sitting on Bryan's bed, her back to the wall, her knees drawn in a protective way, clutching Mr. Fluffykins in a death grip. She was dressed in her Powerpuff Girls nightgown. Her bare toes, recently painted blue, peeked out from under the hem. Bryan sat next to her, patting her knee, his sleepy expression a mixture of concern and annoyance. He looked up at me, obviously relieved that I had arrived to take his sister off his hands.

"Sheesh, Mom. She's totally freaked out. Says you had red eyes and fangs and swords."

Crud. She'd seen the swords. I swiped my tongue across my upper teeth, relieved to note that my incisors had retracted. I glanced in the mirror above Bry's cluttered dresser. My eyes weren't glowing red, but they did look haggard.

"Jenny, baby. C'mere."

"No!" She scuttled closer to her brother.

Bryan looked down at his sister in surprise, and then at me. "Stop being a butthead," he admonished Jenny, but without his usual rancor. His arm went around her and she huddled against him, her accusing gaze locked on to me.

Knowing that my baby was scared of me ripped me to shreds. I willed myself not to cry. Even without the ability to produce tears, giving in to the desire for a nice, dry cry would make the situation worse.

"I'm not a monster," I said, in a reassuring voice. "Or a robot." I smiled.

Jenny did not smile back. "You're not my mommy."

"Jenny!" She flinched at the censure in my tone.

Damn it. I tamped down on my temper. She was scared and lashing out. I was the adult here. I was the protector. "I have to tell you both something. Something very important."

"I want my mommy!" wailed Jenny.

Bryan's eyes were as round as plates. He absently rubbed his sister's shoulder. He looked confused and no longer sure that his sister was telling a tale. I noticed they'd both managed to squirm farther away from me. My heart rippled with pain. I was a vampire. I couldn't change that fact any more than I could change the color of the sun. An object I would never see again with my own eyes. God in heaven. What had I done?

Nothing. You had no choice. I gave you no choice. Tell them that, love. Tell your children I am the monster.

Patrick! For once, I wasn't irritated that he was in my mind. I felt comforted and strengthened and I realized that he was somehow infusing me with those feelings. *Do you really think I would tell my babies this whole situation is your fault? The next time I see you, I'm slapping the shit out of you.*

He laughed. The low sound filled my head, a joyful echoing that made me feel better. *The next time you see me, I will give your hands something more pleasant to do.*

A sensual thrill zipped up my spine. *You're so annoying!*

You have no idea. I felt his playfulness shift into a solemn tone. *Tell your* clann *that I am sorry about what happened. I am sorry that they will be in pain and discomfort as they deal with their new lives. Even so,* a thaisce, *I will never be sorry that you are mine.*

Hel-lo. Who says I'm yours?

"Uh, Mom?"

Patrick had closed his mind to mine. One day, I was gonna figure out how to do that, too. He poked around enough in my head without me knowing it.

I looked at Bryan and found him staring at me with a funny expression on his face.

"You look different," he said.

"I know." I heard the pounding of his heart and of Jenny's. Those little organs were beating a mile a minute. Fear rolled off my kids as they gaped at me.

"I'm not a monster," I said, looking at Jenny. She met my gaze, but still seemed distrustful. And she was so scared. *Oh sweet baby girl. It's okay.* "But something very bad happened to me . . . and because it did, I've changed."

Bryan frowned. "You mean literally, right? Not emotional, but real. Something physical."

I raised my eyebrows, surprised at Bryan's intuitiveness. And that he knew how to use "literally" in a sentence.

The time had come to tell them the truth. I squared my shoulders and looked at Bryan and Jenny. Then, I admitted, "I'm a vampire."

Chapter 10

Bryan and Jenny looked at each other, then at me, then at each other again.

They burst into laughter.

While this reaction was certainly preferable to screaming and wailing, it was disconcerting. And weirdly unsatisfying.

"I'm serious. I'm a vampire. I'm even one of Seven Sacred Sects."

The tongue twister brought on fresh gales of merriment. Bryan brushed his sister's hair behind her ear. "See, Jenny? She's just playing a trick on us."

For all her giggling, I noticed that Jenny hadn't moved away from her brother's protection. I was nonplussed. How did I convince them I was a vampire without scaring the crap out of them? How did I tell them I was one of the undead . . . that I would never grow old and never change appearance? That I would outlive them?

These worries cut me to the very quick. Maybe my

kids sensed the change in my mood because their laughs faded.

"Were you really sick, Mom? Are you sure you feel better? You look so pale."

Bryan's solicitous comments were surprising. In typical male fashion, he eschewed illness, particularly mine. Like most men, Bryan chose to growl and fuss rather than nurture and show compassion.

At a loss to explain everything that had happened since Wednesday night, I decided it would be better to wait for the Saturday night meeting. At least then all the parents would be together with Consortium members . . . and Patrick would be there. I wouldn't be alone, floundering my way through explanations.

"Why don't you two go back to bed? We'll talk about this tomorrow."

"Will you get up in the morning with us?" asked Jenny in a polite little voice she reserved for Sunday school teachers and boys who doubted her ability to throw a baseball.

"No. I . . . uh . . ."

"Dr. Stan is taking us on a picnic," she said in the same awful tone. "Damian promised to catch me a frog."

I heard her message. *If you won't be there then how can we count on you? You've let us down. How can we trust you? You've abandoned us, just like Daddy.*

"Jenny, cut it out. You're acting stupid." Bryan yawned. "I'm going to bed. Get out of my room, squirt."

"I want to stay with you."

"No way."

"Please, Bryan. I don't want to go out with . . . *her.*"

Hurt was a lightning strike in my heart. I tried to tell myself she was just upset, but still . . . I was her mother. She should never doubt my love. Never.

Before I could decide what to do, I felt an alteration in the air. A silver mist formed, shimmering into a neck-biting gorgeous male. Patrick. He stood next to the bed, looking at the children. "You will not remember me," he commanded softly. "Neither of you saw your mother this night. Sleep, *clann*, and enjoy wonderful dreams."

The kids closed their eyes, slumped against each other, and fell into an immediate, deep sleep. Sheesh. Why hadn't I thought about doing that? I had the ability.

"You're still getting used to your powers," said Patrick. "Once you learn how to use your new skills, they will become second nature."

Patrick looked at Jenny and to my amazement, my little girl rose into the air, Mr. Fluffykins dropping from her loose grip. As she drifted toward me, Bryan sprawled onto his stomach and snored lightly.

I wrapped my arms around the floating Jenny and buried my face into her hair. Terror ripped through me. I never wanted to lose my children. How did you survive such a thing?

Day by day. Moment by moment. Sometimes, you do not get by at all. You wish for death. You wish for a second chance. You beg God and bargain with the Fates and in the end, you understand that your heart will always feel empty, that your soul will never heal from the wound.

Oh Patrick.

He looked at me, those terrible memories still in his eyes, and offered a small smile. "It was hurting you to talk to your children. It was not possible for you to enlighten them and protect them."

Patrick's gaze caressed Jenny's face. "Aine had seen her second winter before . . . ah, before she left this world. For her birthday that year, I carved her a horse from a *leamhán sléibhe*—a Wych Elm."

"She wasn't your only child?"

"No, but she was my only daughter. My sons were older." He looked at me. "Three. I had three children."

Patrick had been a father. And he still mourned his babies. My heart broke for him and I wanted to weep.

"I don't need your tears, love." His fingers brushed my cheek. "But I thank you for your grief, for your understanding. Go on, now. Put your daughter to bed."

"Will you stay?"

It's not wise to stay near the one I want so very much and yet cannot have.

He glimmered silver for an instant.

Then he was gone as if he'd never stood there.

For the first time in three days, I tucked my little girl into bed. It always amazed me how the mundane details of life were the ones that meant so much.

Her room was tidy. Jenny was naturally fastidious, which meant she never had to be told to clean her room and she always had an opinion about the cleanliness of other rooms.

I pulled the pink bedspread up to her chin and stroked her alabaster cheek. There was nothing in the world more enchanting than a child asleep. Just like there was nothing in the world more frustrating than a child awake.

After I made sure her glass of water was full and the night-light was still on, I retrieved Mr. Fluffykins from Bry's room and left the stuffed bunny near Jenny's shoulder.

I resisted the urge to climb into bed with her and cuddle. Both my kids were affectionate, though Bryan often pretended to merely tolerate hugs and smooches. But day by day they needed me a little less. I felt that separation keenly and yet, I also encouraged those seeds of independence. Reluctantly, I might add.

I kissed Jenny's forehead and left her bedroom. I wandered downstairs. I no longer felt like going into the basement to purge the boxes gathering dust. Did vampires have garage sales or give stuff to Goodwill?

Probably not.

Restless and bored, I flopped onto the couch, and reached down to grab the remote from the coffee table. Instead, my hand glided across the parchment pages of an open book.

A book that was not mine. It looked like a medieval text—the kind only seen behind glass in museums. *Legends of the Seven Ancients, Ruadan the First* was written in calligraphy at the top. Around the edges of the story were beautifully inked pictures of creatures I'd once thought were mythical. The writing was precise and straight—the hand of a thoughtful man. I traced one of the creatures—a male fairy with gossamer wings who wore a green tunic and a mischievous smile.

Well, then. There was nothing left to do but read . . .

Chapter 11

Legends of the Seven Ancients
Ruadan, The First
As written by Lorćan, Filí don Tuatha de Danann

Once there was a great warrior-magician whose name was Ruadan. To know a man, you must know his story, and all the stories of men begin with their mothers . . .

Ruadan was the son of magician-healer Brigid and warrior-prince Bres.

Brigid was born the daughter of Dagda, all-father to the Tuatha de Danann, and of Morrigu, the crow queen. Bres was born the son of Fomhoire prince Elatha and of Tuatha de Danann princess Eriu. So, the families bound together their children so that earth and sea magic might rule as one.

The Fomhoire were of the night. They were cunning warriors who knew the secrets of sea magic. Some called them deamhan.

The Tuatha de Danann were of the day. They were wise magicians who had mastered earth magic. Some called them sidhe.

Many believed Bres would bring peace to the troubled nations. When he became of age, he married Brigid to solidify his bond with the Tuatha de Danann. In time, he was made King of Eire.

But Bres was a foolish ruler, ignorant of his people's suffering and unjust in his judgments. The sons of Tuatha de Danann rose up against him and took his crown, banishing him. In defeat, Bres returned to his father's kingdom.

Brigid sought to soothe her husband's wounded ego. "Why does a prince of the Fomhoire need to rule an island?" she asked of him. "You are Elatha's son! Will you not be king of a continent?"

Yet, Bres was too prideful to turn away from the dishonor shown to him by the Tuatha de Danann, no matter how deserved. He vowed to take back what had been taken from him and to once again rule Eire.

Brigid wanted peace between the Fomhoire and the Tuatha de Danann. Without her husband's knowledge, she sought her mother's council. Morrigu foresaw the future and told her daughter the truth: The Tuatha de Danann would triumph over the Fomhoire, but not before Brigid lost her husband and their sons, Ruadan, Iuchar, and Uar.

"If Bres wishes to die in a war of his own making, I cannot stop him," said Brigid. "But he will not have my sons!"

Brigid extracted a blood oath from Bres that he would not send their sons to war until they wed and sired children. Brigid hoped that the war would end before the oath's conditions could be met, but as their sons grew into manhood, the battle for the Isle of Eire raged on.

Though a mother may hope no harm befalls her children, Brigid was not a fool. Her father had taught her the skill of smithing gold, and so she forged two half-swords made of the precious metal. The handles were bejeweled with precious stones and the blades enchanted with sidhe magic. Never had such weapons been seen by either Fomhoire or Tuatha de Danann.

When their eldest son, Ruadan, celebrated his sixteenth year, Brigid gifted him with the swords. And Bres gifted him with a Fomhoire bride whose name was Aine.

Afraid Ruadan would impregnate his young wife and thus fulfill the blood oath, Brigid brewed an infertility potion. Every eve, she put the potion into Aine's tea and sat with her, chatting, until every drop was drained. For twelve moons, no children were born.

Bres grew impatient with his eldest son's lack of heirs. He asked the crow queen for fertility magic, that Ruadan might father a child. But Morrigu, who prospered in turmoil and ruin, offered not a spell, but a secret: She revealed her daughter's treachery to Bres.

Infuriated by the duplicity of his wife, Bres secreted away Iuchar and Uar in a mountain fortress, telling Brigid that the boys would be educated by holy men. Instead, his sons were given into the care of the best Fomhoire warriors, who taught them every needful thing about war.

Another twelve moons passed. Now, Iuchar and Uar

were old enough to wed and Bres let them each pick a bride from twenty virgins stolen from the Tuatha de Danann. Within a cycle, the women bore their husbands each a daughter.

Triumphant, Bres returned home with Iuchar, Uar, their wives, and their daughters. Grief-stricken by Bres's sedition, Brigid entered her rooms and wept for a sennight, for now Morrigu's prediction about her children's fates would come to pass.

Ruadan's wife fell into despair. Here, the lesser sons of Bres had fathered children on enemy women, and yet she remained childless. Aine refused to eat and to drink and took to her bed, allowing only the comfort of her husband. Without the potion working its magic on her womb, she soon conceived. Ruadan would not leave his wife to bear their children alone and so, Bres, Ruadan, Iuchar, and Uar spent the next nine moons planning campaigns against the Tuatha de Danann.

The Tuatha de Danann had a magical well that instantly healed their warriors so long as they had not suffered a mortal blow. Created by a goldsmith named Goibniu, the well was safeguarded by spells and men alike. "Kill the builder of the well," said Bres to his sons, "and destroy its magic . . . and the Tuatha de Danann will fall."

So it came to pass that Aine bore twin boys, Padriag and Lorćan. Ruadan wept with joy and placed a blessing on his sons, that they should have long, happy lives. Then he and his brothers sailed to the Isle of Eire to fulfill his father's plan and his grandmother's prophecy.

The brothers used stealth and cunning to break

through the defenses of their enemy. While Iuchar and Uar battled those that guarded the well, Ruadan stabbed Goibniu with the fae swords. But Goibniu, though mortally wounded, thrust his spear into Ruadan's chest and felled the warrior.

Iuchar and Uar retrieved their brother and bade their finest warriors to take him home so that Brigid might heal him. When they returned to finish the task set upon them by their father, they were captured and killed. The Tuatha de Danann, fearful the brothers might live again should sea or earth touch them and invigorate their magic, cut the bodies into eight pieces and burned them at eight separate locations on the Isle of Eire so that they might never be resurrected.

Near death, Ruadan arrived in his homeland and was taken to his mother. She used all her magic and healing arts, but could not save her son. The very same night Ruadan breathed his last, Brigid received word of the fates of Iuchar and Uar. She fell to her knees and wailed with such sorrow, that anyone who heard the sounds knew a mother's heart had been rent from her. It is said that Brigid was the first to keen and ever since, so does any woman who suffers the loss of her loved ones.

Morrigu heard the keening of her daughter, so she turned into a crow and flew to the land of the Fomhoire. Though the dark queen craved chaos over tranquility and war over peace, she felt pity for her daughter and offered one chance for Brigid to regain her son.

"Give Ruadan a cup of my blood, but be warned! When he awakes, he will not live as a man, but as a

deamhan fhola. He will never again walk in the light. He will not consume food or drink, but shall siphon the blood of the living. Neither will he have breath nor beat of heart. Never will he sire another child by his own seed."

"Is there no good to be wrought then, Mother?"

"Where there is dark, there is also light. Ruadan will never age. He will heal from even the most grievous of wounds. He will know the thoughts of those he loves. And he will be a warrior none can defeat. He is of the Fomhoire and of the Tuatha de Danann and those skills and magic will always be his to wield."

So blinded by grief was Brigid, so badly did she want her son to live again, that she agreed to her mother's terms. But still, Morrigu was not satisfied.

"Should Ruadan drain a man and replenish him with tainted blood, he shall Turn. Your son will create others and he will rule a master race long after all whom you know and love turn to dust and ash. Even knowing this, will you still give him my blood to drink?"

And again, Brigid agreed without hesitation. Morrigu cut her wrist and bled into a silver goblet. Brigid lifted her son's head, opened his mouth, and poured every drop of her mother's blood into him.

When Ruadan awoke, he was deamhan fhola.

Bres, devastated by the loss of his sons, went himself to the Isle of Eire to wreak vengeance on his enemy, but he, too, was killed. Finally, the Tuatha de Danann triumphed over the Fomhoire, and there came to pass an uneasy peace between their peoples.

But Aine was frightened of the creature her husband

had become and refuted him, calling him demon and eater of flesh. She plotted to kill herself and their infant sons, but Ruadan knew her thoughts and stopped her. He wished only happiness for his family and so, he bartered with Aine. If she returned with his mother to the Isle of Eire and raised their sons as Tuatha de Danann, he would leave them alone for all time.

For twenty-five cycles, Ruadan roamed the Earth to search for his place in it. It is said that he kept journals of his travels and collected great treasures and knowledge. It is also said that he Turned six others in different lands, creating the seeds of the master race foretold by his grandmother.

Then, because he longed to see his family, he broke his promise to Aine and went to the Isle of Eire to visit his sons. He found that Aine had married a fisherman and she lived, if not happily, at least securely, in a little cottage near the sea. Her mind had suffered greatly since their parting, and it had been his mother Brigid, immortal sidhe, who'd kept watch over his sons.

Padriag lived on a simple farm with his wife and their three children. Lorćan had a more spiritual and thoughtful nature and became a draoi-filí. His sons knew that Ruadan was deamhan fhola, but they were not afraid, and welcomed him.

When Aine discovered Ruadan had returned, her sanity completely gave way. She feared his monstrous nature, and she told her husband, who was a suspicious and mean-spirited sort, about the deamhan fhola and how it visited her son's farm every eve. One afternoon, the husband whiled away the hours drinking with his friends and telling them Aine's stories of the deamhan fhola. Made brave by the drink, they went to Padriag's farm to destroy the creature.

Because the men were drunk and riled up by their fear, they dragged out all who were in the house. They burned the building to the ground and, finding no deamhan fhola, decided Ruadan had taken the guise of a human. The villagers tortured Padraig until he collapsed, unconscious. Then the angry villagers killed his wife and children.

When Aine learned what her husband had done, she cursed him and the village, then weeping, threw herself off the cliffs.

Ruadan awoke from his rest and found the destruction of his son's farm and family. As his son passed from the mortal realm, Ruadan drained him, and tearing open the vein in his own neck, forced his son to drink his tainted blood. And so Padraig was Turned.

Ruadan took Padraig to the cave where Lorćan lived and bid him to care for his brother. He instructed Lorćan on the ways of the deamhan fhola, and warned him that his brother was no longer a man, but a creature destined to walk only in the night.

But Lorćan did not heed his father's warnings. When Padriag awoke, he was mad with grief and hunger. He tore open his brother's neck and drained him 'til the point of death. When he realized what he'd done, Padraig saved Lorćan in the same manner Ruadan had saved him.

Now both of Ruadan's sons were deamhan fhola.

Ruadan took his sons from the land of the Tuatha de Danann. He summoned his first six Turn-bloods to a meeting, and they created the Council of Seven. The

Council labored to create laws for their people and bound all deamhan fhola with magic and oath to uphold these laws. Those who broke faith with their Families faced banishment . . . or death.

And so it was that Brigid's son fulfilled her mother's prophecy.

He was the creator of the deamhan fhola.

He was ruler over all.

He was Ruadan the First.

Chapter 12

Had I been able to cry, the first teardrop would've fallen onto the drawing of two red-faced creatures reminiscent of Ninns—the soldiers who did the bidding of evil Lord Sparr in *The Secrets of Droon*.

I closed the book and pushed it away, then lay down on the couch and dry-wept. Patrick had lost everyone . . . his mother, his wife, his children . . . and his dad bestowed a monstrous gift without his consent. What would he have decided if Ruadan had asked him? Would he have gone to the afterlife? Or chosen to live as a vampire?

I wondered what Ruadan might've chosen if Brigid had asked him rather than pour her mother's blood down his throat. Hadn't he, too, been turned into a vampire without the chance to choose his fate?

Ah, but the theme was the same, wasn't it? Parents who loved their children so much they couldn't let them go. How far would I go to save Bryan and Jenny if anything horrible happened to them? What if it was the worst thing ever . . . would I Turn them? Would I save them or doom them? Would I hold on or let go?

I cried a little more. Well, a lot more. After I was finished, I picked the remote up and turned on the TV. I was ready for mindless entertainment. My brain was in full meltdown. And I still felt horribly sad.

An infomercial touted a knife that could cut through a tin can and then slice a tomato. *Click.* Lieutenant Columbo pretended to bumble his way to solving another murder. I watched Peter Falk for a few minutes. *Click.* Another infomercial blared the wonderful qualities of an exercise machine. Hah. *Click.* A horror flick played on the Sci Fi Channel and I watched some muscled no-name actor blow the head off a slimy gray alien. Okay, enough of *that.*

"So, is this what you do with eternity?" I asked the empty room. "Watch bad television. And without any good nibbles to distract me."

I wondered if vampires took donors to the movies. The donors would eat popcorn and drink soda and the vampires would eat nothing and drink donors. Popcorn-flavored blood. I snickered at the idea of inviting Sharon to the Olde Tyme Theatre to be my snack.

After going through all the channels a third time, I settled on *Columbo.* I sighed. I'd have to get a satellite dish or a subscription to Netflix. Then again, with the whole town switching all activities to nighttime, I'd be busy again with mommy duties. We'd have to start over. School would never be the same. And what about the PTA? Everyone Turned, except Charlene and Ralph, had belonged to it. We'd have to change the name to Preternatural Association of Parents. PAP? Uh . . . no.

I wasn't sure how to spend the rest of the night. Either I was stuck watching reruns and infomercials or I had to face the basement and its contents. Or . . . I could procrastinate. It's not like I wouldn't have the time in say, oh, a hundred years, to worry about it.

Patrick? I waited, but didn't receive any response. He'd shut off his mind again and I probably wouldn't hear from him. I thought about his children. His wife. My heart ached for him and for all that he had lost over the centuries.

Patrick? Are you okay?

He didn't answer though I swear I felt a fingertip brush my temple. Maybe it was my imagination. Or maybe it was him, trying to let me know he was there. Or maybe it was nothing at all and being a vampire was making me nuts.

I felt so restless . . . so hollow. Well, damn. I missed Patrick. The only thing I knew for sure was that I lusted like crazy after him. What would it be like to have actual intercourse with Patrick? I'd probably implode.

But man-oh-man, what a way to go.

As I lay on the couch daydreaming about sex with Patrick, the low drone of the television was a constant lullaby. Though I wasn't tired, I felt drowsy. The drowsiness melted into a kind of euphoria. After a moment, I felt almost giddy. Then floating . . . happy . . . free.

When the TV went dead and all the downstairs lights flickered off, I didn't feel compelled to disturb my elation. Despite the sudden and total darkness, I could see perfectly well. Granted, I should've been alarmed at the big, furry man-thing that appeared next to my couch. Huh. How had he gotten into the house?

"You're really tall," I said.

He leaned over me and snarled.

"Phew!" I waved a hand in front of my face. "Two words, honey. *Breath. Mint.*"

His maw opened, saliva dripping from razor teeth, and roared. The garbage-stench of his breath made me gag and the loudness of his roar vibrated through me. On some level, I knew I should be terrified. Yeah. I should've been pissing my freaking pants. *This isn't real,* whispered the soft voice of reason, *you're dreaming. And dreams can't hurt you. Ssshhh.*

"Go away," I murmured. "Bad, bad dream."

The monster's blue eyes flashed with triumph. He lifted a huge, hairy arm and swiped down. The ugly yellowed claws raked open my chest.

Pain ripped through me, but I felt so disconnected, I couldn't comprehend what was happening. I felt a warm sticky liquid splash my neck and face. Oh, right. *My blood.* It splashed him, too, and matted the fur coat he wore.

"That hurts," I pointed out. "I would really appreciate it if you'd stop."

I heard glass shattering and wood snapping. I thought about the French double doors that opened from the breakfast nook onto the patio. Rich had installed those a few years ago. I *loved* those doors. Those were some great freaking doors. Gone now. Such a shame.

A loud, angry roar echoed through the house . . . then ricocheted inside my skull. Heavy footsteps thud-

ded and then I saw another furry creature lope into the
living room. Familiar. Tall, brown, and fanged . . . oh
yeah. That guy. He attacked the one still trying to paw
my flesh into ribbons.

Ssshhh, precious one. You're fine. Everything's okay.
No need to think. No need to worry.

I relaxed as the soothing voice rubbed away my
headache, the throb of my wounds. I was okay. Sucky
dream, that's all.

The two beasts ripped into each other, pounding
with fists, kicking with legs, biting with teeth. It was
like watching two fierce lions battling for the zebra.
Hey, wait a minute. *I* was the zebra. I laughed at my little joke, and felt the rusty flavor of blood fill my
mouth. It dribbled off my lips. Shit. I couldn't lift my
arm to wipe my mouth, either.

I watched, bemused, until the creatures battled their
way out of my line of sight. I heard crashes and growls
and fighting. And lots of roaring. Oh for Pete's sake!
Enough of the roaring, already. Really, those two
should take it outside. How the hell would a bigfoot
pay to replace broken furniture and shredded curtains?

Suddenly dizzy, I felt a distinct POP in my mind.
The rapture wrapping me in a nice, fluffy cloud of in-
difference abruptly dissipated.

Pain roared through me. Horrible, throbbing,
sharp . . . I was bathed in fire. In acid. In broken glass.
And there was a terrible keening that made my head
ache.

Then I realized the long sad noise came from me.

I was screaming.

I bit on my lower lip hard and swallowed those

awful sounds. I mentally sought Bryan and Jenny. Patrick's command to sleep had not been broken. They were safe. Thank God, they were safe. So much for Damian, the bodyguard. So much for any guards. Where the hell was everyone?

It didn't matter. Nothing mattered. My kids were safe. I was ready to let go now. I didn't have to fight anymore. I didn't have to hold on.

"Jessica."

"Bigfoot," I croaked. "I'm sleepy."

"No, Jessica. Stay." He stroked my cheek with the back of his hand. The feel of silky fur against my skin felt so soft, so nice.

"I'm not afraid," I said. "It's okay." That was the truth. The pain had faded into nothingness. I felt like a bubble, about to rise and float away, and I looked forward to the journey.

"Stay," he demanded. *You are Patrick's happiness. I will not let you go.*

Don't bully me. And stay out of my head. You're as bad as your brother.

I rose up, up, up . . . through the ceiling . . . the roof . . . the sky . . . I rushed toward the bright and beautiful stars.

The last sound I heard was the anguished howl of Lorćan O'Halloran.

Jessica. Jessica? Jessica!
What?
Where are you?
I don't know. I'm safe. I'm okay. It's nice here.
Come back.

No.

Come back, love.

I can't. I don't know where I am. I don't know how to return.

I'll guide you, a thaisce.

I don't think I'm supposed to leave.

Please, Jessica. Please come back to me. To Jenny and Bryan. Is t mo shonuachar.

I don't speak Gaelic, you doofus.

Jessica . . . you're my soul mate. Come back to me.

I woke up without opening my eyes. My body felt so heavy, so clunky, I could barely stand to be inside it. I took several deep, cleansing breaths. Wait a minute. I could breathe.

"A dream," I muttered. "Just a dream."

I wasn't a vampire. There'd been no ravaging beast eating citizens for dinner. Broken Heart wasn't turning into a community filled with paranormal residents. I'd had a very realistic, long-lasting nightmare. I was in my own bed, snuggling under my thick, warm comforter, dreaming of the weird and the wild.

Stretching my arms above my head, I slowly opened my eyes.

And looked straight into the face of Satan.

"Aaaaahhhh!"

"So you *are* awake," said the Devil.

"You're a woman." I pointed weakly at her nose, which was closest to me.

"Yes, I'm a woman. It's delightful to know that you recognize gender." She peered at me, her green eyes narrowed. She had skin like fresh cream, the sort of cheekbones most women had to buy, and a full mouth as red as fresh-picked cherries.

Strange gold patterns pulsed on her face. I swear the color shimmering on her flesh seemed alive. But even with the markings on her face, she was utterly gorgeous.

Satan is a woman. She's a tall, tattooed, redheaded woman. And she likes to wear pearlescent white robes. And she has minty fresh breath.

"Padriag has been pacing outside the door since sunset."

"What for?"

"Hmmm." She straightened and I realized how tall she was. Wow.

"Are you an Amazon?"

"I'm a healer." She smiled. "My name is Brigid."

She had a lyrical, soothing voice. Her accent reminded me of Patrick's, but though she was probably Irish, too, I wasn't sure. Brigid . . . that name sounded familiar. Oh, wow. Was she *that* Brigid?

"Are you related to Patrick?"

"Yes." She waved her hand at me to forestall other questions. I realized the gold patterns covered her entire body. They swirled and changed into different symbols and shapes.

"Holy shit. How are you doing that?"

"The *draíocht* senses what spells you need and changes to accommodate your health."

I felt the magic. I didn't know how to describe it. A tingling in the air around me, I guess. As a kid, whenever I got sick, my grandma would arrive with her stock of cures. One thing she always did was rub menthol on my chest. The magic produced by Brigid was like a menthol full-body rub. I looked at the ever-shifting gold designs in total awe. "It's alive? Like a . . . a parasite?"

Her eyebrows arched. "It is a sacred gift, one that I am honored to have and duty bound to use. I will allow Padriag to enter and speak with you. There are many others who wish to see you, too. But they will have to wait."

"My kids? Are they okay?"

"They're fine. They have come in every day and whispered prayers for you."

I felt relieved that Jenny and Bryan were okay. I felt weak and dizzy and very, very thirsty. I scooted around to find a comfortable position. A nap might be in order. What had happened to me? Vague images flashed, but nothing fit together in a way that made sense. Then what Brigid said penetrated my thickheadedness.

"Wait a sec. What do you mean my children came in *every day*?"

My question remained unanswered. Brigid opened the door and beckoned Patrick inside. As he strode across the room, she left and shut the door behind her.

Patrick stood over me, his silver gaze sweeping across my blanket-covered body. Then those eyes settled on my face. He said nothing, just gave me the Inevitable Doom Look until I wanted to squirm all the way under the covers and hide from him.

Instead, I managed to squeak, "Uh . . . hi."

"You will feed."

"I'm fine, thanks for asking." I pouted at him.

"Brigid is the best healer in the world. Of course you

are fine." Then why did he look so damned relieved? What had happened to me? I'd been viciously attacked. Panic wormed through me.

"Stop thinking about what happened," said Patrick. He climbed into bed and gathered me into his arms. "There will be time enough to figure out the details. You will feed now, Jessica."

"You're in my presence for five seconds and you're already bossing me around."

"Get used to it." He cradled my head and adjusted positions so that my mouth pressed on the pulse that beat in his neck. "Take what you need, love."

"What about spontaneous combustion? I can't control myself around you. My lust meter goes off the charts."

"Jessica . . ."

My fangs had already elongated in anticipation of feeding. I punctured the vein and almost moaned when Patrick's blood gushed into my mouth. I drank until my thirst was assuaged. Then, reluctantly, I pulled away. The holes healed instantly; I licked away the tiny dribbles left behind.

"It's not quite as good as the thigh," I said. "But it'll do."

I pushed back so that I could look at his face. He looked so sad. I brushed my knuckles across his cheekbone. "Are you all right? I didn't slurp you dry, did I?"

A small smile curved his lips. "No, love."

"What happened?"

"I don't know." His jaw clenched. "Everyone was glamoured. Damian, the security guards in the front and rear of the house, the kids, and . . . you. The electricity was shorted out. Then you were attacked." His hand burrowed under the covers, under my pajama top, and flattened on my belly. I shuddered at the contact, relishing the warmth of his palm, the coiled strength I felt in the sensual flexing of his fingers against my skin. "I will never shut you out again, *céadsearc*. If I had not closed my mind to yours, I would've known you were in trouble."

"It's not your fault."

"Yes, it is." His seeking hand found the curve of my hip. He traced it with the tip of his forefinger. "I Turned you and it is my duty to protect you. I failed in that. But you are so much more to me, love. We belong to each other. You are my soul and I abandoned you."

"Patrick, please. . . ." I wasn't sure I could think about the whole soul mate thing. I enjoyed how he made me feel, but handing over my heart to another man, to an immortal no less . . . No, I couldn't face that kind of commitment.

"You amaze me, Jessica." The wandering hand found my buttock. He cupped it and squeezed then decided to explore my thigh. "I vow that I will not fail you again."

"Could you stop with the self-guilt trip already? I'm not blaming you. Sheesh." I thought about how Patrick seemed to fall back into formal speech patterns, which also seemed to increase his brogue, when he was emotional. I found it really sexy that he could talk like modern-day guy then go all warrior-king on me.

Or maybe I was just getting hot and bothered by the skirting of his fingers along my inner thigh. A few inches to the left and the man would touch the sweet spot.

"There is one more thing I must tell you," he said in a low voice that sent a sensual thrill zipping up my spine, "and then I will touch your sweet spot."

"Patrick!" I wiggled closer, content to let him touch me. Even though I'd fed, I still felt tired. I knew that feeling exhausted and feeble was probably a bad thing. But I was alive (mostly). Obviously, I hadn't gotten the whole story out of Patrick yet. "Don't keep me in suspense. What's this 'one thing'?"

His hand stilled for a mere second. Then his gaze snared mine. "I would've never thought my brother capable of such brutality. Before he was changed, he would've plunged a knife into his own heart rather than harm an innocent. I know now that the soul of Lorćan is dead. I cannot risk that the creature might hurt you again."

The languorous desire spreading from belly to nipples instantly fizzled. Dread weaved through me. "Oh my God, Patrick. What did you do?"

Chapter 13

"The Consortium council has charged Drake and Darrius with hunting Lorćan—and when they find him, they will destroy him," admitted Patrick in a strained voice.

The dark and painful images of the attack swirled and coalesced until one moment stood out in sharp relief. I gave Patrick the equivalent of a mental brain poke and showed it to him:

"Jessica."

"Bigfoot," I croaked. "I'm sleepy."

"No, Jessica. Stay." He stroked my cheek with the back of his furry hand.

"I'm not afraid," I said. "It's okay."

"Stay," he demanded. You are Patrick's happiness. I will not let you go.

Don't bully me. And stay out of my head. You're as bad as your brother.

The last sound I heard was the anguished howl of Lorćan O'Halloran.

Patrick stared at me, shock and hope etched on his face.

"There were two," I said. "The first one hurt me. Then your brother showed up and saved me."

"I don't understand," said Patrick. "Surely we would've known if there was another lycanthrope in Broken Heart."

"Who cares! If Drake and Darrius are tracking Lorćan, you gotta stop 'em. Then come back and tell me what the hell happened after I passed out and why I feel so wonky."

"A thaisce," he whispered gently. He brushed his lips against mine and sparkled out of sight.

"I've been out a week!" I yelled. "An entire friggin' week?"

After Patrick left, I closed my eyes to take a little nap. And woke up the next night. Once again, Patrick let me feast on his neck until I was sated. Then I was able to sit up without feeling woozy and I no longer felt like baked dog shit. I checked mentally on Bryan and Jenny several times and they were fine. Worried about me. Missing me. But okay.

I wasn't up to seeing them, not yet. I hadn't gotten my balance back, emotionally or physically. And . . . well, I was afraid they'd be scared of me. Scared of what I'd become. I'd been out of their lives for a full-on week. I'm sure they felt abandoned. What would I do to ever make it up to them?

I'd have to think on it later. Right now, Linda and Stan and Drake and Darrius and Brigid and the dark-haired French dude, François, who had watched over

Emily's body, were all in my bedroom. Patrick lounged next to me, his arm loosely draped over my shoulders.

"So how did the your-parents-are-vampires meeting go?" I asked.

"We did it, just like we planned," said Linda. She sat on the end of the bed. Stan hovered behind her like an agitated ghost. "I brought Jenny and Bryan. We explained everything. Took some doing, I tell you. But it's settled now."

"We've started the children on the night schedule," added Stan. "It's not easy for them. I think it'll be better when they return to some sort of routine. We're working on getting a school set up for the fall, but we don't yet have qualified teachers."

"I can't wait to see who shows up for that job." I worried my bottom lip. "I'm sorry I missed Emily's memorial."

"It was a beautiful service," Linda said softly. "She's resting next to Mama now . . . and we've said our good-byes." She sounded stronger, like the old Linda. I was glad for it, too. Then she snorted. "Girl, you about had a memorial of your own. Your man wouldn't let you go. He stuck to you like frosting on a cake." Her gaze met mine. "It was bad, Jessie. It was real bad."

"Yeah. Sorry I scared the bejeebers out of everyone." I sighed. "I'm kinda tired of waking up dead."

Everyone laughed and it broke the tension that had been building among us. We had a lot to worry about—not the least of which was figuring out what to do about the rogue werewolf running around Broken

Heart. If Lorćan was self-aware enough to save my life—he wasn't a mindless beast.

"My friends, we must discuss what happened to Jessica." François pushed off from the wall he'd been leaning on and crossed to the bed. His pale fingers curled around one of the cherrywood posts as his blue gaze met mine and then Patrick's. "You say there were two creatures?"

"It's kinda jumbled up. But there were definitely two creatures." I remembered the flash of his blue eyes, filled with anger and madness, right before he ripped off my skin. "Its eyes were blue. Lor's are silver."

I saw the look that François and Patrick shared before they both looked at Stan. Then Drake and Darrius joined in all the caveman oh-ah-ugh eye language. I could practically hear the Morse code being tapped out among all the males in the room.

It bothered me that I couldn't remember the details of the attack. Maybe it was best that I didn't. Who wanted to remember getting killed for the second time? Reliving the first attack at weird moments was bad enough. Then again, looked at through the perspective of a creature that had been starved, that was beyond control, and that needed to feed until it regained its senses made me understand Lor's behavior. He'd fed on eleven people. But he hadn't killed them. Well, he hadn't meant to kill them. That thing that had attacked me in my living room had murder on his mind—not a quick and convenient dinner.

"Why did all eleven of us Turn?" I asked. Everyone looked at me. I waved my hand impatiently. "Patrick told me most humans don't make the transition to vampire. But Lorćan drained eleven of us. And we all made the Turn. Why?"

"It has to be something to do with the lycanthrope blood transfusion," said Stan. "Ten females and one male . . . so we don't think it's gender related. You're all different blood types. As for DNA . . . none of you are related or have any common genetic factors or flaws."

As Stan attempted to bore us into another universe, I felt an Oprah-worthy aha moment.

"We're all parents," I blurted. "We're all *single* parents."

Stan looked at me, surprised. He seemed to mull over my brilliant observation before he shook his head. "Coincidence. Or laws of probability. Broken Heart has the highest number of single and unwed mothers in Oklahoma. Seems only a matter of odds that he'd get eleven single parents."

"Why *does* Broken Heart have the largest number of unwed mothers in the state?" mused Drake . . . or Darrius. I still wasn't able to distinguish between those two.

"Because it's named Broken Heart, I figured," said Linda. "Maybe people move out here after relationships go bust because they like the irony of it. Maybe they wanted to be reminded why love sucks so they wouldn't fall for it again."

"You think love sucks?" asked Stan, his tone wounded and confused.

"Oh, honey," said Linda, looking over her shoulder to talk to him, "I think I'm too old, too tired, and too dead to worry about falling in love again."

When Linda faced me again, I saw the expression on Stan's face. He was hurt by her words. Well, hell.

"What if we Turned because we are parents?" I asked, partly to distract Stan from becoming too over-wrought.

Stan frowned. "I don't see how it's relevant."

"How many moms and dads have been Turned in the last few hundred years?"

"Not many," admitted François. "It is against the Consortium's Code, though not all vampires follow our guidelines. Even so, rare is the vampire who Turns a mother or father."

"I noticed you didn't say rare is the vampire who *kills* a mother or father."

François shrugged. "Not all vampires share the Consortium's vision."

"Especially the Wraiths," said Patrick. "They want to rule over humans."

"Superiority complex," said Stan, nodding. His gaze strayed to the back of Linda's head. The look of tenderness and longing he directed at my friend reminded me of a puppy's adoration for a soup bone. Oh-ho. *Interesting.* Did Stan really have a thing for Linda? Or maybe he just suffered from hair envy. I bit back a laugh. *Yeah. Right.*

François shook his head. "Ron and his Wraiths cause us more and more problems."

"Ron?" I laughed. "You're kidding. Their leader's name is *Ron*? That doesn't exactly inspire fear, does it?"

"He decided a few decades ago that Ronald was better than Ragnvaldr," said Patrick, "which was the name his mother gave him three thousand years ago."

"Oh," I said. "I see his point. Is he . . . *droch fhola*?"

"No. He's just an asshole," said Drake.

"Where's the rest of the Brady Bunch?" I asked. The room was missing several Panel of Doom members, including Nasty Nara. "Why is it just you guys in this powwow?"

There was another male-to-male exchange via significant glances. I sighed. Hey. Finally! "Something's going down in the Consortium, right?"

"Few can be trusted, *liebling*," said one of the D-men. "We believe some of our problems stem from our own community. Unfortunately, there are traitors among us. They work for the Wraiths to discover what we know about the Taint and they wish to sabotage the Consortium's efforts."

I found it really interesting that Nara wasn't part of this inner circle. Did they suspect she was a traitor? Or did they realize how much I wanted to pull out her hair strand by strand? Probably the latter.

"Tell us about the Wraiths," I said. They sounded like a pain in the ass. Like I wanted to be worried about *another* group of vampires marching into Broken Heart and wreaking more havoc.

"As Stan said, the Wraiths have a different view of the world's pecking order," said Patrick. "We thought they were inconsequential. Unorganized. We were wrong."

"We received intelligence that they were planning an attack on our facility," said François. "Since we'd decided to move to Broken Heart, we had already moved many of our personnel and equipment out of the buildings."

"Most of the RVs were already in transit," added Patrick. "But the Wraiths infiltrated our underground chambers and set off flash bombs. Those vampires still inside were incinerated. They set fire to everything else and destroyed it all."

"But if the Wraiths know you're searching for a way to stop the disease," I said, "why would they kill your people and set fire to a place that might house the cure?"

"Unless they have a cure," said François, his gaze thoughtful. *"C'est possible?* We know that the disease does not transmit to humans or to werewolves. Hmmm. Did you hear about the recently discovered temple in the Sudan?"

I stared at him. "Yeah. I'm a regular reader of *National Geographic*."

Ol' Frankie's brows quirked. "You wield sarcasm, madam, as well as a master swordsman does."

"Gee, thanks." I smiled at him and batted my lashes.

Quit flirting. Patrick flicked the command into my head. He sounded half-annoyed, half-amused.

I'm not flirting.

Quit being cute and likeable.

An impossible request. I've always been too adorable for words.

"The temple was dedicated to Set," said Patrick. "He's an ancient Egyptian deity not known for being a nice guy. In fact, he was the god of chaos."

"So he's like the devil?"

"Close. One of the symbols used for his name," said François, "was 'illness.' He was also thought to be infertile. Unlike other gods, he had no children. He had a battle with his brother's son, Horus. Set's testicles were torn off."

"That's kinda Anne Rice, isn't it?" asked Linda, who had loved Rice's vampire series up until *The Tale of the Body Thief.* I had to admit I had been thrilled when she'd given up her obsession with the Vampire Lestat. "Or even *Blade 3: Trinity*," she continued. "I mean, every vampire plot I've ever read about or watched in a movie seems to point toward some sandy forgotten place in Africa."

"Why is it surprising that fictional accounts so closely mirror the reality? The root from which mankind has grown can be traced to Africa," said François. "Why not this recent outbreak of an ancient plague?"

"Who discovered the temple?" I asked.

"Some of the Consortium's archaeologists," answered Patrick.

"You guys have archaeologists?" I took a sec to think about this revelation. "Why would the Consortium have archaeologists out in the Sudan, which I know is a dangerous place to be, for humans anyway, unless you were looking for something specific and you knew where to look?"

"I wish Kam was here," said Stan, once again gazing at Linda. "He's better at relaying this information." Aw. The only expression sadder than the doc's was the liquid, big-eyed look of a baby seal about to be stabbed by a hunter's spear. How could a guy look so pathetic?

"Kam led the expedition," said Patrick. "Even with what we managed to get from the temple, we haven't been able to trace the origins of the disease. Our research indicates that a similar plague happened in ancient times. Our hope was to find out how it was cured."

"If it was the equivalent of the Black Death . . . well, that was never really cured," I said. "It just decimated half the world's population."

"I remember the Plague," said François. "It was horrifying beyond belief. Many vampires went to ground for a half-century or so rather than risk feeding on bad blood."

"You mean your *food* was poisoned so you took a nap until you could get fresh meat? Well, if that don't make a gal feel like a piece of prime rib," grumbled Linda in a disgusted tone. I guess Linda still felt human—and so did I. It was going to take a while to acclimate to being an entirely new species.

"A crude, but succinct way to describe the situation, madam," said François. He bared his fangs and ran his tongue along his teeth as if talking about famine made him want to feast. "Nature has her ways of balancing the scales. Perhaps the disease needs merely to run its course."

"Not necessarily," I said. "If we have the tools and the means to cure the disease, we damn well should."

"Y'all are creeping me the hell out," said Linda. "I never did like all those forensic shows. Science is beyond my scope and boring to boot."

I saw Stan blanch. Oh poor Dr. Michaels. I felt sorry for him. He couldn't handle Linda. She'd stomp his heart flat then use his credit card to buy herself new shoes.

"The disease only thrives in a vampire's body," said

Stan dully. He rubbed a hand over his head, his fingers skating across his bald spot. He blanched again and dropped his hand. "Most vampires live through the deterioration of the organs, but when the bacteria attacks the brain, they go slowly, painfully insane."

"Most choose to greet the dawn before that happens," said François in a low voice. "There is no cure. So, to turn to ash in the sun's rays is preferable to the consuming madness."

I was horrified by Stan's description of the disease. Dread clawed at me with scabby fingers. "Lor bit us. Jesus God. He gave it to us."

"No, love," said Patrick. "You were human when Lor bit you. The bacteria cannot live in a human's body. It dies instantly. And all of you were Turned by Masters without Taint."

"Lor isn't crazy," I mused. "The cure you attempted with him worked . . . sorta. Is that what you found out from the guys who were digging around in the Sudan desert?"

"No. The Consortium received several crates containing papyrus scrolls, statuary, photographs of the temple, and wall etchings. Then we stopped receiving information," said Patrick. He gathered me close and the sudden show of protection made me realize I wasn't going to like what I heard next. "Before they had excavated even a fourth of the temple, they were killed and the entrance to the complex was destroyed."

"Killed?" I asked. Cold fear snaked up my spine.

"Four were caught, tied to posts, and left outside. When the sun rose, they burned to death," answered François in a tight voice. "It will take months to dig out the temple entrance and begin our work again. Until we find out who does not want us to know the truth, we dare not risk anyone else to pursue this endeavor."

"Kam was scouting another location and went to ground where he was instead of returning to the dig site," said Patrick. "We're lucky he survived."

"Good Lord. So he found his colleagues the next night?" I asked, horrified. "That sucks!" I chewed my lower lip. "Do you think the Wraiths did it?"

"We don't know," said Patrick. "But it is probable."

"We are preparing for battle," said Brigid in her lyrical voice. She sat in a cherry-red wingback that had been placed in the left corner of the bedroom. Everyone turned to look at her. Her expression was solemn and beatific as the gold symbols on her face shifted. Damn, that was weird to watch. She was so resplendent that looking at her was like staring at the sun and not caring that you'd go blind. "The Seven Sects are worried about this disease, too. However, they ignore the Consortium's efforts. The Sects protest our goals because they don't want to involve themselves in the world of men."

"So . . . *they're* killing Consortium members?" I asked, confused.

"It is not the ancients," said Brigid. "Not even they wish to destroy a five-hundred-year-old legacy, all that Patrick and Lorćan created to bring good and peace into the world. It is the Wraiths who wish to establish a new order—which includes ruling over the humans. They're using the disease and the vampires' fear of it to wage war against the Consortium."

"They're winning, too," said Patrick bitterly. "The

Council of Seven continually throws words like 'fate'
and 'destiny' around as if they have no control over
events. They refuse to help us, to help themselves. We
don't deny our customs or traditions. We don't dis-
count the sacrifices of our creators. But progress re-
quires change. If we stay mired in the past, we cannot
move forward to build a better future."

I was getting a larger picture of the situation. Good
heavens above. The world was much bigger and so
much more different than I had ever imagined. Yeah,
all right. I was a throwback to the 1950s. I was a
housewife. I cleaned and cooked and cared for my
family. Let me tell you something: It was a difficult
damned job and the pay *sucked*. But it's what I knew
how to do and I liked doing it. Well, as my grandma
used to say: *Stop chewing your cud and get on with it.*

What I had *been* wasn't nearly as important as what
I had *become*. I thought I had problems before. Now, I
was worried about a freaking vampire war, a freaking
vampire plague, and a freaking vampire marriage. In
addition, we had a vicious unknown monster on the
loose, a Lorćan to catch and to cure, and a whole town
to re-*vamp*. I was overwhelmed. And when I start feeling like I'm going to drown into the murky waters of
obligations, expectations, and needs, there's only one
way to keep from going under.

Tequila. And lots of it.

I'm kidding. (Mostly.)

"I need paper and a pen," I said.

The next thing I knew I had three different kinds of
notepads and three kinds of pens materializing on my
lap. Brigid, François, and Patrick cleared their throats.

"Vampires are such show-offs," said Darrius . . . or Drake. He sounded more amused than envious.

"Uh . . . thanks everyone." I lifted a pink pen with a fuzzy feather on it. "Who made this one?"

I eyed Brigid. I didn't think she was the pink fuzzy type. She shook her head and confirmed my suspicion.

"I fear, madam, that creation is mine." François smiled, his eyes twinkling. "You like?"

"Immensely." I picked up one of the notepads and scribbled out my list.

"So, the first thing we need to do is find Lorćan."

"Oh gawd," groaned Linda. "We're doomed. When Jessie starts making a list, she won't rest until every item is checked off." She fell forward onto the bed and punched the covers. Then she moaned melodramatically.

"Suck it up, woman. You've survived Christmas shopping with me at the mall, you can survive this."

Linda popped back up and rolled her eyes. "I barely survived. The only reason I never collapsed was because you kept me supplied in peppermint mochas."

"Whiner. Next, we need to find the asshole who attacked me and make sure he dies." I bit my lip. "I mean, um, make sure he doesn't try to kill anyone else."

And if he's dead, that problem is solved.

I heard that, a thaisce, *and I heartily agree.*

"Third on the list, is to find a cure for the disease." I tapped the end of the pen against the notepad. "Then we need to figure out how to take out the Wraiths, too."

"Think you can put something on the list that we can actually accomplish?" asked Linda drolly.

"I need a whole separate list for the town. We have to make sure all the houses are emptied and the former residents are gone. We have to find merchants willing to run the necessary businesses. The most important task, of course, is setting up a school. The kids will need to keep to the same routine and they need an education. Then again, if we train 'em to sleep during the day and stay up all night, they're going to be ill-prepared for college." I thought about that. "Well, maybe it'll prepare 'em for college, but not the real world. They still gotta live in it even though we don't."

"There's always Las Vegas, honey," said Linda. "Or Alaska. Right now, the kids are in the this-is-cool phase as we adjust to the nighttime schedule."

"Good point." I looked at the list. It was basic, but even though the tasks were daunting I felt better. "Okay. Let's go get Lorćan."

Patrick's hand cupped the back of my head and tilted it back. His eyes were filled with merriment. "Surely, *a thaisce*, you do not expect to simply go out and find Lorćan when the best trackers in the world are unable to catch his scent?"

Chapter 14

I blinked up at Patrick. "Well, no, I don't plan to go prancing through the woods and expect your brother to be waiting for me. But I thought I would just, you know, do the mind meld thing."

"What mind meld thing?" asked the twins.

I had everyone's attention, especially Patrick's. A knot tightened in my belly. "I showed you my memory. Lorćan and I communicated mentally."

"Mon dieu!"

I looked at François. "What?"

"No one's been able to reach him," said Patrick. "Not even me. And yet you . . ." He frowned, obviously pondering why I could connect to his brother while he couldn't. Well, that made two of us.

"It takes a profound connection to reach into someone else's mind and communicate direct thought," explained Brigid. "Most vampires use energy to soften the will of others, to make them open to verbal suggestions. True compulsion and the ability to easily glamour are talents usually found in the Family Romanov."

"You mean you can't make people do things just because you're a vampire?" asked Linda.

"Each Family has its own strengths," said Brigid, her thoughtful gaze on Patrick. "A Family's particular powers are passed along to Turn-bloods, but it usually takes a century or two for a vampire to call upon and effectively wield those powers."

"The ability to glamour includes limited telepathy—to put suggestions into the victim's mind. However, it is also true that strong bonds, such as those created by mates, allows telepathic communication between vampires," added Patrick.

"We're not mates," I said, sounding churlish.

"Our bodies do not know that," Patrick said in a low voice. His brogue thickened with every word. "The binding is not yet performed, but the soul knows its other half. You belong to me, Jessica. And I to you."

"Oh gawd! He's such a dickhead," said Linda in a dreamy voice, "but I love the way he talks. So possessive and arrogant and yummy."

"Don't encourage him," I said. "He's bad enough as it is."

"Perhaps," said Brigid, who looked like a queen sitting on a royal throne instead of a garage-sale wingback, "during the attack, you remembered things differently from how they really happened."

"Are you calling me a liar?" Outrage made me bristle. I sat up and shoved Patrick's arm off my shoulder.

Brigid only smiled. "I refer only to the idea that you

were still under the glamour. Sometimes, its lingering effects cause faulty memories."

"Fine!" I snapped. "I'll prove it." I shoved off the covers and rolled over Patrick. I was wearing a decent nightgown, which meant Brigid probably picked it out. "Hel-lo. Meeting adjourned." I turned on my heel and hurried into my bathroom. I locked the door and leaned against it.

Patrick shimmered into being in front of me. His finger and thumb gently clamped my chin, tilting my face up so that I would look at him. His eyes were gorgeous. Mercurial with emotion. It amazed me how his gaze could seem so cold, like a sword point, or so hot, like molten silver.

"I like how you think about me," he said. "You make me feel . . ." He shrugged as if that careless gesture could replace the word he couldn't articulate.

"Actions always speak louder than words," I said. This was a piece of motherly advice I dispensed every day to my children. My mother had said the same thing to me growing up, only her phrase was: *If you're gonna talk the talk, sweet pea, you better be able to walk the walk.*

Patrick's handsome face descended toward mine. He stopped when he was just a whisper away. "You have a beautiful mouth."

God, he was magnificent. Such harsh, sensual beauty. The luck of genetics and vampirism and gym time? Who knew?

He watched me watching him and I knew he was probably in my head, listening in on my thoughts, my confusion. He grinned, just a little, and I knew that *rotten, ugly, fat troll* was reading my mind.

He laughed, unrepentant, and his breath plumed my lips. How the hell did he do that? How could he pretend to breathe? Or better yet, *why* did he pretend to breathe?

"You are getting distracted by unimportant details." He flicked his tongue over my lips. My thoughts suspended immediately. I focused on him, on his movements, and nearly died (again) from the want of it. From the want of him.

His tongue traced the outline of my mouth. He dipped into the seam and licked across . . . and back again. This light teasing was an artist's rendering, a paint stroke against canvas.

My arms crept up his shoulders to wend around his neck. He gathered me closer still; his hands caressed my sides. Flames seemed to erupt wherever he touched despite the fact he hadn't made contact with my skin. His palms cupped my hips and there they stayed, clenching as if he were afraid to continue on.

Oh wow. Did he know how to make me melt or what? *You make me crazy, you know that? Drive me stark raving bonkers.*

Then we are even. Kiss me, Jessica. Please.

'Twas the please that caught my memory. I sensed his confusion and sent a low laugh into his mind. *The Princess Bride.*

I didn't give him time to ponder the meaning of me quoting my all-time favorite movie. I pressed my lips to his. My tongue darted out, swiping his lower lip. He took the invitation, and apparently weary of skirting our lust, thrust his tongue inside my mouth.

Everything whirled away.

Everything but Patrick.

He was merciless in his tongue-and-lips assault. He'd had centuries to perfect kissing. It was all I could do to keep up with his expertise, to meet each tender assault with one of my own. After a while, I surrendered to him, conquered by the intensity of my own need.

The man made my thighs quiver and his hands hadn't moved from my waist. An erotic all points bulletin went out to my body. My nipples answered the call immediately, tightening into aching peaks. My nightgown was thin and so was the shirt Patrick wore. He noticed the scraping of my breasts against his chest and let out a half-groan, half-growl.

I thought I knew what lust felt like. But the emotion whipping through me attested that anything I'd felt before this moment was just a shadow of longing, a desert shimmer of yearning. White-hot fire consumed me until I was only craven desperation. Primitive and animalistic.

Our mouths parted and met again and again.

"Just a little taste," he murmured.

"Yes," I agreed, though I didn't know to what. I would've gladly handed him the keys to my car, the deed to my house, the secret location of my Godiva stash. Anything he wanted as long he promised to stay right here and make me feel this way forever.

His lips left mine and I cried out in distress. He scorched a line down my throat. Yes. That's what he should do. *Bite me.* I went dizzy, my fingers digging into his shoulders. My fangs extended in anticipation though I had no intention of taking his blood.

Did I?

Do you see why we must bind? I wore the chains for you, céadsearc, *because I almost mated with you that first night . . . I have not taken from you because I burn for you . . . I wanted you to have a choice. Every day that I am near you . . . every day that I share your thoughts . . . it becomes more difficult to resist you.*

I heard his words. I detected the urgent tone, too. But I didn't care. Patrick was my world. My whole, beautiful world.

His fangs sank into my neck. I felt pressure, not pain. His snarl vibrated against my skin as he drank. I clung to him, unable to stand, and felt the floor tilt under my feet.

My eyes closed as he tightened his grip. It was almost as if he wanted to join with me. Almost as if we were two halves that needed to be a whole. I tried to laugh away the insanity of that thought, but I couldn't. I had never felt this way. Not ever. This was not lust. Or love. Whatever bound Patrick and me was far greater than any emotion that could be named.

I should've been scared out of my wits.

Instead, I felt pre-orgasmic. My whole body tingled as if he'd spent hours touching and kissing my entire being into a sensual frenzy. An ache throbbed between my thighs and I moaned.

Patrick knew that I teetered on release. He pushed up my nightie and slid his hand into my panties. He pinched my clit between his thumb and finger and sent a command into my mind: *Come for me.*

I did.

You know how you read in romance novels that a

woman saw fireworks? Or stars? I'd never had that
kind of orgasm. I figured that kind of delightful explosion was reserved for fictional heroines with perfect
complexions and no cellulite on their thighs.

I was wrong.

Pleasure detonated from my core and flowed over
me as thick and rich as the sweetest nectar. (I haven't
had nectar, but it's a damned fine word to use here.)

Colors blasted behind my eyes. I rose up to the stars,
basking in their heat and light and eternal beauty, until
I floated back to Earth.

Patrick still had me clutched in his arms. He was
trembling, his mouth against the spot where his fangs
had pierced me. "Do you see?" he asked hoarsely. "Do
you understand now?"

"Yes," I murmured. "Yes."

"Your scent drives me wild," he said. He licked my
earlobe. "I smell your sex. Your need. If we were
mates, I would kneel before you and worship you as a
goddess. I would pierce your flesh and drink from you
in a way no other ever has or ever will." His gaze was
fierce silver . . . a warlord's armor glinting in the
morning before battle. "I would taste you until your
essence filled my mouth and your screams of pleasure
filled my ears."

Okay, I admit it. His words were working some
good mojo. I was getting wet again and he knew it. If
my heart still had the ability to hammer, it would've
driven right out of my chest. My fingernails dug into
my thighs, a desperate attempt to keep from accepting
those wicked promises.

"I have a present for you," he murmured. He held

out his hand and a black holster appeared. Inside the loops on each side rested the Ruadan swords.

"Oh Patrick!" I was damned near giddy as he belted the holster around my nightgown.

"How does it fit?"

I did a hip wiggle. The leather stayed put. The swords tapped against my thighs. I walked toward the bathtub, then I turned quickly, whipping out the swords. They didn't snag. They felt good in my hands, like they belonged there. "This rocks!"

"Wear the swords when you go out. And practice!" Patrick chuckled, but his eyes were still filled with the need for the one thing I wasn't ready to give him. "I must go, love. Before I do something . . . permanent."

In the blink of an eye he shifted to silver mist and before I could manage a response, he dissolved into nothingness.

I marched out into the woods with the twins and Mr.-Get-The-Last-Word-In-And-Melt-Into-Thin-Air trailing behind me.

Patrick closed the distance between us; it was wide enough in this section of woods to walk side by side. His expression was bland, but I figured he was still feeling pissy. I know he didn't want me to jump into the binding. But I glimpsed his hunger for me, his need that went beyond anything else anyone had ever shown me. Was that love? Obsession? Infatuation?

I didn't know how to feel.

I found myself in the same mire of emotions I'd felt since I got Turned—overwhelmed, scared, worried . . . and interwoven into the mix . . . *horny*. I wanted to lick and touch and kiss Patrick. I wanted to slide over him and take him and bring him to the edge. I wanted to be naked with him. I wanted to find his favorite spots and show him mine. Where were his sensitive areas? Behind the knee? Yeah, that's where I should flick my tongue, maybe a nip up his thigh, I'd love to coast down between his legs, wrap my lips around his big—

Jessica. God in heaven, stop.

I grinned. *What's wrong? Getting too hot for you?*

You have a skill in torture that rivals a Spanish inquisitor's. You know that I will not break our connection again. Even if that means being tormented by your impure thoughts.

If having sex with you didn't mean a hundred years of marriage, I would happily spend the night with you.

There are ways to pleasure each other without consummation. But to taste you, to know you . . . it isn't enough, love. If you cannot bring yourself to commit to the binding, we cannot bed together.

Fine. Leave me alone, okay? You can stay out of my head since you're a foot away from me. I want to see if I connect with Lorćan.

As you wish.

I blinked. Did he know that phrase was from *The Princess Bride*? Nah.

I watched the twins scope out the area in a strange, precise tandem that was almost militaristic. It didn't take much to figure out that their senses were more attuned to sounds and sights and smells. Vampires had extraordinary sensory skills, but the way Drake and Darrius behaved made me believe that they were in sync with nature. Drake and Darrius found an old

walking path and stayed about three feet ahead of me.
Patrick trailed behind, alert, his footsteps eerily silent.
Me, I stomped forward with all the skill and grace of a
lumbering bear. Nothing for it but to see if Lorćan
would pick up the mental phone.

*Hey, Lorćan! Nobody wants to kill you anymore. We
know there's another lycanthrope. Just c'mon out so we
can experiment on you and find a cure for the disease.*

You sure know how to tempt a man. Or a beast, a
droll voice whispered through my mind.

Lorćan! Hoo-wee!

*Don't get excited, Jessica. I'm not revealing my lo-
cation to you. It's not safe for me to be near anyone.*

*Oh shut up. This isn't about you, it's about me. I
have to show up your tight-assed brother.*

Laughter echoed in my head. *I see why he likes you.*

*Yeah, he really enjoys how prim and proper I am.
Why can I talk to you? You didn't Turn me.*

No. I murdered you.

Don't worry. I'm over it.

Another chuckle rippled. Then I felt the ache of his
regret, the cold horror of what he'd done. Shit. I was
losing him. He was going to hang up on me.

*Look, we gotta find a cure. You're the key. Whatever
they did to you stopped the disease.*

*And turned me into Cousin It. I don't think most
vampires would appreciate the side effects.*

*We can't fix the problem or you unless you meet with
us. C'mon, Lor. I won't let anyone hurt you.*

My hero. Okay, bean-shithe, *I will meet with you and
Patrick, but no others. No one can know about it.
Agreed?*

Damn straight I agree. When and where?
The hour before dawn at Putt 'Er There.
We'll be there. And Lor?
Yes?
A girl really hates to be stood up.

His amusement swirled in my mind, then he was gone. I stopped walking and looked at Patrick. "It's time to go home."

"You talked to him?"

"Yeah."

"I didn't hear a whisper. I've always been able to connect with him."

"Maybe it has something to do with the physical changes he's gone through," I said, putting my hand on Patrick's arm. I hated that he was so distressed about his brother. "Maybe it's messed up his brainwaves or something. His channels got flipped."

Something close to humor glittered in Patrick's gaze as he looked at me. "You mean he tuned into you?"

"Yeah. The weird woman network. He's entered my own personal episode of *The Twilight Zone*. Lucky him."

Patrick brushed his knuckles along my jaw. "No, *céadsearc*, lucky me."

When I entered the house, I heard the delightful sounds of Bryan and Jenny fighting over the TV's remote control. For a second, it was so normal, so like my old life, I felt as if time had shifted backward and dumped me on my ass. Then Patrick's fingertips grazed my elbow and I jolted into the present moment.

"I'll meet you upstairs," he said. Then he actually

walked up the carpeted stairwell like a normal person instead of turning into mist or a bat.

I can't turn into a bat.

So you say.

I knew Patrick was ducking out of a familial moment. There was a wall between him and my children, one that he erected. I understood why. That kind of pain . . . well, I guess "time heals all wounds" just wasn't the case for a father who'd lost his children.

But there was no me without Bryan and Jenny. And Patrick's reluctance to even sit in the same room with us all meant . . . what? Could Patrick be a dad again?

Brigid glided from the living room into the foyer. "Are you well?" she asked.

"I'm peaches and cream," I said. "Those two been at it long?"

"No." She laughed and the sound was the peal of church bells on Sunday morning. "Any luck finding Lor?"

"Uh . . . sorta."

Her green eyes sparked with curiosity, but I knew she wouldn't nag me about the vague reply.

I cleared my throat and met her gaze. "Thank you, Brigid. I know I was dead. I mean, for real, and you saved me. And I know you're a special kind of . . . uh, person."

"I am not a vampire, you mean," said Brigid. "And you wonder what I am."

"Yeah."

"I am *sidhe*," she said proudly. "And Padraig is my grandson."

"What? You're his . . . *what*?"

"Grandmother," said Brigid, amused at my reaction. "You read the story, did you not? The one Lor left for you?"

"He put the book on the coffee table?"

She nodded. "Lor likes to write down the legends, prophecies, myths, and other stories. He has hundreds of those volumes . . . and that doesn't include what he's managed to type into a computer."

My mouth dropped open. "You're the Brigid from the legend?"

The screeches of my still arguing children rose in urgency and tone. Brigid smiled her enigmatic smile and rested her palm against my cheek. "You must not give up on him, Jessica. He didn't give up on you. If there is anyone to thank for your life . . . it is Padraig."

"I know that." I sounded sullen. I rubbed a hand over my face as if I could wipe away my glowering. "God, I'm so bitchy. I owe a number of people for saving my butt. I won't forget."

"Good." As she sparkled out of sight, she waved her hand in farewell.

Chapter 15

I headed into the living room and witnessed a remote-control tug-of-war between my kids. Bryan managed to yank it out of Jenny's grasp. She put her hands on her hips and stomped her bare foot.

"Just because you're older, doesn't mean you can boss me around," wailed Jenny. "I'm going to tell Mom that you're being a butthead."

"I'm not watching the Bratz movie," retorted Bryan. "You've seen it like, a billion times, and it's stupid. *You're* stupid."

"I'm not stupid. I get A's. You get F-minuses plus infinity."

"Shut up."

"You shut up."

"Make me."

"Oh make yourself! Give me that remote, Bryan!"

My son, an expert in torturing his younger sibling, held up the remote and invited his sister to "go on and take it."

"How about *I* take it?"

"Mom!" they chorused.

"Bryan's being a jerkazoid rex," announced Jenny. "We watched *The Matrix* and now it's my turn to pick a movie."

"She wants to watch some dumb Bratz movie. I hate Bratz."

I silently agreed with him. I wasn't fond of those apple-cheeked, pillow-lipped, bug-eyed dolls, but I respected Jenny's right to like them. Okay. Respect was probably the wrong word. I tolerated her obsession with the creepy plastic fashionistas.

Jenny jumped like a frenzied Chihuahua as she tried to grab the remote from the hand of her smirking brother.

"How many televisions do we have in this house?" I asked. Who-gets-the-remote-control was an old, ongoing argument. It didn't seem to matter that Jenny and Bryan both had TVs with digital cable in their bedrooms; they were forever battling for territory and privileges in the living room.

"I know, Mom. We have four TVs," said Bryan. "But we wanted to sit on the new couch."

"The new couch?"

"Yeah," said Jenny, momentarily distracted from trying to best her brother. "It's *way* better."

I had been focused on the kids and the Remote War, but considering the size of the new couch and the obvious rearrangement of the living room to accommodate the piece, it wasn't exactly hard to miss.

"It's got a *chaise*," said my daughter primly. One end of the red behemoth was a long rectangle—a suitable space for Cleopatra or a nine-year-old who enjoyed feeling like a princess.

"What happened to the old one?" asked Bryan.

"Bigfoot ate it," I said. "Give me the remote, Bry."

He tossed the remote to me as if it was the football and I was the quarterback. I caught it, but he got the Look for A. throwing it and B. throwing it in the house. He plopped onto the couch, his socked feet stretched out just close enough to Jenny to annoy her.

"Get your stinky feet away from me!" she cried, crinkling her nose in disgust and scooting into the corner of her chaise as if Bryan's toes had turned into snakes. "Moooom! His feet smell like lima beans."

Jenny hated lima beans so she equated anything disgusting to the offensive vegetable. And who could blame her? I'd always thought Bryan's feet smelled like lima beans, too.

"Can you two cool it for a minute?" Nausea crowded my throat as I looked at the couch and thought about why the old one had to be replaced. God. Oh God. I knew that Patrick had made sure the couch soaked with my blood had been taken away and replaced with something better. He had taken care of cleaning the downstairs and getting rid of the evidence of the attack. My babies didn't have to wonder why things were trashed or have to be afraid for me.

Patrick.

Who won the remote?

I did.

His laugh caressed my mind.

Um . . . Patrick? Thank you. I didn't think about

what happened to the room . . . the house . . . you took care of it. Of my kids. Of me. Thank you.

A thaisce. I felt his fingers drift down the curve of my cheek. Then he was gone.

When I blinked back into the moment, both of my kids were staring at me over the top of the couch. "What?"

"You, like, totally zoned," said Bryan.

"Is zoning out a vampire thing, Mommy?" asked Jenny.

"No. But I'll show you something that is a vampire thing." I rose a few feet off the carpet and flew over the couch to settle between them. Bryan jerked up his feet as I landed on the fat, soft cushion.

"That was so cool," said Bryan, his eyes wide. "Can we do that?"

"No," I said. "And don't you try it, either. Okay, guys. I know you have questions. Our lives have changed big time. And you know . . . well, I'm a vampire now."

It was weird to have a second conversation with my kids about my undeadness, although this one was going a lot better than the first one.

"We understand," said Bryan. "Dr. Stan explained it to everyone when you were sick. You've been sick a lot. Is that normal for vampires?"

"No. Just for me. Don't worry about it, baby. I'm fine now."

"Okay." He shrugged. "It's weird to be awake at night and sleep during the day."

"Having a hard time adjusting?"

"Naw."

I looked at Jenny and saw her serious brown gaze on me. "Does it hurt to be a vampire?" she asked.

"No, honey."

"Dr. Stan said you had to drink blood," said Bryan.

"Yeah," said Jenny. "Whose blood do you drink?"

"Jenny. Ew." I cleared my throat. "Got any questions I want to answer?"

"Prob'ly not," said Bry. "Who's your donor?"

Oh shit. Embarrassment forced me to look at the floor. Why did it feel like Bryan had asked "who's your lover"? "What the hell did Stan tell you guys?"

"You cussed," said Jenny. "You gotta put a quarter in the Cussing Jar."

I cussed all the time. Jenny, who was industrious as well as persnickety, had taken a Mason jar, colored a pretty label for it, and put it in the kitchen. Every time she or Bry caught me saying a bad word, I put a quarter in it. Needless to say, they'd earned quite a chunk of change from my potty mouth. Yeah, I know. Some mother, right? Well, every mother has a flaw. Or three.

"All right, squirt. I'll put a quarter in the jar."

"Keep it up, Mom," said Bryan. "We almost got enough to buy another Xbox game."

"Har de har."

"Mommy?"

I turned to Jenny. I wanted to hug her. I wanted to hug them both. But I knew Bryan's hands-off "you're embarrassing me" policy and I was still worried my daughter thought I was a monster.

"What is it, Jenny?"

"Will you read me a story before bedtime?"

Relief cascaded through me. Normalcy. I didn't

think it was possible to ever have it again. Maybe it was just redefining the concept of "normal." I looked at her and tapped my chin thoughtfully. "Hmmm. I don't know. Can you afford my superior reading skills?"

"Maybe," she said. "What do you charge?"

"Two hugs and one kiss."

With tilted head and pursed lips she considered the cost. "That's kinda steep."

"Got a counteroffer?" I raised my brows at her.

She grinned. And I grinned back. Then my sweet baby launched herself into my embrace and wrapped her little arms around my neck. "I can afford your askin' price," she said.

I held on to her and squeezed, trying to gather her warmth, her love into me. I wanted it to soak into my skin. I never wanted her to doubt, to worry, to fear. Oh, the things a mother wanted for her kids. The things we couldn't ever really give them. Because to be human meant you doubted, worried, feared. No matter your age. Not even being a vampire would help me protect my kids against the disappointments and the hurts the world offered.

I looked at Bryan. He was watching us, a longing in his eyes that battled with his obvious pride. I loosed one arm and beckoned him into the cuddle. He hesitated. I realized he didn't fear getting close to me, but he hadn't decided if it was worth letting go of his manliness for a minute to enjoy an old-fashioned, girl-infested hug.

He scooted close and I enclosed him with us. For a few perfect moments, we sat there on our new couch, my family and I, and reaffirmed our faith in our bond.

"I love you," I said. "I love you so much."

"Aw, Mom." Bryan broke free. He didn't move away, but his face pinched with revulsion. "Don't go mushy on us."

"Too late."

"She loves *The Secrets of Droon.* So did Bryan when he was her age. I kept his collection for Jenny and we started reading them a few weeks ago. We're on the seventh book," I told Patrick.

"How many books are there in the series?"

"I dunno. A zillion, I think."

"Ah. It might take a while to finish the series."

I laughed. "Yeah, probably."

Hand in hand, Patrick and I walked down the block, like a regular couple out for a nightly stroll. After the kids were tucked into bed, all the while complaining about their 4 A.M. bedtime (but Moooom, Wilson and Miranda and Joey and Sue Ann all get to stay up until 5 A.M.), it was nearly time for Patrick and me to meet Lorćan.

"We should probably fly there," I said.

"Fly where?" asked a petulant female voice. Nara the Nasty shimmered in front of us, blocking the path.

Oh goodie. My favorite person. Her ensemble screamed "vampire slut." The tight red leather minidress barely covered her vagina. The bustier pushed up and put together her generous boobage and caused what I called the Jell-O Effect (. . . *watch them wiggle, see them jiggle . . .*). The high heels she wore were ankle busters; the red straps crisscrossed all the way up her calves. She looked exactly like a vampire chick on the prowl for a human snack.

"Isn't this cozy?" She sent Patrick a blatant do-me-now-big-boy look, obviously pretending I didn't exist.

Patrick's thumb stroked across my palm and pleasure tingled through me. He was mine, right now anyway, so I kept my mouth shut. But being quiet didn't mean I had to be nice. I moved closer to Patrick, dropping his hand to snake my arm around his waist; my thumb hooked into the loop on his 501s. His arm settled around my shoulders. This was a move that Nara noticed. And didn't like.

"Where are you going?" she asked. The "with that bitch" wasn't spoken, but I knew she was thinking it.

"Why do you care, Nara?" Patrick asked politely.

Her eyes widened and her lower lip trembled. Wow. I wondered how long it took her to perfect that move. "Of course, I care. I have always cared. It is you I love, Padriag."

Love? She *loved* him? Yuck. I should've figured something had gone on between them after the Alexis Carrington treatment she bestowed on me. If we were going to have a real *Dynasty* moment, we'd start bitch slapping each other soon. I relished the idea of smacking Nara.

"You love only yourself," Patrick said, his voice weary. I got the impression this was an oft-repeated discussion. And Nara didn't seem like a girl who took hints to leave. Hell, she didn't seem like a girl who took "no" for an answer.

Her gaze slid to me then up to Patrick's face. I saw the calculation in her eyes, the slight smirking curve of her lips. "You know I don't mind sharing. Not for a night. And it's not like we haven't done a threesome

before." One slim pale shoulder lifted. "I'm not at-
tracted to her, but I will do as you wish. As always."

Patrick tensed, holding on to me so tightly I couldn't
move. That bitch. That arrogant, stupid bitch. *Let me
go. I'm going to claw out her eyes.*

Be still, love. Will you give her what she wants?

*You're damn right I will. I'll break more than her
fucking hand this time, too.*

*Please, Jessica. We have more important worries
than Nara's petty attempts to tear at our bond.*

Argh! Fine! But . . . argh!

"Don't talk that way in front of Jessica," Patrick
warned in a low voice. "You think to embarrass me,
but you will only embarrass yourself."

I felt Patrick's weariness. Yeah, this was definitely
an ongoing battle. How long had he been putting up
with this woman? And why?

"What do you want?" he asked, his tone uninterested.

"You." She sashayed toward him, her hips undulat-
ing in a way most men probably found sexy. It reminded me of the way clothes tumbled around in a
dryer. "For seven hundred years, I've paid penance for
my mistake. When will you forgive me?"

"Never."

Her nostrils flared and I saw the flash of temper in her
eyes. She got ahold of herself, though, and allowed her
mouth to curl into a sensual smile. "You haven't claimed
her. She claimed you and you did not reciprocate. She re-
fuses to bind with you." Her voice dropped into a sexy
purr. "We claimed each other, lover. I happily completed
the binding with you. And I would again."

The words echoed in my mind like a blast of

dynamite. Nara . . . and Patrick . . . and the binding? Anger burned through me as I turned to Patrick. "Please tell me that she is not your ex-wife."

"Jessica." He loosed himself and stood next to me, his fists clenched at his sides, his gaze begging me to understand, to accept.

Triumph flared in Nara's gaze. "You didn't tell her that we had been bound?" She tapped a red-painted nail on her lips. "Ah. I get it. You're trying to make me jealous, aren't you? I know she looks like Dairine. But sweetie, that doesn't make her your *sonuachar*."

"She is my *sonuachar*. But I will not force her to live a life she doesn't want to live or be with a man she doesn't love. Her happiness is worth far more than my own. This is a concept you have never understood."

She rolled her eyes. "You've always been difficult. But I enjoy a challenge, as you well know."

"Are we done?" I asked. "Because I'm really bored."

Her lips peeled back into an ugly scowl. Her pretty face twisted with her hatred. "You will regret taking Patrick from me. You will pay with pain and with blood."

"You're pathetic," I said. "A sad, bitter woman who seriously needs some therapy. Three's a crowd and I'm tired of sharing my space with you. Go the hell away."

I looked at Patrick. Maybe I wasn't sure about the soul mate thing or if I wanted to marry him or if it was wise to do the mattress mambo with him. But I had never felt more safe, more cherished, more beloved than when I was with him. I worried about the future, about my kids, about so many things. But I knew that I wanted Patrick. I really, really, *really* wanted him. And so, I whispered, "Claim me."

Chapter 16

"Jessica." My name was a prayer issued from his lips—and that tender refrain whispered through me like a silken promise. Patrick placed his hand on my neck and murmured, "Mine." I felt a tingling heat bloom and fade. Another honeysuckle? Or was Patrick's symbol different?

"No!" Nara's arm went up, her open palm swinging toward my cheek, but Patrick grabbed her wrist and flung it away.

"You cannot have him. He is mine!"

"No, he's mine," I said. "Fuck off."

Realizing she'd lost this round, she screamed in fury then . . . sparkled away.

"What a bitch!"

"Jessica . . ." He shook his head, smiling. "You are impudent."

"It's a gift."

"You are the gift."

"Patrick, you're twisting me into knots. You're all

smoochy and lovey and saving-my-life one second and all brooding and dark and driving-me-crazy the next. I don't know what to do with you."

"I could think of several things you could do with me."

"Yeah. Tell me about it." I nibbled my lower lip. "So . . . Nara . . . you, uh, were married to her."

"It was more blackmail than marriage."

His eyes went distant and I could feel him go back through the centuries. "She was beautiful. Seductive. Yet the only reason I agreed to the binding was because she had my father's swords."

"What?"

He nodded. "The swords had been stolen from my father—no one knew what had happened to them. Then, seven hundred years ago, Nara showed up and bartered with me. If I would bind with her, she'd give me the Ruadan swords. It's tradition with vampire bindings for the couple to exchange gifts—usually these objects have great emotional value."

"What did you give her?"

Patrick's jaw clenched. "Nara would settle for nothing less than the coin made from Dairine's *fede.* She hoped to force me into another binding to regain the coin."

I thought about the *Legend of Ruadan the First* and I realized why Nara would try to blackmail Patrick into marriage. "You and Lor are the sons of the first vampire. You said the vampires had a class system. So, she wanted the power and prestige that was part and parcel of being your mate."

I really didn't like her. She had taken advantage of

Patrick. She was vindictive, greedy, and coldhearted. I sooooo wanted to hurt her.

"I can't undo the past," said Patrick. "I spent a hundred years in hell . . . I wouldn't give Nara another hundred, not even for the last reminder I had of my life with Dairine." He cupped my face and looked into my eyes. "I am connected to you. You are the one I want. You are *mo chroi*. My heart."

In the depths of silver, I saw the truth of his emotions for me. What I saw there scared the crap out of me. It was like gazing into eternity and knowing that I had a place in it. That I would never be alone and always be loved.

"Holy shit."

"Yeah. Holy shit." He kissed me lightly, silencing my questions. "Let's go meet Lor."

"Okay."

We broke apart, and holding hands again, rose into the air.

"Lor?" called Patrick. "Lor!"

"He didn't respond the other forty times," I said. "I don't think shouting it another forty will get you different results."

"How many times have you tried to connect with him?"

"Way more than forty . . . with the same results. My mental mojo is failing. Or he's ignoring me."

We circled the golf course of Putt 'Er There for the second time. Even with the tall grass, overgrowth, and untrimmed trees, it would be hard to miss a seven-foot-tall hairball.

At the broken windmill, we paused in our searching.

Maybe Patrick felt what I did, which was seriously creeped out. It seemed unnaturally quiet, the silence not even broken by the singing of crickets or the flitter of bird wings. The air was thick with moisture and heat, and heavy with the scent of honeysuckle from bushes that half-rimmed the small pond to our left. I looked at the water, the cool, strange calm of it, and saw the glimmer of something round and pale.

"What's in the water?" I asked as I leaned over the gray murk. I grasped a primitive understanding of the shape and size of it, but I wasn't ready to give name to what I saw lurking below the depths.

Patrick waded knee-deep into the water and reached in to grab the body. He pulled it out by the arms, and dragged it away from its iniquitous grave, until it flopped against the weeds and untamed grass of the golf course. I watched, my tears mute, as he knelt down and gently, lovingly pulled down the pink muumuu to cover the chubby white knees.

He wasn't thinking. Couldn't be thinking. Why cover her legs when her torso was ravaged, the dress hanging in shreds around the ugly gashes?

Like Emily, her face had been untouched. Her pretty, round face tinged blue, her eyes open and filmy, and . . . God. Oh God. Her neck was pristine, as white and strong and beautiful as I remembered. And below that perfect column of flesh lay blood and gore and ruin.

I felt sick and dizzy and sank to my knees next to her, my hand drifting over her leaf-strewn red hair. I stroked away the strands clinging to her cheeks and murmured, "Oh, Sharon."

Chapter 17

Patrick used his cell phone to call Stan. He told him to bring Damian to the golf course and to take care of Sharon. He also made Stan promise not to tell anyone about her death until we awoke and could handle the fallout.

"My kids," I said. "Are they okay?"

Patrick covered the mouthpiece. "Yes. Damian put extra guards around the outside of the house. Drake and Darrius will guard Bryan and Jenny's doors. I swear to you, nothing will get to your *clann*, Jessica."

"Thank you." I kissed his cheek and nuzzled his jaw. "Thank you."

He pressed his lips to my forehead and I wandered away so he could finish the phone call.

Everyone would think Lorćan killed Sharon. Though I didn't want to, I wondered . . . did he? Not even Brigid had believed me when I said there'd been two creatures. Had Lor implanted a memory to fool me? Had he invited me and Patrick to the golf course to show us his latest kill? I didn't know.

I couldn't help it. No matter where I put my gaze—on the sky, on the windmill, on Patrick . . . it was always drawn back to Sharon. I found myself reluctantly kneeling next to her again. My stomach felt queasy, but I managed to push down her eyelids. It made me feel better, as if she'd gone to sleep instead of dying so horribly. Had she known her killer? Had she fought? Or had she succumbed to glamour before getting mauled?

I stood up and hurried away. Patrick leaned against the windmill, watching me. He was still on the phone with Stan. I smiled and waved away his concern. I needed some space, but I wouldn't go out of his sight. Fear chilled me. Maybe as a vampire I should've felt brave and invulnerable, but I was scared shitless.

It was appalling to face the mortality of someone I knew. It wasn't the first time I'd seen a dead human body. Before Sharon, I had seen Emily, and before her . . . Rich.

Going to the morgue that night had been like walking into hell. After I got the phone call, the one that shattered a world already fragmented, I dropped off my kids at Linda's and drove to the square-bricked, two-story hospital. The coroner was one of three physicians who worked in Broken Heart—the other two rotated between other towns, but Doc Wallis was permanent and changed professional hats when needed. Our little town had one or two deaths a year, and none from murder. No one had died from homicide—that we knew about—for at least twenty years.

I trudged into the small room where autopsies were done. It didn't have big picture windows or TV monitors—devices used to distance the living from the dead. It smelled strongly of lemon-scented cleaner, but not even industrial-strength 409 had the ability to mask the underlying miasma.

Nausea crowded my throat; grief sat in my stomach like a bag filled with sharp stones. But I tucked in those emotions, wrapped them tight inside me, as I watched Doc Wallis open a square metal door and roll out my husband.

Rich's skin was waxen and pale. He didn't look asleep. He looked dead. I couldn't remember the last words we'd said to each other, but we'd done nothing but argue—about alimony and child support, visitation rights, whether to sell the house or fight over who got to live in it. We'd gotten to the point where every conversation ended with, "Talk to my lawyer." And yet, here I was, still his wife, completing the final, awful duty that befell me as his legal spouse.

I identified his body.

I didn't cry until I had gotten into my car.

Rich's death offered no closure. Death never did, did it? I wasn't finished being angry with him. Just because he'd died didn't mean I could automatically and easily release my hurt or let go of the depth of the betrayal I felt.

And yet, not even I, who had relished every petty satisfaction derived from hurting him, wanted him to die.

I had been too swathed in my pain, my anger, and my cowardice to tell Charlene that her lover was gone.

She labored two floors above the morgue to have that baby, unaware that she'd never lay eyes on Rich again, and I walked out without checking on her. I asked Doc Wallis to drop the bomb after Charlene had recovered sufficiently from giving birth.

That was bitchy of me. Guilt still pricked me with sharp edges that I hadn't made the noble gesture. It was cruel to not build a temporary bridge to Charlene and her child—to acknowledge her right to grieve Rich's loss.

The divorce proceedings had been a slow and painful process and hadn't been close to completion. Instead of becoming Rich's ex-wife, I became his widow. And so, Charlene didn't get the casseroles and sympathy cards and daily help.

I did.

While Charlene learned the weary tasks of caring for an infant, I planned Rich's funeral. While she struggled to find a job to support herself and her baby, I collected his health insurance and sold his business. While she endured the censure of my friends and family, I enjoyed empathy and companionship.

Oh, I sucked. On a grand scale. For a long time, I hadn't had the emotional space to think about Charlene as a human being. She was the Other Woman. At some point, there had to be healing and forgiveness and getting-the-hell over myself.

All these revelations spun in my head while Patrick paced and talked to Stan and I paced and tried to avoid looking at Sharon's violated body.

The click of Patrick's phone snapping shut pulled me out of the memories. We looked at each other, both of us feeling the weight of Sharon's death, feeling how it enchained us to other deaths, to other losses.

"Is this what it means to be a vampire—witnessing these horrors over and over?" I asked.

"I wish I could tell you something comforting that would not be a lie."

"Yeah. Me, too."

The sun would rise soon. I knew this not because of the changing colors of sky, but because of the weird malaise squeezing me into unconsciousness.

Patrick scooped me into his arms. "C'mon, love. I know you're tired."

We had to leave Sharon, alone and ravaged, beneath the broken wood shards of the windmill. It felt like a final indignity to her, to abandon the one who'd been friend to Patrick and might've been friend to me.

It was pure psychology to suddenly feel the need for physical connection. I snuggled into Patrick's embrace and he held me tightly. He flew me all the way home and he didn't let me down until he had taken me upstairs and into the bedroom.

I worried about Lorćan. And I wondered about my memories of the night I had been attacked . . . was I wrong? Had there been two creatures? Or only one? Had the last human vestiges in Lorćan allowed him to talk to me? Maybe he'd only wanted to tell us that he'd killed Sharon and that's why he wanted to meet at the golf course.

But what if someone had managed to "listen in" on our conversation and set up Lor? Maybe whoever it was killed Sharon and dragged her to Putt 'Er There. Lor discovered the body before we arrived, panicked, and left so that he wouldn't be accused of her murder. Or maybe he'd been hurt or killed.

"Damn," I said. "This sucks."

"Whoever killed Sharon and Emily will pay." Patrick made sure the bedroom door was locked. "For now, we are safe. The *clann* are safe."

"That means children, right? *Clann?*"

"Yes."

"What about those other words you're always calling me?"

His eyes glinted with mischief. "I probably shouldn't admit what they mean."

"I knew it! You're insulting me!"

His laughter rolled over me. "You are too easy, love." He looked at me, his amusement fading. "*A thaisce* means 'my treasure.'"

"You call me that? Wow. That puts the usual 'honey' and 'baby' endearments to shame. What about the other one? Kay-uh-es-whatever?"

"We must work on your Gaelic pronunciation," he said. "*Céadsearc* means . . . first love."

Admittedly, I was already feeling mushy toward Patrick, but to be called his first love? Forget mush. I was goo. "Why, Patrick? How can you love me? Don't we need time and dates and long conversations and . . . and . . . I don't know? We can't just love each other because you say we're soul mates."

"I know what I know. If you opened your heart to mine, you would know the same."

"And my children? Do I abandon them so that I can love you?"

"Never!" He looked shocked that I would even

• make the suggestion. Relief flooded me. Not even true soul mate-forever love would drag me away from Jenny and Bryan.

"Thank you for taking care of them, even though . . ." I shrugged.

"Even though what?"

"Nothing." I didn't want to hear his response to the questions I couldn't yet voice. Soon, we'd have the my-kids-are-first conversation, and soul mates or not, I figured we'd part ways. He'd lost his family and his own life in a terrible, brutal way. How did I ask a man to open his heart to that pain again?

"I'm really tired," I said because I couldn't think of anything else that would fill up the chasm between Patrick and me.

Patrick crossed the room and rubbed my shoulders. Knots loosened under the wonderful pressure of his fingers. Sheesh. I had no idea I was *that* stressed. "Are you staying with me?" I heard the whine in my voice and flinched.

"Yes."

"That's good. That's really good." I felt cold and so exhausted, I could probably sleep standing up. I thought about Sharon, her serene, bloated face, her unseeing gaze. Those images interposed on Emily's young face then melded onto Rich's waxen complexion. Death. So much death.

"Do vampires dream?" I asked. "I don't remember dreaming. But I don't want nightmares. I don't want to feel sad or afraid anymore." I sighed. "That's selfish, isn't it? You know what? I'm tired of feeling selfish, too. I've been a terrible person, Patrick. You have no idea."

He turned me around and gathered me into his arms. "You are willful and strong and beautiful, love. Do you want dreams tonight? The kind of sweet fantasies that make you forget that you are sad and afraid and selfish?"

"Hell, yeah." I grinned. "Is it possible for you to control my dreams?"

"Not the way you think." He stepped back and gave me a heated stare. In an instant, my clothes disappeared and I stood before him naked and shivering.

"Stan told me vampires could do the disappear/reappear thing because of their molecules or whatever."

"The removal and creation of clothing is something else. It's *sidhe* magic. The Family Ruadan's power includes magic, healing, and flight."

"Not all vampires can fly? Hmmm. But everyone can go all misty."

"It takes years to learn how to break down your essence into energy, transport to another location, and return to solid form."

His gaze transferred to the bed and the covers peeled back.

"God, that's sexy," I said. "You getting naked, too?"

"No. It's temptation enough to sleep next to you with my clothes on."

"Hey! I've woken up twice with a naked Patrick next to me."

"Hmmm. The longer I'm around you, the less I'm able to control myself."

He could easily keep me in ooey-gooey do-me mode if he kept up with those kinds of compliments. "What's that they say about Irish men? Silver-tongued devils? You kissed the Blarney stone, right?"

"Who has need of a stone when I have the beautiful lips of Jessica Matthews to warm mine?"

Oh gawd. Seriously, Patrick was going to turn me into a puddle. People would point and say, "Look, there's where sex-starved Jessica met her end." Exhaustion weighed on me. I crawled between the sheets and sighed at their coolness as my eyes shuttered. I felt the bed dip then Patrick's still-clothed body wrapped around mine. "Tell me, *a thaisce*, do you want to dream with me?"

"Yes," I said. "Oh yes."

I awoke in a thatched-roof cottage. The bed was a simple mattress on rough-hewn logs. In the corner was a hearth, the fire reduced to red embers. I rolled onto my side and noticed a long wooden table situated a few feet away. Above the table was a series of hooks on which hung pitchers and cooking utensils.

Something about this setting seemed familiar.

I swung my legs off the bed and noticed I wore a brown cotton dress with a cinched waist and square-cut neckline. Not exactly my usual sleepwear.

After I stood up and explored the one-room cottage, I wandered outside. The sun was shining from a sapphire sky. I basked in its warmth, in its light for a long, wonderful moment.

On either side of the little farm were rolling green hills. Nothing but lush and quiet surrounded me. Again, I felt that weird sense of déjà vu. I knew this place . . . and yet, I didn't think I had ever been here before.

A few yards away, I spotted another thatch-roofed

building—a barn with two horse stalls. One was filled with hay and the other was empty. As I walked inside, I spotted a tall, black-haired Irish god leaning against a post and waiting for me.

"Patrick?"

He looked at me, a lazy smile curling his lips. His silver eyes gleamed with pleasure. He wore a loose white cotton shirt, the kind you see heroes wear on the covers of romance novels, tight black breeches, and black riding boots.

He was the kind of gorgeous you wanted to lick.

"This is the dream you chose?" I asked as I walked to him. I couldn't resist touching the crisp, black hair peeking from the vee of silk.

Lust careened through me.

"I can have you, right?" I asked, sounding desperate and horny. "Because we're only being naughty in our minds."

Both my hands tucked inside the shirt and trailed up to his pectorals. His skin was warm and those muscles . . . Drool City, baby. I leaned forward and placed a kiss between his pecs.

"Patrick?" I breathed on the spot then darted my tongue across it. Then I flicked his nipples with my fingernails. I felt him quiver under my palms. "Please tell me I can have you."

His thumb slid under my jaw, lifted my chin. "As you wish."

It clicked into place then, the familiarity of this setting. I grinned at him. *"The Princess Bride?"*

"I pay attention, Jessica." He leaned forward and nipped my lips. "Is this where you want to stay?"

"Where would you take me?" I asked. "And what would you do with me?"

He smiled wickedly. The scene around us melted away like a watercolor that had gotten rained on. When the scene righted, we were in a new place.

He let me go and I explored his chosen setting for our rendezvous.

In the huge room draped by shadows, the stone walls drew my notice first. A castle? How medieval of Patrick. I grinned. I had never been in a castle before, though I'd hoped to one day travel to Europe and visit a few before I died. Well, maybe I would get to visit 'em now that I was dead.

The only visible piece of furniture was the biggest bed I'd ever seen. Piled with pillows, the lush red velvet spread only hinted at the decadence underneath it.

Across from the bed was a large fireplace. It too was faced with gray stone. The blaze warmed the room and created the only light. I smelled sandalwood and cedar.

"This is . . . do you own this place?"

"I did once. The castle doesn't exist anymore."

"And this room? Is it your make-out room or something?"

"Oh yes. I ravished all my women on that bed."

"Patrick . . ."

"Jessica . . ." His gaze caressed me.

"So you ravished your women somewhere else?"

"All over the place," he said dryly. "By the way, did you know that you're naked?"

I looked down. Whaddaya know. I *was* nekkid. I blinked and realized that my darling Irishman was deliciously nekkid, too. My gaze took in his clothing-free, lust-inducing bod. "I just want to eat you," I said.

"Really? Because that could be arranged." He stalked me. "I know just where you could begin such a feast, too."

I yelped and jumped away from his playful pounce. Laughing, I dove onto the bed and rolled around on it. "Oh my God. This is so soft. It feels like . . . like melted butter."

"Butter?" Patrick groaned. "You. Naked. In melted butter."

"Are we real here?"

"Ah. You mean human. Yes, if you like. It is a dream. And everything we do to each other will feel real and we will remember it, but love, it will unfold in our minds. Do you understand?"

"Yes. We're dreaming it. Not living it. So . . . does it count for the ritual?"

"No. We must share our bodies and our blood."

He crawled onto the bed, grabbed my calves, and pulled me to him. The red velvet skidded underneath me, the material sensuously rubbing my skin.

Patrick knelt between my legs, his hands wrapped around my ankles, and he looked at me like I was the last chocolate in the box.

"What . . . what are you doing?"

"Ssshhh." He sat on his haunches and brought one imprisoned ankle to his mouth. His lips were soft, warm. His tongue flicked the bone, encircled it.

Little flames of sensation erupted. It had been a long, long time since a man had touched me . . . since I had felt the want, the need, the desire of another. *For* another. Patrick's minute attention tortured me deliciously. And scared the hell out of me.

Rich hadn't been my first man. He'd been my second. The only guy I'd ever married. The last guy I'd ever screwed. We weren't what anyone would call adventurous, but we seemed to do all right. At least, I had thought so. But what did I know?

The fear of disappointing Patrick nibbled away at my confidence. God, what if he discovered that I was a sucky bed partner? What if I didn't turn him on? What if I did something that just . . . *just what, Jessica? Made him go to another woman?*

No matter how many times your best friend or your therapist or your nosy neighbor says it's not your fault that your spouse was faithless, you don't believe 'em. If only I had tried harder. Been different. Attempted more.

"What are you thinking about?" asked Patrick.

"You tell me."

"I'm not reading your mind," he said. "This is a dream. We're sharing a mental connection, but your thoughts are your own."

I wanted to blurt, "Nothing! Keep doing that thing with your tongue!"

But he deserved my honesty.

"It's . . . uh, been a while. The last time I did this was with . . . Rich. My husband. And you know, I probably wasn't that great because he—um . . . with Charlene."

"Ah." He rubbed his jaw on the curve of my foot then his lips dragged along my heel. Talk about melted butter! I felt my throat catch, my heart pound. "Jessica, what am I doing that reminds you of Rich?"

"Nothing. He never did anything with my feet."

"What a shame." He nipped at my tendon. My belly jumped at the sudden violence, the cruel tenderness.

"Whoa. Wow." I grabbed hold of the velvet covers and held on. His attention turned to the other foot. More kissing . . . licking . . . nipping. "What are you doing to me?"

"I'm worshipping you."

What a beautiful thing to say. I turned into mush. I know, I know! I'm such a lame-o. If I had read about a hero saying that in a romance novel, I would've rolled my eyes. But hearing it from the perfect lips of a handsome man who had his mouth on my calf . . . well, it made me quiver.

And damn it, I was entitled to quiver.

"I'm sorry, Patrick. I'm really sorry."

"Jessica?"

I didn't want to meet his gaze. He'd know my shame, my fear. But I looked at him, anyway, and all I saw in his eyes was desire, was need . . . and that Emotion I Will Not Name. "Never apologize to me for how you feel or what you think or who you are." He kissed my instep. "You turn me on, Jessica. I will always want to touch you, to kiss you, to make love to you. I will never get enough of you. Never."

His words brought daggers of heat plunging into my core. All thoughts of inadequate bedroom techniques, all images of dissatisfied husbands, all doubts of self faded.

Only Patrick existed.

Chapter 18

I wiggled my toes. "You know, the top part of me likes to be worshipped, too."

"I will get there, love." His promise sent a flutter of anticipation through me. I already felt edgy, hot.

"I want to touch you."

"There will be time," he said, "to do as you wish."

He discovered my knee. He kissed every centimeter of it, flicked his tongue at its dimple. I enjoyed his exploration of what I used to think of as a mundane body part. *Lord-a-mercy.*

I almost jumped out of my skin when he lifted my leg to taste the underside.

"What's the back of the knee called?" he asked.

"Uh . . . I don't think it has a name."

"It should." His tongue wiggled across the sensitive flesh. I gasped as heat twisted from that spot all the way to you-know-where.

"We could just call it the oh-wow spot," I offered weakly.

He chuckled and the sound whispered on my skin. His fingers danced down my thigh, skimming close to woo-hoo zone. My breath hissed out as I was denied touch where I really wanted it.

"Who's the Spanish inquisitor now?" I grumbled.

Patrick was unmoved by my complaint. He continued to explore my flesh in excruciating detail.

I opened for him as he leaned down to pay homage to the inner slopes of my thighs, his tongue tracing a sensuous pattern. My whole body ached, trembled.

"You're so soft," he muttered. "And you smell like honeysuckle."

"Yeah, that's me—a delicate flower." I smiled widely, an idea perking. "You know how to get honey from a honeysuckle flower, don't you?"

Patrick's silver eyes were molten passion. Oooh, baby. My heart giddyupped something fierce.

"Do tell, love."

"You gotta pluck the flower from the stem."

His gaze dipped between my legs. "Hmmm."

"Then at the bottom, there is this little green knob."

Patrick slid onto his stomach, belly-crawling between my legs. I put my calves on his shoulders as he slid his hands under my ass and pulled me close. He breathed on my . . . uh, flower, and I nearly lost consciousness.

"You were saying something about a knob?" he asked, like he was a good student who was listening to the lecture instead of a bad student fantasizing about the hot teacher.

"Uh . . . yeah. You pluck the knob, but you gotta be careful and patient or you'll break it off. Then, you draw out the green thingie."

"Thingie?"

"Whatever the long green part is . . . oh, shut up. You're interrupting my very educational speech."

"Sorry." He breathed on my neglected nether regions again. The whoosh of warm air made me tingle and heat and forget what the hell I was blabbing about.

"What do you do next?" asked Patrick. He studied me like an anatomist mapping female genitalia.

"If you've pulled out the green thingie correctly, there is a drop or two of honey. You get to lick it."

"All that work," he mused. "And so little reward."

"Oh it's worth it," I said. "I'll show you sometime."

"I have an idea," said Patrick, as if suddenly inspired.

"Yeah?"

"I'll show *you* my honey-licking technique." He looked down, as if surprised to find himself staring at a woman's vagina. "And look! A flower I can practice on . . ."

The first sweep of Patrick's tongue made my hips arch off the bed.

Holy God!

He took another taste and another. He created a slow, sweet torment. One that he seemed to like. His moan vibrated deliciously against me. Yeah, he liked it.

I could count on one hand how many times a guy had given me this kind of intimacy. Rich hadn't liked giving oral sex to me (though he'd loved to be on the receiving end) so I'd rarely gotten such a yowzer gift.

"Tell me what you want," demanded Patrick in a husky tone. "Tell me what you like."

"You. This. More." My fingers tunneled through his hair and scraped against his skull. I wanted to pull him closer and to push him away. Tremors rippled, unbearable and exquisite.

"I want to please you," he said.

I don't think I'd ever heard anyone say that to me before. *I want to please you.* My head spun with the possibilities of that phrase. Of what it meant to hear Patrick say it . . . and mean it.

"You are pleasing me," I managed. My voice sounded shaky. "I like what you're doing."

"I like what I'm doing, too." He rose up a little and met my gaze. "But I want to make you come. I want to taste you. I want to feel you. I want to give you pleasure, love. Tell me how."

"Keep talking like that and you won't need to do another thing." Sweat pearled my skin. I felt hot, so damned hot, and it was because Patrick could stoke my fire just by *talking.* It might've been stupid to fall for such slick, too-pretty words, but I was happily doing it. Falling for the words. For the man.

Patrick leaned forward and traced a lazy line to my *knob.* He flicked it repeatedly.

"Oooh. Um . . . yeah, good. Definite thumbs-up on that move."

"Would you like me to do it again?"

"Yeah. And do it a lot."

"As you wish." Patrick took my hands and guided them to my pubic area. "Open for me."

I did. Oh hell, did I ever. I slid my fingers along my vulva, my breath catching at the intimacy of such an act, and parted myself for him.

His mouth descended . . . and devoured.

Raw pleasure jolted through me as his tongue did

wondrous, unimaginable things. As that wicked, gorgeous mouth created a maelstrom of sensations, my fingers trailed up to his temples, caught in his hair. Rational thought evaporated. Joyfully, I matched his rhythm with tiny movements of my own.

Everything turned to heat and to ecstasy.

The rapturous feeling built, rising, and I reached for it, wanting it . . . I arched, moans echoing, and bless his lustful heart, Patrick nipped and licked and suckled.

I burst into a thousand, white-hot stars.

Vaguely, I heard Patrick groan, felt his tongue lap at me, but I was floating in beauty, in light.

It was quite possible I had left my body altogether. I hadn't responded this way to making love for a very, very long time. I had to admit that not even Rich had brought me this kind of all-encompassing, mind-losing bliss.

When I regained my senses, Patrick had risen to his knees, one hand fisted against his thigh, the other wrapped around his hard cock.

He was trembling, my handsome lover, and I nearly wept at the sight of his desire.

"A thaisce."

I opened my arms, beckoning him, and he slid on top of me. He nuzzled my breasts, his tongue swiping each puckered nipple. "So beautiful," he murmured, drawing one taut bud into his mouth. He released it, grazed the tip. "Jessica. My Jessica. If I lived another thousand years, I could never pay enough homage to your breasts."

"But you'll try, right?"

"Yes." He grinned, scraping his jaw along my

collarbone then catching my chin between his teeth. His silver eyes sparkled. (I know, I know, you're thinking enough with the silver eyes, but if you had a lover who had eyes like Patrick's, you'd go on and on, too . . . so there.) "Is there something else you would like?"

"Yes," I said, "I would like very much if you would . . . oh, I dunno . . . fuck me."

He drew in a sharp breath, his gaze darkening. He said nothing else. He didn't have to now, did he? Instead, he wrapped his hands under my shoulders and positioned himself above me.

The first warm, hard slide of his cock tested our compatibility. I nearly swallowed my tongue at the amazing feel of his penetration. He kept his movements slow and careful and I met each of his thrusts, bumping my still-humming clit against him.

His head dropped to my shoulder, his uneven breath skittering against my neck.

I wrapped my legs around his waist and tilted up my hips. I knew Patrick was capable of bringing me to another orgasm and by golly, I wanted it. My nails dug into his back as I encouraged him to pick up the pace.

"You're killing me," he whispered. "I don't want to hurt you."

"It's a dream," I reminded him. "You can't hurt me. I want you, Patrick. More than anyone I've wanted *ever.*"

He lifted his head so that he could look into my eyes to see the truth of my words. "You mean that, don't you?"

"Yes. I've never felt this way. How could I?"

He kissed me, his tongue thrusting into my mouth. It was a possessive kiss, and maybe a hint of the way he really wanted to take me. I shuddered to think of

how much he was holding back, of how well he protected me from the full force of his passion.

"I want you to come again," he said. "I want you to
come on my cock and scream my name."

"Well, then . . . let's give it a whirl, shall we?"

He let go then. Just gave in to primal urges. It was the
difference, I found, between making love and mating.

The ability to think once again deserted me.

Teeth nipped, nails scratched, and flesh slapped
against flesh. He brought me to another breath-stealing
climax and as the pleasure rolled through me, I sure-
as-hell screamed his name.

As I convulsed around him, he thrust hard, deep . . .
he buried himself inside me, filled me completely.
Then his big body tightened over mine, his eyes went
blind, and the last word he uttered was, "Jessica."

When I awoke, I was alone. I stretched, feeling replete after the va-va-voom dream.

Patrick had slipped out of bed and out of the room
entirely. I would've known if he was near, and he
wasn't. Sniffle. I wanted to cuddle. My hand swept
across his pillow and knocked something off it. I rolled
onto my side and reached for the object.

Honeysuckle.

He'd picked me several flowers and left them next
to where I'd been sleeping. A reminder then . . . and
maybe, a promise. I pressed the petals to my nose and
took in the sweetness of the scent and of his gesture.

Patrick?

Hello, love.

Thank you for the honeysuckle.

A chuckle rippled. *I look forward to a demonstra-tion of your honey-licking techniques.*

You'll be surprised what I can do with a long, hard stem.

Too bad I don't have a stem. What can you do with a big thick limb?

I rolled my eyes. Patrick was *such* a guy. *Where are you?*

With Damian and Stan. They think the same creature that killed Emily also killed Sharon.

Maybe I've watched too many episodes of CSI, *but if it was Lor going freakazoid . . . why would he change his method of killing? He didn't claw me or any of the others that first night. Why such destruction of the torso without any sign of feeding?*

It's a good question, love.

I have another one. What or who has Lorćan been feeding on for the last two weeks?

Maybe if you can connect mentally with him again, you can ask him. By the way, the Consortium will meet at the high school gym in two hours. See you there?

Oh yeah. I love hanging out with the Panel of Doom. They're a laugh a minute.

I felt the stroke of fingers along my jaw. *Until then,* céadsearc.

I followed my mental connection to my kids to check in on 'em. They were awake, ensconced on the new couch in their jammies, and watching Cartoon Network. They were eating big bowls of Count Choc-ula cereal. Oh, ha ha. I wondered which jokester had purchased that sugar-coated junk and served it to Bry and Jenny for breakfast.

I took a quick shower, put on a pair of shorts and a tank top, and shoved my feet into a pair of flip-flops. It was nice to see my pedicure had held up. I also put on my new belt and swords. I really needed some sexy pants to go with the swords, too. Wearing the gold blades with jean shorts seemed silly somehow, but I had promised Patrick to always wear the weapons. Silly or not, I wanted the protection.

Hunger tightened my stomach. Uh-oh. No Patrick. No donor. My fangs extended and I poked at the incisors with my tongue. Well, shit. I couldn't go into the living room looking like the creature on my kids' cereal box. Hmmm. Okay. I was a mom. I was a vampire. I could improvise.

By the time I'd gotten to the stairs, I still hadn't a clue about a way to find vamp food. I sat on the top step, hoping inspiration would strike. *Um, Patrick?*

Sorry, love. We're moving Sharon to another location. Can you wait?

Yeah. Sure. See you soon.

"Hi."

The deep baritone startled me. I jolted to my feet, my hands against the swords, and whirled around. A man lounged against the wall behind me, looking tough and bored, like Sodapop Curtis from *The Outsiders*. Only this guy was much better-looking than Rob Lowe, and quite frankly, that shouldn't be possible.

"Uh . . . hi there," I said. "Who the hell are you?"

"Johnny Angelo."

Oh. Well, that said it all, apparently. I knew that he wouldn't be standing in my house unless he was Patrick-approved, so I wasn't afraid of him. Besides, he didn't put out "evil guy" vibes.

He wore jeans, a white T-shirt, and a black leather jacket. His Converse sneakers were black and scuffed. He had dark blond hair, sad blue eyes fanned by thick lashes, and pouty red lips. Why did he look so familiar?

Gawd. He was impossibly handsome. The kind of handsome that defined a *GQ* model, or a royal prince, or a movie star. Movie star. Whoa. That was it. But . . . oh, no *way*.

"You seen Lucifer?" he asked. "She's missing."

"The ruler of hell? That Lucifer?"

"My cat," he clarified, "though it's likely she's also the ruler of hell."

Something about his voice finally clicked. "*You're* Johnny Angelo?"

"Said so, didn't I?"

"The 1950s movie star . . . oh my God! My mother *loves* you. I can't tell you how many times she made me sit through *Rebel's Cause*. She told me the story fifty-million times about how you disappeared after filming *West of the Garden Divine*."

His lips hitched into a half-grin. "Won a posthumous Oscar for that one."

"You got turned into a vampire?"

"Yeah." He looked at me, those blue eyes taking me in. "Haven't fed yet?"

"Uh, no."

He tilted his neck and tapped the vein. "Don't mind offering."

I hesitated. What was the etiquette for drinking from other vampires? Especially vampires of the opposite gender when one was, like it or not, attached to a particular male? Crud. I was starving, but I didn't want to accidentally do something against policy or tradition. Again. Worse, I didn't want another lecture from Stan or Patrick.

"Only drink vintage?" he asked.

"Vintage?"

"Jessica Matthews. Pat's girl, right? He's vintage. You picky like that?"

It took a second to interpret his meaning. "I'm not a blood snob," I said. "I'm new to the vampire thing and I've already flubbed up."

He grinned and tapped his neck again. "C'mon, Jess. Drink."

"Fine. But only a *little*. And if Patrick kills you because my fangs were in your neck, it's not my fault."

"Whatever."

Well, he *was* one of my mother's favorite film stars. Mom was on another cruise—to Alaska, this time— and I wasn't looking forward to saying, "Hey, Ma! Guess what? I'm dead!" when she returned. But as soon as she'd recovered from fainting, I was soooo telling her that I noshed on Johnny Angelo's neck. Maybe I should ask him for his autograph. I bet that would make a fortune on eBay.

He waited, patient. Or bored. Maybe both.

"You've fed, right? Because if you don't have enough to share, really, I'll be okay."

"Drink."

I stood in front of Johnny and gazed longingly at his neck. I stalled the urge to gouge and gnaw, but it was a hard-fought battle. Since I'd only snacked on two people, I wasn't exactly versed in vampire table manners.

"What?" asked Mr. Verbose.

I did a quick mental check on Jenny and Bryan. They were watching an old episode of *Dexter's Lab*. Good. They would stay occupied a few minutes more. I licked Johnny's neck. He shuddered then adjusted his position so that there was more space between us. I didn't feel any sensual tension, though. Patrick seemed to be the only guy in my lust zone.

Johnny's hands crept around my waist. His fingers stabbed my hips, but he wasn't getting fresh, just anchoring himself. Though I recognized how good-looking Johnny was, I really didn't feel any sexual attraction for him. Still, we were in an intimate position and I'd just licked the man's skin . . . and I felt guilty. Like I was cheating on Patrick.

"Ready?" he asked.

I pressed my fangs into his neck. A quick stab then . . . *nirvana*. Oh man, I was starved. I gulped Johnny's delicious, warm blood until my hunger pains faded. Finally, I felt sated enough to release him.

"You taste really good," I said, wiping off my mouth in a very unladylike way. "Thanks."

"No prob." Johnny unhooked himself from me. I felt like I'd had sixteen cups of coffee. Woo-hoo! Nothing like some breakfast to rev you up for the day . . . er, night.

"Oh sorry. Got some blood trickling." I reached out to swipe away the residue of my sloppy eating, but Johnny slapped a hand on his neck.

"Got it, Jess. Thanks."

My back hit something solid at the same time I saw the direction of Johnny's gaze. Arms slid around my waist and yanked me backward against a rock-hard chest. I looked up and saw the stern jaw of Patrick. He glared at Johnny as if he was considering the most painful way to make him implode.

"Hey honey," I said weakly. "Johnny . . . uh, let me snack on him."

"That's why I'm here. To offer what you've already taken from him."

The tone of his voice made the hair rise on my neck. I had never heard him sound that pissed off before. And I had given him plenty of reasons to get mad in the last two weeks.

"She is claimed," Patrick said. "You know what that means."

"For now." To my astonishment, Johnny's gaze raked me as if I was a choice steak and he was an expert cook. Seconds before, I'd been positive that he had no intention of putting the moves on me, but for some reason he wanted Patrick to think that he desired me.

"If you don't bind with her, then she'll be up for grabs again." Johnny smiled lasciviously at me. "And I have to tell you, Pat, I sure like the way she bites."

"Hey!" I protested. "That sounds really smarmy!"

Patrick released me, then picked me up by the waist and set me aside. He grabbed Johnny, slamming him against the wall. Patrick's hand wrapped around the actor's throat and shoved him upward, holding my mother's idol at least two feet off the floor.

"What are you doing? Stop that!" I batted at Patrick's arms. "He was teasing. Weren't you, Johnny?"

"Nope," he wheezed. "If Pat . . . doesn't . . . want . . . you . . . I do."

Patrick growled. He actually freaking growled. He

pressed so hard on Johnny, the wall cracked as the poor vamp was pushed literally into the paneling.

"Are you suicidal, you liar?" I yelled.

"Jessica. Go away." Patrick turned to stare at me, eyes glowing with rage and his fangs bared. I realized, belatedly, that he wasn't exactly feeling rational.

"Uh . . . sweetie . . . put down the moron, okay?"

"He wishes to claim you. And you are mine!"

Possessive *much.* Sheesh. I looked at Johnny, who wasn't struggling. In fact, he seemed content to allow Patrick to choke him. I was fairly sure that since vampires couldn't breathe, Johnny couldn't suffocate. However, it was possible that Patrick had the strength and the desire to squeeze off his head and I didn't want to watch that happen . . . or clean up the mess.

"My mother will kill you if you decapitate her favorite film star."

Patrick frowned. "What? Where is your mother?"

"Alaska."

He blinked down at me and the red glow in his eyes dimmed. "Alaska?"

"You're still choking him," I pointed out. "Maybe you could stop."

The tormented yowl of a cat followed by vociferous barking echoed through the house. Since we didn't have any pets—not since the Hamster Incident—I wasn't too happy to hear those sounds. Kids always knew when to ratchet up the stress another notch. It's like they enjoyed playing poker with their mother's mental state: She's getting ready to crack, ante up!

Now, with my lover on the verge of murdering the star of *Rebel's Cause,* my kids had found a way to make the situation worse. Or rather, they'd found a way to introduce a new situation while I was still trying to deal with the first one.

Ain't motherhood grand?

The noise increased in volume then I heard clattering, breakage, and children's delighted screams. I didn't have to worry about going to the mess, however, because it came rampaging up the stairs.

A sleek golden cat zipped past me and tore around the corner toward my bedroom.

"I found your cat," I said to Johnny.

He smiled faintly. Patrick had lessened his grip on the guy's throat, but he was still trying to push him through the wall.

Two huge black-furred mongrels raced up the stairs, their maws snapping and growling. "Are those *dogs*?" I shouted. "In my *house*?"

Jenny and Bryan, shouting and laughing, hurried after the animal chaos. While Bryan hurried into my bedroom, Jenny skidded to a stop and turned around. She put her hands on her hips and looked at me, lips pursed. "Hi Mommy."

"Hello, monkey britches." I smiled brightly as her gaze took in Patrick and Johnny. Shit. I tried to remember how to work the you-are-not-seeing-this magic, but I drew a blank. Oh, that's right. Nobody had taught me how to do memory-wipes.

"Hello, Mr. O'Halloran," she said politely. "Are you trying to kill that man?"

Chapter 19

Jenny's sweetly delivered question snapped Patrick out of his fury. He let go of Johnny. The actor flopped to the floor like a tossed puppet then leaned against the cracked wall and closed his eyes.

"I'm sorry, Jenny," said Patrick, his tone formal. He bent down on one knee and gestured to her. "I didn't mean to frighten you."

"I wasn't scared," she said. She looked at Johnny, and then at Patrick. "Mommy says physical violence is for the weak-minded."

I flinched. I did say that, but mostly to her and to Bryan after they'd engaged in one of their slap-pinch-hit fights. This was what always happened when your kids listened to you—they tucked away certain tidbits to say when you least wanted to hear them repeated.

"Sometimes a person is forced to violence when he or those he loves are threatened," said Patrick.

"You mean that guy tried to hurt you?"

Patrick paused, obviously thinking about his answer.

He was in no mood to apologize for defending his claim on me, but I knew that he realized he couldn't give Jenny carte blanche to knock the snot out of anyone she perceived as a threat. I understood the issue he was trying to skirt, but Jenny was literal-minded. I knew my daughter. She was thinking: A smack for a smack. Now, Patrick was trying to explain, badly I might add, why an emotional hurt required a physical response.

"He hurt me . . . in a way," said Patrick carefully.

"What way?" She gasped and narrowed her eyes at Johnny. "Did he kick you in your woobies?"

Patrick blinked at her, opened his mouth, and snapped it shut.

"If he didn't kick you, then what did he—"

"You know what, Jenny?" I interrupted. "Why don't we go see if the kitty is still alive, hmmm?"

Bryan darted out and shouted, "The cat climbed up your bedpost, Mom! It's on the top railing. The dogs are going nuts."

Jenny dropped her interrogation and ran to join her brother. I would not think about the state of chaos that currently reigned in my room. Or what destruction was being wrought. Or how I was going to rub out claw marks from my cherrywood finish or get animal hair off my sheets.

Patrick stood up, his expression filled with both temper and chagrin. I helped Johnny to his feet and immediately removed myself from grasping distance, in case he decided to do something else stupid.

"Was that cat wearing jewelry?" I asked.

"Yeah," said Johnny. "It's an ankh."

"Oh." What the hell was an ankh? Did I care? I

searched the depths of my soul. No, I did not. "And the dogs?"

"Not mine," said Johnny. He ambled down the hall and into my bedroom.

Well, day-amn. Was everyone going into my personal, private space? Add some dance music and a pitcher of margaritas and it would officially be Party Central in there. Alas, I had bigger fish to fry. (And my blender was busted, anyway.)

"What the hell is wrong with you?" I yelled at Patrick. "You can't go all caveman on me every time I try to eat."

"Yes, I can. Especially if you're fang-deep in Johnny Angelo's neck." He glanced down the hall. We heard a round of growls and "hey, that's my mom's underwear!" I rolled my eyes. I mentally added new lingerie onto Patrick's tab.

"I hope it wasn't the sparkly pink teddy," he murmured. "I really liked that one."

"Patrick? Focus, please." We walked toward the open door of my room, though truth be told, I did not want to look inside. "Stan didn't buy the kids a pair of slobbering dogs, did he?"

"No. Those mutts are—"

The cat bulleted between us.

"Lucifer!" shouted Johnny as he hurried after her. "That's enough, you crazy bitch!"

"You gotta put a quarter in the Cussing Jar," yelled a delighted Jenny, who was hot on his heels.

Bryan shot past us, followed by one of the big, black dogs. I frowned at the fuzzy, wagging tail. "They look like wolves."

"They are." Patrick grabbed my shoulder and put a finger against my opened mouth. "Ssshhh! Trust me, Jessica, your children are safe."

"Okay." I trusted Patrick. He would never put my kids in danger. I knew he would sooner give up his own life than endanger theirs. That thought hit me like a lead fist. Wasn't that a helluva good quality for a parent?

"Why don't you like Johnny?" I asked.

"I do like him. I just don't like him anywhere near you."

"Why not?"

"He wants you."

"No, he doesn't. He wants you."

"What?"

"Not like that. Probably. I don't know. You're really cute."

"Jessica . . ."

I shrugged. "He wanted to piss you off. Why?"

Patrick gauged my expression and realized I was going to annoy the hell out of him until I got answers. A muscle ticked in his jaw. "I know the location of his Master and I won't tell him. No one will."

I crossed my arms and stared at him.

"He wants to kill her."

"He won't tell us why," said Darrius as he strolled into the hallway, his waist wrapped in a towel. He held up a shredded purple teddy. "Sorry."

"You don't look sorry," I said, releasing my grip on Patrick to grab the mangled silk out of Darrius' hand.

Patrick took the teddy from me. "I never got to see you in this one," he said morosely.

"You've been gallivanting around my house with your brother—as *dogs*—chasing a cat?" I fingered the swords at my sides, drawing Darrius' amazed gaze.

"We're wolves," corrected Darrius. "And chasing a cat is a lot of fun. Especially when it's Lucifer. She hates us."

"I can see why." I poked Patrick in the arm. "Why aren't you all over him about being practically naked in my hallway? Huh? Your guardians flirt with me all the time and you don't try to kill them."

"Ah. Patrick knows we cannot pursue you. A shape-shifter can only mate with another shape-shifter. We are not compatible with other humanoids." Darrius' smile faded. "It is one of the reasons our species is dying out."

"One of the Consortium's goals is to figure out how to revitalize the lycan population." Patrick put his arm around me and pulled me into another embrace. I have to admit, it felt great to be held so securely.

"Darrius, I'm sorry." I wasn't sure what else to say. *Hey, it totally sucks that you're part of an almost extinct race of mythical beings?*

"Thank you, Jessica. We are hanging on, though there are only a few thousand of us left, and we don't have many females. Our children . . . we are lucky if they live a year."

"That's horrible!" My heart ached for him, for Drake, for the wehrs. "Is the Consortium close to finding a cure or a horde of females or something?"

"We're working on it," said Patrick, "and it's one of the reasons we want to create a community here. So we can raise families in true security."

Surely he was thinking of Dairine and their children—how he'd lost them to ignorance and violence. I wrapped my arms around him and tried to wish him free of all misery. He'd lost so many people whom he loved. I was so sad for him. I wanted him to never suffer again. But that wasn't the way life worked, not even the life of a vampire.

Is fear rith maith ná drochseasamh.

And that means what?

A good run is better than a bad stand.

Oh. And that means what?

It means, Jessica, that life is about choices. Sometimes you fight, sometimes you flee, but you never surrender.

"We understand, *liebling,*" said Drake. "Truly we do."

In the high school gym, I sat with Drake and Darrius on the bleachers. Patrick was off with Stan doing something with the evil PDAs. As we waited for the rest of the Consortium members to arrive, I lectured the D-men on how to act in front of my kids.

"Let's go over it again, shall we?"

"We will not shape-shift in front of your children unless it's an emergency," said Drake.

"And if it is an emergency, we will try to find a place to hide, or, if that isn't possible, we will change so that they see our backsides," added Darrius.

I stared at Drake. He rolled his eyes. "I did not 'flop around' in front of Jenny. I was behind the couch and she was on the stairs. She saw only my head." He pointed at his skull. "This one! On *mein* shoulders!"

"I know." I waved at them. "Continue."

"We will keep shorts or jeans stashed in many locations so that when we shift back into human form, we'll be able to cover our woobies," said Darrius.

"Excellent." I looked at Drake and smiled benignly. "How's your rear end?"

"Sore," he groused. "Not even Brigid would heal the scratches from that damned cat."

"She was too busy laughing," said Darrius. "It's a good thing your daughter didn't charge him for the German curse words, too. *Mein bruder* is a wealthy man, but Jenny could very soon make him a poor one. She is an excellent entrepreneur."

"That's one word for it," I agreed.

"Jessica?"

The soft female voice had me clenching my teeth. Drake and Darrius' hands strayed to the weapons on their hips and I was oddly grateful for that slightly disturbing gesture of friendship. I scooted around to face Charlene Mason. She stood next to the bleachers, looking up at me on the third row.

"Hello, Charlene." I managed to sound civil. Goodie for me. "Guys, would you mind giving us a sec?"

Drake and Darrius looked at me, and then at Charlene with blatant curiosity. They got up and sauntered away. The urge to yell, "Kill her! Kill her now, my minions!" was so strong I had to bite my tongue. I doubted they would have taken their dirks to her on my say-so. Probably.

She twisted her hands, nervous as all get-out, and nibbled her lips. "I've applied to be the teacher for the new school that opens in September. I'm not accredited. Not yet. But I've been taking online courses and I'm close to getting my bachelor's degree."

I was stunned. I had no idea Charlene had been trying to get an education while working at a low-paying job and raising a baby. I didn't want to be, but I was impressed. Impressed enough to almost respect her efforts. But I don't suppose I had enough forgiveness in me to gloss over the fact she'd been my husband's mistress.

"I was taking online college courses before I started working for Rich. That was just supposed to be a part-time job . . . and well, it turned into a full-time job and I quit college."

Her words reminded me that almost twenty years ago, I had been the receptionist at Matthews Insurance. I worked there part-time, too, while I attended community college, which had been a long drive to Tulsa three times a week, and decided who to date next. Rich's daddy owned the little business and as soon as his son earned an MBA, Mr. Matthews brought him in as a full partner. Rich and I started going out, we fell in love, and I quit college and married him. A year later, I was pregnant with Bryan, and happy to be little Suzy Homemaker, complete with a husband who didn't want me to work a 9-to-5 job.

And here was Charlene, living her future the way I had lived my past. Except now, she was doing it alone. She didn't have a husband or a house or a cent. But she had gumption and plenty of it.

"Why didn't you leave?" I asked. "Surely life would've been better for you somewhere else."

"My son will never know his daddy except through

this town and these people." She hesitated. Maybe she thought talking to me was wrongheaded. Maybe it was, but for once, I wanted to hear what she had to say. "I guess that's not the case anymore, not with all the humans moving out and the other folks moving in. All the same, Rich was born and raised here. I figured his son should be, too."

I didn't want to like her. Or rather I didn't want to remember that I liked her. How many times had Charlene eaten dinner with my family? Or taken my kids for ice cream? She helped me plan Rich's fortieth birthday party. By that time, the affair had been going on about two months. Rich turned forty and a month later, we were supposed to celebrate sixteen years of wedded bliss.

"You want me to say that I wrecked your marriage?" asked Charlene. "That you and Rich were happy and I seduced him away from his family?"

"Did I ever say those things to you? I don't recall." Somehow I couldn't quite work up the usual fury. "I'm not a fool, Charlene. No matter how I felt about my marriage to Rich, he obviously wasn't happy. He never once told me he wanted something different. I think that's what pissed me off the most. I never got a chance to fix whatever was wrong between us."

"I did seduce him."

I looked at her sharply. She met my gaze though I could see it about killed her to do it.

"He was a good man. A handsome man. And I wanted what you had, Jessica. A family. A home. A husband who loved me and took care of me."

"It takes two," I said, shaken by her confession.

"Or it takes one who's really damned persistent. I've lived with my shame. The shame of what I've done. He told me at his birthday party that night. Ended it. Said I could keep my job, but only if I never made another move on him."

I tried to take in what she was saying, tried to understand her reasons for admitting to me what wasn't true. Rich had given in to temptation. Did it matter if he initiated the affair or simply gave in to Charlene's offer? "I appreciate you lying—either to make me feel better or to get that teaching job. You might as well stop, girl. What's between me and Rich is gone. And I can't change the outcome."

"I'm not lying," said Charlene. Her lower lip trembled. "I'm selfish. I wouldn't give you the comfort of a lie. I wanted Rich all to myself." She rubbed her hands on her jean shorts then clenched her fists. "He was going to take you to Hawaii for your wedding anniversary. A surprise. But I had one for him, too. I made him meet me at the Motel 6. I knew Linda's little sister worked the night shift and made sure she'd seen us so that she'd call you."

Emily had called me that night. I remembered that now. And Charlene had planned it? She had not only tried, but had actually managed to pry apart my marriage. What did that say about me and Rich? That we were human and prone to stupid mistakes? Or that we didn't love each other enough to trust or to forgive?

"He was a good man. But he was still a *man*," Charlene continued. "Enough temptation and even a good man will do the wrong thing. He caved, and you got there just in time to see him do it. I'd already dropped my little bomb. I was pregnant—two months along. Even when he stood there and told you he was leaving, the minute you walked out the door, he changed his mind. He wanted to go to you. Wanted *me* to tell *you* how I trapped him with his own lusts."

She sounded disgusted, but I didn't know if it was because she felt the weight of her own actions or because Rich had wanted her to face up to the consequences of what they'd done.

"God, Charlene. I threw him out." I pressed my fingers to my temples. "I was so angry. Lord-a-mercy, I'd never felt that kind of anger before in my life. Everything shattered. Because of you."

"Yes," said Charlene. "Because of me. Rich moved in with me and tried to make it work. He got a lawyer because you got one, but I knew he didn't want to divorce you. Didn't want to lose his family. He loved y'all."

My insides crumbled into dust and the cold hollow left filled up with acid. It burned me, burned me until I wanted to scream, but I clenched my teeth together and swallowed the barbed knot lodged in my throat.

"He would've done right by me if I had let him go. He'd've supported the baby, took care of me financially. But I kept hanging on, tooth and nail. I was scared. So scared, I couldn't admit I was making him miserable," said Charlene. "What's worse? Killing a man or killing his spirit?"

"I don't know," I said softly. How should I feel about Charlene's disclosure? Everything I had believed about Rich . . . everything I had allowed myself to think about him . . . hadn't been true. Well, he *had* fucked Charlene. Was that something that could've been forgiven? He hadn't left us, hadn't wanted to end our marriage. *He hadn't wanted Charlene.* At least not forever. All this time, my anger and self-righteousness had clouded my mind and poisoned my heart.

"The night he died? He wasn't going to the hospital." Charlene sounded like every word was being pulled from her by force. Her jaw clenched, but she got ahold of herself. "We had a terrible argument. He told me that he loved you, that he wanted his life back. He said he'd rather beg your forgiveness for the rest of your days than spend another minute with me."

I saw the truth in her eyes. And I knew it was the truth, because glittering along with it was a big ol' helping of shame. All this time I'd felt like the bitchy wife who hated the poor, young, single mother who'd committed the sin of loving the same man I did. No matter how young or how pretty or how conniving she'd been, Rich had wanted me.

"You tell me this now, when I can't take back what I said, what I did. We were so hateful to each other. That's what I had in my heart for that man. Hatred. And before you, I loved him. Together, we had created something good together. Something wonderful."

"That's true enough," she said softly.

Hadn't I just been thinking about building a bridge to Charlene? Wasn't it time to heal wounds and begin again? I had to rethink what happened with Rich and what that meant to me.

What about Patrick? I loved him. In a desperate, terrifying, oh-my-God way. My feelings for him weren't comfortable or serene. But maybe love wasn't supposed to wrap around you like an old comfy robe all the time. To love strongly meant taking risks. Was I ready to risk for Patrick?

"I figure you'll protest."

I blinked down at Charlene, startled out of my thoughts. "Protest?"

"Yeah. I understand why you wouldn't want me teaching Bryan and Jenny same as I understand why you don't want 'em to know their little brother. But I'm applying for the teaching job," Charlene reiterated, with steel in her tone. "You go on ahead and try to stop me."

She turned around and stalked away, chin tipped and shoulders straight. I watched her leave, feeling like she'd punched me in the stomach.

Well, now. Charlene sure had issued a challenge.

So what was I gonna do about it?

Chapter 20

"We cannot keep protecting your brother just because he is the son of Ruadan!" roared Ivan Taganov.

Patrick looked at the big Russian, one brow quirked. Ivan reminded me of a snorting bull, pawing the ground, just waiting for the hapless bullfighter to step into the ring.

The meeting had been in session for ten whole minutes and it wasn't going well. The announcement about Sharon's death had been received poorly, particularly by Linda, who kept siding with Ivan. I didn't know if she agreed with him because she figured Lorćan was the bad guy or if she felt compelled to support her Master's viewpoint.

We all sat in a circle of chairs like we were having group therapy for the damned. I sat between Patrick and Darrius. On Patrick's right was Stan and on Darrius' left was Drake. Stan, Linda, Marybeth, and Ivan filled up one side of the circle. François, Brigid,

Johnny, and the rest of the Panel of Doom members filled up the other side. Completing our little Dante's ring was the Broken Heart Turn-bloods. (We were thinking of starting a band with that name. I've always wanted to play the drums.)

Ivan held up one of his huge hands and counted off on his sausage-shaped fingers. "Lor kills eleven people that the Consortium is forced to save. He mauls innocent humans, including his favorite donor. He even tries to kill your mate and still you wish to save him!"

"Hey, asshole," I interrupted, my temper snapping, "I'm the mate in question and I want to save him, too. I don't think Lorćan killed Emily or Sharon. And he didn't try to kill me, either."

Ivan's glacier blue eyes raked me. "Yes. We heard the tale of another lycan. Pah!"

"Oh no, you didn't. You did not just *pah* me!" I launched myself off my chair with every intention of marching across the gym and ripping off Ivan's balls, but Patrick grabbed my shirt and yanked me into my seat.

"Apologize to Jessica," he said mildly.

"This is not the council of ancients," sneered Ivan. "I say what I like, even to you. Here, you are not a prince."

"And you still owe Jessica an apology," said Patrick patiently, ignoring Ivan's jibe.

Obviously, the whole apology thing was a pissing contest between two males with egos the size of Montana. Even if Ivan did apologize to me, it wouldn't be sincere.

"You are not a prince here!" yelled Ivan.

What is he talking about? Are you a prince? I sent the questions into Patrick's mind. *Your father is . . . is . . . a vampire king? Holy shit! Does this mean you'll shower us with caviar and diamond tiaras?*

You know very well I'm not a prince. Ivan still thinks too much like a Romanov. They run their sect like a royal court.

Huh. Well, lucky for you that I hate eating fish eggs and wearing things that pull my hair. But Jenny would love a tiara.

Then she shall have one.

"Where is Nara?" asked François suddenly. "Should she not be here?"

Silence descended as thick and cloying as a bad perfume.

"When did she go missing?" asked Ivan, distracted from his temper tantrum. "Did no one search for her?"

I found it interesting that only François had noticed Nara's absence. Why? Had he noted that she was missing because he was involved with her in some way? Oh, c'mon. I couldn't see him and Nara doing the horizontal bop. Maybe he'd been put in charge of keeping track of her movements in case she was a Wraith trying to bring down the Consortium. I liked that idea better.

"Forget Nara!" said Ivan. "She is empty-headed and useless."

My irritation at Ivan had an instant reversal. A guy who insulted my nemesis wasn't all bad.

Ivan surged to his feet. He was one of the few vampires I'd met who wore facial hair. His goatee dripped off his chin like frozen black tar and it was pointy, which made him look sinister. "We must decide what to do about the Wraiths. And whether or not Patrick agrees—we must also hunt Lorćan."

"Someone else is attacking and killing innocents. Jessica barely escaped with her life."

"Pah!" yelled Ivan.

"Sit down, Ivan," demanded Brigid softly.

He glanced at the woman sitting primly in her chair, her serene gaze zeroed in on him. The gold symbols on her skin flared brightly as they swirled into a new pattern. Ivan looked as if he might be willing to take on an armada, but no man was brave enough to argue with Brigid. He slunk back to his seat, obviously unhappy but at least he kept his trap shut.

"I don't believe Lorćan attacked Jessica or killed Emily and Sharon," said Patrick. He stood in the middle of the circle, looking all strong and cute and leaderlike. "I believe there is another creature . . . maybe one that lived in this area and was drawn to us. Maybe one that is already among us."

"Diseased vamp," drawled Johnny. "You think one of us has the Taint."

"It's possible," said Patrick. "Though I find it strange that a vampire would kill without feeding."

"Progression of the disease," mused Stan. He was tapping information into his PDA. "If the vamp is in the dementia phase . . . who knows what he's thinking. But once that stage is reached, it's not possible to hide the effects."

"Everyone's accounted for," said a guy that I remembered seeing briefly at the first meeting. He had an exotic accent I couldn't place. I had no idea what his name was, either. "And no one has exhibited symptoms of the disease," he added.

I studied him while conversation weaved around me. His skin was the color of chocolate and he was so big and tall that he looked capable of snapping Ivan in half. He wore casual, but expensive clothes. He had a shaved head and while I've never found skulls particularly alluring features, this guy's was *sexy*. But the most fascinating thing about him was his eyes. They looked like burnished copper.

"Let's just say that we buy your theory about Lorćan not being the murdering bastard," said Linda. She leaned forward and gave Patrick the stink-eye. "If all the paranormal folks are accounted for and vampires aren't showing signs of the Taint, then we're left with the humans. Most of 'em have already packed their bags and headed to greener pastures. That being the case, we're left with believing there's an unknown attacker running around Broken Heart and clawing people to death."

Damn. Her logic was almost irrefutable. And I wasn't the only one who thought so. I saw people nodding and heard murmurs of agreement.

"I saw two creatures that night," I insisted for the gabillionth time. At least, I was ninety-nine percent sure I had seen two. I was certain Lorćan hadn't attacked me. He had rescued me. But what if I was wrong? What if the glamour had screwed up my mind? And if Lorćan was innocent, why hadn't he contacted me again? Was it because he couldn't . . . or wouldn't?

"No offense, Jess, but we can't count on you being in your right mind when you got hurt." She looked at me, her gaze entreating, but her expression was set in no-bullshit stubborn. "Honey, Patrick's brother is just about the only one who could be murderin' folks. We can't forget he's the reason eleven of us are sitting here, part of the blood-suckers bandwagon."

"We vote," commanded Ivan. "Should we track and kill Lorćan?"

"You are proposing," said Brigid in a quiet, deadly tone, "that we vote on the cold-blooded murder of my grandson?" She rose to her full height, which was at least six feet, and swept her arm out, as if to encompass all who sat in judgment of Lorćan. "Who will cut off the head of Lorćan O'Halloran and show it to Ruadan the First?"

Nobody answered and very few could meet Brigid's gaze. Her fury encompassed the entire room, so much so that I felt like a little girl wrongly sent to the principal's office. Brigid strode across the room until she was toe to toe with Ivan. "Would you do such a thing, Ivan? You, who owe Lorćan more than any man here! You would kill him?"

"My debt to my friend is paid," said Ivan, though his baby blues flashed with regret and pain. "The monster who does these things is not Lor. How can it be so when we all know he would rather greet the dawn than hurt a living soul? No, *vedomye zheny*, you cling to hope where there is none."

I watched as Linda laid a hand on Ivan's arm. To my amazement, the bluster went out of Ivan like a popped balloon.

"I honor Brigid," Ivan said in a worn voice. He rubbed a hand across his jaw. "But if Lorćan is innocent of killing the humans . . . why doesn't he turn himself in?"

"Ivan's right," I muttered as I paced the high school parking lot. Patrick leaned against one of the big, white RVs parked near Sharon's pink Twinkie. "If he's innocent, why is Lorćan staying away from everyone?"

"I'm sure that my brother has his reasons," said Patrick.

He sounded less than sure so I went to him and slipped my arms around his waist. In his silver eyes, I saw beautiful, terrifying emotions. "What are you thinking about?" I asked.

"You."

We lifted into the air. Just like that, he flew me up and away. It was joyful to feel the wind against my face and to see the ground zoom by. I wasn't afraid of it. Not anymore. This was freedom. This was a gift.

We landed near the entrance to the Boob & Barley Barn. The neon sign, which consisted of two stalks of wheat pressed between a pair of breasts, had already been dismantled. Bulldozers were parked on the surrounding field and half the structure had already been torn down.

Patrick took my hand and walked me around the back of the building. The biggest RV I'd seen yet was parked in the gravel parking lot. The long sleek vehicle was solid black, except for the gold symbols painted on it.

Patrick saw the direction of my gaze. "Protection spells," he said. "Only I, Stan, or Damian can enter alone and others only if they're accompanied by one of us."

"Wow. Good to know."

He waved his hand across the entire bus. The symbols sparkled then changed patterns. He smiled at me. "Now, only I, Stan, Damian, or *you* can enter alone."

I looked at the RV then at Patrick. I was getting those warm fuzzies again. Darn the man. "This is your version of giving me a key to your apartment?"

Patrick laughed. "Yes, love. That's an excellent analogy." He opened the door and ushered me inside.

To the left was a black curtain that blocked off my view. So, I turned right and entered the luxurious domain of an Irish vampire who could afford a custom-built recreational vehicle.

Two gorgeous coffee-brown leather couches faced each other. In the middle of both gleamed ebony tables.

"So, what's back there?" I jerked my thumb toward the closed door.

His gaze glittered with mischief. "Why don't you find out?"

Chapter 21

"What a surprise," I said. "It's your bedroom."

"The bed is big enough for two," said Patrick as he plopped onto the edge of it.

"Are you kidding? It's big enough for five." I wandered around the space. Considering the limited square footage of an RV—even a custom-built, mega-huge one—the bedroom was spacious.

No windows, for obvious reasons. The black walls shone with the same metallic finish that coated the bedroom walls at my house. Everything here was black and brown with hints of gold. I figured the color scheme was probably the same on the whole bus.

Nearly all the dressers were built into the walls. The small, narrow doors that faced the bed, I assumed were closets. And the big door on the right wall probably opened into the bathroom.

"Okay, I've seen it. Now what?"

Patrick stood and walked to the bathroom door. "How about you get naked, wet, and soapy?"

"Yeah, right."

He opened the door with a flourish and, curiosity piqued, I followed him into the room.

"Is that a . . . a waterfall?" I asked. "Holy shit!"

"I should have Jenny make a Cussing Jar to keep here," said Patrick, laughter in his voice.

"Don't you dare." I walked to the edge of the huge, square bathtub. "Is this real marble?"

"Yes."

The tub could probably fit at least eight people in it. Water burbled and bubbled not only from the spray gently arcing from the back wall into the tub, but from jets arranged around its perimeter. On three sides, a ledge with dips and curves offered places to sit or lie down.

"Want to go for a swim?" asked Patrick.

"If you're thinking what I think you're thinking and we've established that thinking is all we're going to think, then . . . uh, I lost track of what I was saying."

"No penetration and no exchange of blood . . . then no binding. Let's pleasure ourselves in other ways." As soon as the words left his mouth, our clothes left our bodies. There wasn't so much as poof or a sizzle. One second we were clothed, the next we were naked.

"I'm so learning to do that!" I said.

"There are other things I can teach you," said Patrick. He stepped into the bathtub and held out his hand. I took it and he helped me across the rim and into the warm, swirling water.

I watched, dry-mouthed, as Patrick slid into the warm water and lounged on a curved seat. His silver eyes were molten—the swirling, grasping heat of magma. His fingers grazed my hips then he drew me onto his lap.

His cock, already half-hard, nestled in the vee of my thighs. Lust knotted my stomach, its fickle tendrils curling through me.

Gotta maintain control. Gotta stay on guard. Gotta make sure I don't lose my mind.

But maybe it was too late. My body went on full alert, a military base preparing for an invasion that wasn't going to happen.

"This is dangerous, Patrick," I whispered as I leaned down to lick water beads from his collarbone. "Really dangerous."

"I know, love." His head lolled back and allowed me access to the strong column of his throat. He was so beautiful. A living sculpture that deserved worship.

I nibbled his neck. And evil nymph that I was, made sure my breasts scraped his lightly haired chest. My nipples tingled and tightened. Down, girl! No . . . not like that. And yet, my hands refused to obey my responsible, not-going-down-there commands. As I explored his jaw with my lips, I stroked the muscled ridges of his chest. Didn't stop, either. Just kept going until I reached the hard length of him. *Stop, naughty hands. Well . . . maybe you can do that for a minute.* One hand wrapped around Patrick's fully hard cock while the other dipped under and squeezed his balls. Like friggin' juicy plums.

I loved plums.

Patrick moaned, his hips flexed, little movements that matched my rhythmic adulation.

"Jessica, love. You're going to kill me."

"You're already dead."

"Ah. Good point." His hands slid down to my buttocks and squeezed. "Fantastic ass," he murmured. His fingers kneaded my flesh and I wiggled closer, tormenting us both.

I shuddered at the sensations of heat and wet and naked Patrick. We sat mercilessly unjoined and stroked each others' bodies. Hands and mouths created fire, passion, need. Patrick cupped my breasts and paid homage, suckling my nipples until I panted and moaned and begged for more.

Then . . . slowly, I slid against his cock.

"No penetration," I reiterated as I rubbed against him.

"No," he said, his voice hoarse.

The sloshing water and the press of Patrick's cock against me made me quiver, made me want. Craven desire bloomed in my belly, flowering within me and burning away good sense. (Like I had any to start with. Hah.) I wanted to feel Patrick inside me for real. No dreams. No pretending.

I wanted his cock plunging into me as we found bliss.

Oh yes. This white-hot, unbearable yearning inspired all kinds of delightful and regretful ideas.

The voice of reason, however, could not be drowned out. I wasn't a do-or-die horny college student. I was a mother who held not just my own future, but that of my children, in my hands. I couldn't give that up, not yet, not until . . . well, not until ever.

Oh but I wanted to . . . with Patrick's scent in my nostrils and his fingers dancing along my spine . . . I wanted him. Forever.

Grabbing his shoulders for leverage, I rubbed against his cock harder, faster. I ground against him and he held on to me, thrusting against my clit.

"Drink from me," I said.

"*Céadsearc . . .*"

"You haven't eaten. I know you haven't. So, drink, damn it."

He bit the flesh above my breast and as my blood flowed into his mouth, pleasure crashed through me from breast to clit. The merging feelings were too much.

"Patrick!" My cry of release ricocheted off the marble. He groaned as I arched against him, contracting fiercely.

As orgasmic aftershocks rumbled through me, Patrick's fingers dug into my hips as he pressed against me, groaning, his face tight. I felt his cock jerk as he let go, the hot spurt of his release ghosting across my stomach.

Then there was only the feel of water around us, tainted with love . . . and with regret.

Later, Patrick reluctantly put clothes on us again and we returned to the driveway of my house.

The glow that resulted from fantastic sex still infused me, but reality was a bitch who wouldn't shut up.

"I don't think it's fair to either one of us," I said.

"What?" Patrick brushed a kiss across my knuckles, his gray eyes glittering with . . . *gulp* . . . *love*.

"This almost-but-never-really stuff we're doing when we make love."

He shrugged. "There are many ways vampires find pleasure without binding."

"Yeah, but it seems like . . . cheating somehow. Not going all the way. Sometimes, you gotta shit or get off the pot."

"You have the strangest way of putting things," he said, chuckling.

I wasn't in the mood to chuckle. My stomach dipped in terror as I realized the truth about me and Patrick. Either I choose the binding with him . . . or we would spend our days almost making love.

"You've shown me some great stuff . . . some terrific things . . . but Patrick, my kids are my world. What kind of mother would I be to bring you into our lives when you don't want all of us?"

Patrick stepped away to glare at me. "Who says I do not want all of you?"

I crossed my arms and hugged myself, miserable. "I do."

"Have I once asked you to be less to them so that I might have more?"

"No." I swallowed the knot of dread in my throat. "I figure you've lived four thousand years. What's a few more?"

He frowned at me. "I don't understand."

Damn it. I didn't want to have this conversation. Apprehension iced my throat, my belly. Oh God. But if not now, when? What would change about the scenario if we had the argument today or twenty years from now? "Patrick, I'm not stupid. What's seven or eight decades to a man who's been around for four millennium? So, maybe . . . you think hey, I just gotta wait it out."

"This is what you truly believe? That I value my happiness over yours?" asked Patrick, his tone warbling with pain. "I want nothing more than for you to always be happy and safe. To always feel loved."

I didn't think I could feel worse, but his words carved out my heart and tossed it onto the pavement. *Way to go, Jessica.* I reached out to touch him and realized that was a bad move. So I shuffled back another step and gnawed on my bottom lip. "I'm sorry, Patrick. Maybe I shouldn't have . . . okay, yeah, I assumed a lot."

"I told you that I wouldn't fail you again, Jessica," he said. "And as long as I walk the Earth, I will honor that vow."

I needed a good curl-up-and-cry and chocolate. Oh, no. Chocolate. The last time I'd tasted it was drinking from Sharon. And she'd eaten champagne truffles because Patrick asked her to give me something I thought I'd lost. Pain lanced me. Poor Sharon.

"Here." Patrick handed me a slim silver device.

I took the cellular phone from him and peered at it. "More technology? Yuck. Take it back."

"A mom without a cell phone? Not possible." He smiled, and I knew he sought to break the tension between us. Too bad it wasn't freaking working.

"One for emergency use that I keep in the car. And I haven't driven a car in forever because, apparently, I have *sidhe* blood now and we have faster modes of transportation." I tucked the phone into the front pocket of my shorts. "So the phone is hooked up to some kind of vampire network?"

"Consortium network," said Patrick. "All the members' numbers are in the address book."

"Thanks."

We stood there, awkwardly staring at each other. Then Patrick sighed, leaned over to kiss my cheek, and whispered, "Good night, love."

He misted into silver and faded away.

Well, fine. Go brood. Suddenly restless, I ambled into the yard. The wet grass slapped against my bare toes. I thought about my childhood, about how I used to run through all the lawns barefoot, risking bee stings and stickers, just to feel the summer grass under my feet. Back then, the air was always tinged with honeysuckle, so heavy and thick with sweetness of those blooms it was like you could lick the air and taste syrup. The neighborhood kids would play hide-and-seek until dusk, our laughter and screams echoing into every backyard. When it got too dark, we'd chase lightning bugs, putting them into glass containers with punched-hole lids . . . until our mothers made us dump out the poor insects and berated us for ruining perfectly good Mason jars.

I used to hate the night. Yeah. I hated when the sun went down and robbed us of childhood delights. After daylight abandoned us, we had dinner and homework and baths and bedtime. The night had stolen from me, and I resented it. Now, all I had, all any vampire had, was the night. I guess it was a good case of being careful what you wished for.

I spent some time with Bryan and Jenny. We watched *How the Grinch Stole Christmas*, which was an odd movie for the kids to select, but there's no accounting for taste. Especially ours.

I made meatloaf, mashed potatoes, and green bean

casserole for dinner. It was a favorite meal of the kids, though watching 'em devour it was just a reminder that I would never consume regular food again, especially after they each got to dig into a chocolate pudding cup. I wondered what would happen if I ate real food? I probably didn't want to find out.

Later, after bedtime rituals were complete, Bryan hid in his room to play an hour's worth of PlayStation 2. Jenny and I read another two chapters about the adventures of a trio of best friends in the magical world of Droon.

"Do vampires celebrate Christmas?" asked Jenny as I tucked her into bed.

"Heck, yeah," I said.

"Wilson said vampires have their own religion and holidays and that him and his mom were converting."

Wilson was sixteen and his mother was Patsy Donahue. I bit my lip to keep from laughing. The hair stylist would sooner dye herself pink and run through town naked than celebrate any religious holiday. Patsy said the holidays were excuses for drinking and eating in excess, which she gladly did.

"Is Wilson the one that said vampires didn't celebrate Christmas?"

"Yeah, he said vampires celebrate Yule. And he said that on December twenty-fifth, he gets to say, 'you'll do this' and 'you'll do that' and we have to because it's honoring his new religion."

I laughed this time. That Wilson. What a card. I stroked Jenny's bangs away from her forehead. "No, honey. Yule is a real holiday and it's a very old tradition. And it wasn't started by the vampires."

At least I didn't think so. The vampires had been around a long damned time. I pulled the covers up to her chin and kissed her cheek. "G'night, baby girl."

"'Night, Mommy."

With an hour or so left before sunrise, I sat at the kitchen table, finishing a letter to my husband. Charlene's confession had turned my world upside down. I don't know why she'd admit something that would put her in a bad light unless she thought making me feel like shit was worth it.

At any time during the last year, she could've told me about Rich leaving her, about Rich loving me and our kids more than her. But she'd waited. She'd held on to that knowledge like a miser hoarding gold. Why had she told me now?

The timing bothered me a lot. We were both vampires. We were both building a new community in an old town. We were both Turned by the same Master.

As I folded the letter and tucked it into my pocket, I wondered if Charlene had issued a challenge that related not to Rich, but to Patrick. *I didn't get your first man, but I'll get your second.*

I turned over that possibility in my mind. Would she be that stupid? Why would she care about my love life? Rich . . . well, I could understand her need for him. She worked in his office, observed our lives together.

Had she told the truth? Or had she lied?

I supposed it didn't matter. What mattered is that I had to forgive Rich. I had to forgive myself. And I needed closure to the situation. Life wasn't neat. You couldn't take sections, fold 'em, and put 'em into sealed boxes labeled "finished." Life was messy. Chaotic. Senseless. But you lived it. Every day you lived it. And every day you tried to make it mean something.

I checked the digital clock on the microwave, gauged how much time I had. Yeah, I could do it. Hmmm. I wondered if Patrick was inside my head right now. Sometimes, I felt him in my mind, just a whisper. Mostly, though, I didn't know if he was there or not. I hadn't tried to get inside his head. Handling my own thoughts was hard enough. Besides, I wasn't sure I wanted to run into information that . . . well, I didn't want to know.

Leaving the house, I waved to the security guard pacing my lawn, then rose into the air and headed toward the Broken Heart Cemetery.

Two months ago, on the one-year anniversary of Rich's passing, my children and I brought flowers to his grave. It was a sad day. The tombstone with his name on it was just a reminder that their father was gone forever. And that was why I didn't make them go every week or every month to show their respects. No matter what choices he'd made for our marriage, he loved his children. I knew he wouldn't want our kids to be in pain. I hired a service to maintain Rich's grave and paid extra to make sure fresh flowers were placed in the concrete vases on either side of the granite tombstone.

We didn't need regular trips to the cemetery to remember Rich. I made sure our family scrapbooks were accessible to my kids, that Rich's pictures were in their bedrooms, that keepsakes of vacations and trips were maintained throughout the house. Rich wasn't forgotten. And the love harbored for him and what he'd meant to them . . . and to me . . . still existed. It was still nurtured.

I settled in front of Rich's gravestone. I felt so nervous. My last words to him hadn't been kind. And since his passing, I hadn't tried to talk to him. I mean, he was gone. What was the point?

Grieving was for the living. And, so too, was closure. Here I was, still able to emotionally gnaw on the problems of my life, while Rich had no recourse at all. He couldn't ever reconsider his thoughts or words or actions.

I withdrew the letter and unfolded it. I stared at the words I'd written.

"Crap. What good will this do? It's stupid!" I clenched the paper so hard, it ripped.

It's not stupid.

I blinked away the tears in my eyes. *Patrick?*

Read the letter, Jessica. Your words will carry to the Universe and somewhere in it, resides the one you knew as Rich. He will hear you.

I felt comforted by his understanding and justified in my attempt to deal with my emotions for Rich. Had Patrick felt the same, done the same for his family when they were taken from him?

Releasing grief is necessary, Jessica. And perpetuating love is vital. Do you what you must, love, then come home. The sun will rise soon.

I felt him slip out of my mind. Once again, I looked at the letter. Then I read it aloud.

Dearest Rich,

This is really hard to write. The thing is, I'm not sure now about you and Charlene. It's uncomfortable to think that she was a mistake, that she made you miserable, that things weren't as they seemed.

I was so mad at you! And I was justified! You screwed Charlene. Rich, Jr. is proof of that. But . . . to be honest, honey, even if we tried to pick up the pieces, everything about us, about what we had, would've been changed. How do you rebuild trust? How do you fix love? If our love was strong and we were happy . . . well, Charlene wouldn't have tempted you—no matter who chased who first.

Maybe you died thinking that if I could forgive you, we could re-create our lives. Or maybe you were thinking about building a new life with Charlene and your son.

My mama likes to say that we live the lives we're supposed to live. What if I had been Turned while I was married to you? Patrick would've known I was his soul mate and hell, I would've agreed. That's terrifying, to carry that kind of knowledge around in your heart.

I think that's what bothers me so much now. What if you looked at Charlene and saw your other half? What if you tried to deny it because of your loyalty to me and, one day, gave in to it and it felt right? Then you're torn between duty and honor and true-blue love.

Hell's bells, what a choice.

I sat in judgment of you for so long. The be-

trayed wife. The stoic widow. The loyal survivor. And feeling the way I do about Patrick . . . oh God, Rich. I can't say what I would've done faced with how I feel about him versus the way I felt about you.

That's a terrible thing to say, especially to the dead. But I gotta be honest. What's the point of trying to get some closure if I'm lying through my teeth?

Rich, what I'm trying to say is that I'm sorry. I'm so sorry that the last words you heard from me were angry and hurtful. And I'm sorry that I couldn't come to terms with what happened to us. I held on way too long to my self-righteousness and my anger and my pain. And if Charlene's telling the truth then I'm sorry you were so unhappy. If you felt trapped, and miserable, and unsure . . . I'm sorry, honey. God in heaven, I'm sorry.

If you need my forgiveness, you have it. And I'll just have to live the rest of my days not knowing if you could forgive my hatefulness.

If Mama was right about living the lives we're meant to, then you and I were gonna unravel anyway. You see, even though I can't truly have Patrick . . . I was meant for him. I know it, Rich. Feel it right down to my very soul. And you know, maybe you were meant for someone else, even if it wasn't Charlene.

Then again . . . what the hell does Mama know? You never did like her much anyway. (That's a joke, hon.)

Rich, please know wherever you are, and I hope

that you are somewhere, that the love we created with Bryan and Jenny exists. It's there, always and forever, for you. From us.

So, I guess that's what I have to say. Take care, Rich. Take care.

Chapter 22

So it's not a great leap to think that I would cry, all right? I dry-blubbered as I tore up the letter and let the light breeze carry away the tatters.

After a while, I climbed to my feet and brushed off the dirt that clung to my legs and shorts. I felt better. I really did. And I was surprised that saying to Rich's grave what I never got to say to him unfettered my guilt.

I heard scuffling behind me. "Patrick?"

No answer, but definitely another person moving across the grounds. As I turned to see who was doing a bad job of creeping up on me, a great hairy arm thwapped me. I flew backward and landed ass-first in the line of well-trimmed bushes that ringed this part of the cemetery. I heard a big, loud *roar* that scared the shit out of me. I untangled myself from the scratchy leaves and flew up into the air, hovering.

The bellowing beast growled and slashed its paws at me, obviously pissed off that I hadn't stayed long enough for him to rip me open again.

Even in the dark I noted those mad, hateful blue eyes.

A screeching noise pierced my head. The whistle-wail nearly cracked my skull. *Stop!* I covered my ears, but the unrelenting squeal increased in volume. *Stop it!* I knew, somehow, the creature was causing the horrible noise inside my mind.

I dropped like a stone; pain ricocheted up my side as I smacked the ground. I curled into the fetal position with eyes squeezed tight, teeth gritted. The earth shook as footsteps of Mad-Bad-Ugly pounded toward me. Even through the howling, I heard the air vibrate with its roar of triumph.

Staggering to my feet, I unsheathed the swords. As promised, I had been practicing the moves that Patrick had "downloaded" into my brain. But I wasn't exactly on the top of my game. The first two slashes met only air. He danced just out of my reach, swinging his big arms at me playfully.

Then he lunged for me and I struck; the blade sliced across his abdomen. Roaring, he reared back. And the shrieking ceased.

"Hold!" shouted a man's voice. I didn't recognize it. To my shock, a vampire appeared next to the crazed lycan and placed his big, pale hand on the beast's shoulder. The thing dropped to its knees and bowed its head.

I looked from the lycan to the very tall, very blond, very scarred man. He was dressed in black dress pants, a vibrant red shirt, and black loafers. He also wore a black coat that reminded me of Neo's garb in *The Matrix*. His face might've been handsome once, but it looked as if someone had thrown acid on him. His eyes glowed black.

Let me tell you, he was fucking scary.

"Who the hell are you?" I asked, keeping my swords at the ready.

"My name's Ron," he said. "This is my pet." His brows rose in consternation. "Tsk. Tsk. You've injured him."

"He was trying to kill me. For the second time, I might add."

"He was a tad too enthusiastic the first time I asked him to fetch you," admitted the mysterious Ron. "So we had a little discussion. He was only supposed to rough you up a little and bring you to me."

"What do you want?"

"I want you. *Duh.*" Ron rolled his eyes. "You'll make a good bargaining chip. I believe Patrick O'Halloran will trade anything to get you back. And I want the cure for the Taint."

"There is no cure." I looked at the beast. It was bleeding, its chest heaving, and he was just . . . as docile as a lamb. "What is that thing?"

"We know that lycan blood cures the Taint," said Ron. "So ol' Georgie here agreed to a transfusion. Only it didn't quite work as planned." He looked at me and bared his fangs at me. "I know Lorćan O'Halloran is cured. And I want to know how."

"You've confused me with someone who gives a shit."

Ron's eyes flashed. One instant, he was by the beast and the next, he was two inches from my face. "You're not smart enough to bring your guardians with you to a fucking cemetery. So, I don't expect you're smart enough to know the secret to getting rid of the Taint."

"Well, fuck you, too." I leapt into the air, but Ron merely looked at me with one raised brow. I slammed right back down and my feet seemed to meld with the grass. I couldn't lift my legs at all. *Shit.*

Panic warbled through me. Then, I felt the familiar heaviness that warned me of the sunrise and the sudden fall into unconsciousness. Oh, great. *Patrick? Are you there? I really need you!*

"Now, now . . . don't bother contacting your other half. He's a little busy protecting those brats of yours."

"Don't you dare hurt my kids!" I felt weak and unsteady, but I still held my swords. Unfortunately, I couldn't raise my arms to slice Ron's head right the hell off.

"Oh relax! They're safe. You don't think Patrick would let anything happen to his *clann*, do you? He'd sooner put a stake into his own heart."

Ron might be an asshole, but he was an insightful asshole. Patrick wouldn't let anything happen to my kids. I had to believe that they were safe. I tried to reach out to them, to make sure, but whatever power was blocking my mental communication with Patrick worked the same awful mojo for my kids.

"Tired, aren't you?" Ron's eyes glittered like black pearls as he stared at me, watching me the way a zoo patron might gaze upon the caged lion. "Go on, dearest. Go to sleep. The Wraiths will take good care of you."

Exhaustion slammed me. My eyes fluttered closed and my body went limp. Ron's arms wrapped around me, my feet unstuck from the ground, and we whipped forward. We crashed through brush, limbs tearing at us, and I realized we'd entered the forest that edged the cemetery. Broken Heart was pocketed by tree-filled areas. So, the Wraiths had settled here, in this forest, just waiting to strike.

As my consciousness grayed, we entered a place that smelled like an old basement. I heard dripping water, the suck of feet in mud.

Then I was lost to the silence. And to the dark.

When I awoke, I found myself sprawled on a thin blanket. I sat up and looked around. The cave was dark as, forgive me, a *tomb*, but I could see just fine. I smoothed back my hair and found it full of leaves, dirt, and twigs. I could only imagine what my face looked like.

I rubbed my arms, mostly to get off clinging soil. The interior felt cool, which was a nice change from the humid heat outside. Other than the occasional drip of water, there were no other sounds. It was like being wrapped in cotton.

Patrick?

No response.

Patrick? Are you okay? Are the kids okay? Hello!

Damnation. I was starved. My fangs were already out, my stomach growling.

"Jessica?"

My heart nearly leapt out of my chest. Patrick's voice came from the right so I staggered to my feet.

"Down here."

About five feet away, I saw a man chained to the

rocky wall. He wore a T-shirt, jeans, and scuffed high-tops. He looked like Patrick, but he wasn't. "Lor?"

"Yeah."

"What the hell happened to you?"

"I've been cured from the Taint."

I gaped at him. "What? How? Who?"

"Be careful, Jessica. The Wraiths are watching . . . and listening."

My hands went to my hips. "They took my swords! Those rat bastards!"

He chuckled. "You are left only with your rapier wit to slice at them."

"Oh, ha-ha." I looked at him. "So, you're not dead. They captured you at Putt 'Er There, didn't they?"

Lor's gaze filled with sorrow. "Sharon had been meeting me there every night. I would feed and we would talk for a while. She was supposed to be gone before you and Patrick arrived."

"But the Wraiths got you instead." I chewed on my lower lip as I considered the silver cuffs on Lorćan's wrists. They looked like the ones Patrick had worn the first night I'd woken up sucking on his thigh. My guess was that it was the spells on the cuffs keeping Lor bound.

"Did Ron's vicious pet kill Sharon?"

"I don't know." He grimaced. "They got to me before I had a chance to warn her. This incredibly painful screeching inside my brain nearly made me go mad. Then I was spirited away and locked up here."

"How long have you been cured?" I asked.

"Tonight. I awoke as I am now."

"I'm sure it'll give Stan a real hard-on to figure out

why." I looked around the cavern. "He thinks the Wraiths are into some kind of vampire biological warfare."

"Now, why would we poison our own kind?" Ron said as he appeared right next to me. I yelped and stumbled backward.

He laughed, his black eyes flashing. Today's outfit was the ol' black pants, shoes, coat combo, but the silk shirt was emerald green.

"God, you suck!" I tried to beat back the fear fluttering in my belly. This guy scared me. He had no compunction about killing humans, he wanted to destroy other vampires, and he wanted to rule over the world. "My kids better be safe, buster. If you even *look* at them wrong, I'll gut you."

"Tsk. Tsk. Such melodrama!"

"We'll see how melodramatic you think it is when I put my swords in your woobies." I resisted the urge to stick out my tongue and stamp my feet. I was an adult, after all. "Just let us go already!"

"Of course! It wasn't like I planned to keep you as prisoners or anything." His thin lips curved into an insincere smile. "Tell you what, I'll make a deal. You fight one of my chosen warriors. If you win, I'll let you and Lor go."

I looked at him, my mouth gaping. "You're kidding."

"Yes," he said. "Well, I was kidding about the letting you go part. I fully intend to entertain myself by watching someone else kick your ass."

Before I had time to utter something witty and cutting, I found myself standing in the center of a large well-lit cavern. Vampires, all of whom favored black clothing, ringed the cavern. Some sat, some stood, but all eyes were on me and Ron. He grinned at me and I really wanted to punch him in the mouth.

"We have a guest," said Ron. He grabbed my right hand and held it up. The silver *fede* ring glittered in the flickering torchlight. "The prophesied soul mate of your favorite vampire, Patrick O'Halloran."

Hisses and boos ricocheted off the uneven walls. The atmosphere was heavy with malicious anticipation. I had never felt such ill will directed toward me. The Wraiths blanketed me with their spite, their glee at my probable demise.

Patrick? Pick up the damned mental phone!

"Oh, stop," said Ron, rolling his eyes. "He can't hear you. If it's any solace, he's frantically searching for you, okay?"

"You have a weird idea about how to comfort people," I said, pulling my wrist out of his grasp.

"We're not people," said Ron. "Vampires are better than people."

"Right. Which is why you're trying to kill your own kind."

"Wraiths are better than most vampires. We understand nature. We accept the true pecking order. Humans represent the ultimate dinner-and-a-show concept. First, you'll entertain me . . ." He licked his fangs, his eyes glowing red. "Then I'll dine on you."

"Hey, Sherlock. I'm not a human."

"Human. Turn-blood. Whatever." He shrugged in dismissal. Then he walked a circle, holding his hands up to quiet the still-grumbling crowd. "Who will fight our heroine? Who will risk death at the hands of this fierce warrior?"

Laughter echoed. Okay, so I wasn't Xena, Warrior Princess, but I could fight. Theoretically. The real question, though, was could I win?

"I'll take the chance," said a purring woman's voice.

"Well, *there's* a surprise," I muttered as Nara sashayed around the counter. Her hair had been pulled into a fat ponytail. She wore black leather pants, a black bustier, and black boots with three-inch heels. "Hello, *bitch*.

"Oh, I love charades!" I cocked a hip, my hands reaching for the swords that had been taken from me. "Let me guess. Cat Woman on a bad-hair day. No? A dominatrix with a bad fashion sense?"

"Shut up." She held up her hands and the Ruadan swords sparkled into her fists. "I've been waiting for this opportunity."

"Isn't it interesting that every time the swords go missing, you seem to find them?" I asked in a bored tone. Inside, I was freaking the hell out. I looked at Ron. "I'd like my swords back, please. She can get her own."

"Technically, she had them first."

"Fine. Then give me another weapon."

Ron considered me, a well-manicured finger tapping his chin. Then he smiled maliciously. "Nah."

He popped out of the circle. I tracked him to the right as he sat down in a big, black chair. Jerk.

Nara banged the swords together. The metal-on-metal noise made me flinch. I stepped back, my hands tightening. Her lips curled into a cruel smile. "This is going to be so much fun!"

She lunged toward me, swords extended, cackling

when I leapt backward and crossed my arms up in front of me.

She charged—this time deadly intent on attacking me.

I leapt over her, which really pissed her off. So, Ron had allowed me to fly again. And that meant there was probably no way for me to escape the cavern. He wasn't dumb enough to unbind my abilities if he wasn't absolutely sure he could control my use of them.

Nara spun and thrust one sword at my thigh. The blade glanced off my leg; blood welled across the gash. The Wraiths cheered as Nara raised the swords above her head, grinning in triumph. While she was acting like a dumb-ass, I kicked her in the stomach.

She flew backward, landing in a heap. But the swords remained in her hands. Damn. Flipping onto her feet, her vamp speed put her right in my face. The swords nicked my sides, but I bounced away. I was scared. Really scared. But the training Patrick had put into my brain was working. I didn't have to think. I was reacting to her moves. Yeah, she was getting me here and there, but she was working for my death.

She swiped at me again and again, but I fended her off. She kept grinning, kept clicking the swords together in attempts to intimidate me.

And it was working, let me tell you.

Around her neck glittered a silver chain. As she poked at me again, the chain swung free and revealed Dairine's coin.

Then, a cold mist began to fill up the cavern. The Wraiths murmured their confusion, straightening away from the walls, and looking around.

The fog thickened and the temperature dropped.

"Wraiths!" screamed Ron. "Prepare for battle!"

As everyone scrambled to what I assumed were Wraith attack positions, Nara attempted to ram both blades in my stomach. I whirled away, but not soon enough to prevent two deep gashes. Blood poured from the wounds. She was fast, really fast. If I had been human, I would've been dead.

She went for another round of Stab Jessica In The Stomach. I jumped up and over her. I landed behind her and grabbed her ponytail. She screamed, trying to jerk away and kick at me. I looped my finger around the chain and pulled it off her neck.

Unfortunately, I also let her hair go and she spun around, jabbing the swords into my shoulders. Pain exploded, but I scurried back, shoving my prize into the front pocket of my shorts.

Even with all the mental mojo Patrick had given me and all my "basic package" vampire skills, I wasn't doing too well in this fight.

It kinda pissed me off to realize I was losing. But that anger was nothing compared to, you know, all the *terror* pumping through me.

Chaos reigned as Wraiths scrambled to either escape or prepare to fight. So far, though, there was no one to fight. Then, as Nara tried again to skewer me, I felt a strange tingling sensation. I saw Nara's eyes widen, her mouth stretching as she let out a furious shriek.

Together, we sparkled out of sight.

Chapter 23

Nara and I reappeared in the cemetery. I noted, in major mondo relief, that we were surrounded by a whole lot of vampires I recognized. Somehow, some way, the Consortium had found and rescued me.

"Jessica!" Patrick strode toward me, his graceful movements and stony expression belying the rage pulsing in his silver eyes. *"A thaisce."* He gathered me into his arms and kissed me until I nearly puddled at his feet. At least he wasn't mad at me for being all stupid and getting caught by Ron. And that meant Nara was the recipient of his wrath. Maybe it made me a bitch (and haven't we established that fact already?), but I was a tad gleeful Nara was gonna get in trouble.

When he finally freed my mouth, I asked, "The kids?"

"They are safe, love." He let me go, not even sparing a glance at the heaving-in-outrage, blade-wielding, pissed-off Nara a couple of feet behind me. Instead, he turned to François, who was one of the ten or so vampires circling us. "Do it."

All the vampires broke off from the group and pointed their hands, palms out, toward the forest. No . . . toward the cave where the Wraiths were hiding out.

The wounds Nara had inflicted on me during our battle were still bleeding. I wasn't sure why the vampire healing thing hadn't kicked in, but I felt weak. "What are they doing?" I asked.

"Destroying the Wraiths," said Patrick.

"But Lor is in there!"

"Don't worry, love. We got him out, too. He's at the medical RV with Stan."

The earth rumbled beneath our feet. I grabbed on to Patrick's arm to steady myself as the low rumble turned into a huge roar. In the distance, a gold light mushroomed into the sky. I watched in awe as trees and dirt sprayed upward.

Then, there was a great *whomp*. The light and flying debris twirled downward. I realized that the cavern had collapsed. I could only hope that Ron had been crushed by a really, really big rock. Asshole.

Patrick strode to Nara, stopping a foot away from her. "Jessica is *mo chroí*."

"You don't love her," she screeched. "You haven't even fucked her yet."

Patrick was unmoved by her temper tantrum; he was as cold and distant as a mountain peak. I followed his lead and looked at her icily, as if she were dirt clinging to my feet. Inside, I was seething. Seething because she'd been bound to Patrick for a hundred years. Seething because she was crude and horrible and mean. Seething because she had inflicted so much turmoil and anguish on Patrick.

"You betrayed the Consortium. You betrayed those who called you friend!"

She shook her head, her shoulders heaving with dry tears. "My love is for you, Padriag. I care for nothing, for no one, the way I care for you. And it is *her* that has ruined all that I've worked for!"

"Jessica is my other half. I love her."

I didn't have time to relish Patrick's admission of love. Nara went blind with her hatred. Before I could blink, I felt the two sharp blades crossed against my throat.

"Ouch," I said.

She squeezed until the edges pierced my skin. "You do not deserve him."

The little swords pressed and the cuts deepened. Ever get a paper cut? Well, it hurt a little like that—except a thousand times worse. My wounds were still bleeding and I had gone from feeling weak to feeling faint. So, I stood there like a schlub and let pixie-girl try to scissor off my head.

"Nara," said Patrick calmly. "Drop the swords."

"If she dies, you will see me again. Love *me* again. You will know Dairine is well and truly dead."

"Jessica is not Dairine."

Nara blinked up at him, without easing up the grip she had on my neck. She had the strength and the motivation to just—*clip*—and I would be headless.

"I loved the mother of my children, Nara. I grieve the loss of my family every day. But Dairine chose the Light."

"But—but why do you love *her*?" Nara cried. "Because she wears that stupid ring?"

"No, I'm really good in bed," I managed through chattering teeth. My vision was graying, but I stayed on my feet.

"Shut up, bitch." She pushed forward and reminded me that my head was only attached because of her goodwill.

"Put away the swords, Nara. You must face punishment for your misdeeds. And you must swear to me you will never seek to harm Jessica or her family."

"No."

I figured out her decision a split second before I felt the pressure of the blades bite into my skin. Oh God!

Nara flew backward, the knives spinning across the dewy grass. She skidded onto her ass, her legs flying up like a marionette's.

I fell to my knees, clutching my throat. Blood dripped between my fingers.

Patrick, why haven't I healed? I thought instant health was part of the basic vampire package.

The wounds caused by the Ruadan swords include sidhe *magic. They will not heal . . . at least not without some help.*

Gently, Patrick pried my hands off my neck and put his own on the wounds. He whispered, *"Leigheas."*

Tingling warmth wove around my entire body. Within seconds, the deep cuts on my neck, the gashes in my stomach, and all the other scratches had healed.

"Thanks," I said.

He kissed me and helped me to my feet. Nara sat where she landed, her face red from struggling against invisible bonds. Whatever Patrick had done to get her away from me had included imprisoning her. With a flick of his wrist, the bloody half-swords rose from the ground and floated into his outstretched hand. He clutched them both by their ornate jeweled handles.

Deliberately, slowly, he walked to Nara and stared down at her.

"Free me!" she screamed. "Free me, you bastard!"

"I ban thee, Nara Colleen MacKenzie of the Family Romanov. I ban thee from me and mine. We will never hear you. We will never see you. We will never know thy presence on this earth so long as your heart bears us ill will."

Her shocked expression crumbled into agony. "Do not ban me! Do not do this! I love you. You are mine, Patrick O'Halloran. You are mine!"

"Walk in the place between worlds, Nara. This is your punishment for cruelty and for avarice. So do I will it, and so mote it be."

"Padraig! Nooooo!"

I watched in awe as Nara faded into nothingness. The vampires who still encircled us, watching the action in silent regard, dispersed. It was eerie to watch the undead walk out of a cemetery—almost like I was stuck in one of those Sci Fi Channel movies Jenny liked to watch.

I looked at Patrick. "What the hell just happened?"

"Nara is in a place that exists between this world and the Otherworld," he said. "She will never bother you, or me, or any that are under our protection. And she will stay there for as long as she feels hatred and vengeance toward me and mine."

"She's gone? Just like that?"

"Banning is not done easily or taken lightly."

Patrick returned to where I stood and with one arm, gathered me into an embrace. He held away the knives, but over his shoulder, I could see the gleam of the blades still red with my blood.

"Wait." Patrick held out the swords. The blood sparkled away. Then the swords disappeared like Scotty had beamed them up to the circling Enterprise. Impressive and unnerving that he could do stuff like that.

"I'm sorry she hurt you," Patrick whispered into my hair as his arms wrapped around me.

"Those little scratches? Puh-lease! I've had hang-nails that were worse." I slid my hands into the back pockets of his jeans. I couldn't help a little squeeze. He had a great ass.

"Hungry?"

"Starved."

Patrick drew me into his embrace and gently pressed me against his throat. "Go on, love."

Before I could offer protest, my fangs pierced his flesh almost of their own accord. Yeah, I wanted some nosh, but I loved biting Patrick. I found something erotic about drinking from him, about regenerating because of him. I wish we could do other kinds of piercing.

"Enough," he murmured.

I licked his neck. He shuddered at my touch, his hands drifting up my arms. I heard his thought: *Oh, Jessica. What you do to me, love.*

For a moment, I couldn't remember why I couldn't bind with him. Why I was denying myself his presence, his love. Images of Bryan and Jenny snapped into my mind—instant reminders of my present . . . and my future.

"I really want a shower," I said. His grasp tightened on my shoulders. I knew he was thinking about the last time we'd been together—in that lovely tub with its gurgling waterfall. "Alone," I clarified.

"Damnú air."

"You're cussing!"

"I refuse to admit to uttering bad words in any language." Patrick grinned and his teeth flashed white. "Jenny has been Googling German insults. I don't want her to look up Gaelic next."

Oh Lord. I tried not to think about what kind of information Jenny discovered in her search. "You let her Google curse words?"

"She said it was for educational purposes."

"Yeah, right. You are so fired as the baby-sitter."

Chapter 24

Patrick escorted me home, kissed me until my toes curled, then left to go check on his brother. I was thrilled that Lor was okay and that he was back to normal. Well, normal for a blood-drinking dead guy.

Jenny was ensconced in the living room watching a Bratz movie with her Bratz dolls. Those things creeped me out, especially how their feet were changed out. Their *feet*. If they didn't have shoes on, they had these little knobs at the end of their legs. *Ick, ick, ptooey.*

The blast of music that greeted my vamp ears indicated my son was in his bedroom. My guess was that he had a Pepsi in one hand and a PS2 controller in the other.

I took a quick shower and got dressed in the usual summer attire, threatened to remove Bryan's stereo if he didn't turn down the music, and made it downstairs in time to watch Jenny lure Stan into the evil world of Bratz.

"You switch out their *feet*?" he asked in a horrified voice as he accepted one of the dolls.

Good God. I snuck outside lest I, too, was drawn into the terrors that awaited poor Stan.

"The minute she pulled out those dolls, I ran," said Linda. She sat on the porch swing, gently rocking. She looked like Valentine's Day candy with her pink pants and purple crop top. Her poofy red hairdo clashed, but at the same time, well, it was full-on Linda.

"You okay?" she asked.

"Yeah. Just another day in the exciting life of a vampire housewife."

"Where's your Irish cutie?"

"With Lor." I joined Linda on the swing and for long, sweet moments we sat side by side and swayed.

"Remember when we used sit on your porch in the mornings with coffee, gossiping and eating those cookies from Betty's Bake Shop?" Linda laughed. "Now, here we are, dead as a doornail, swinging in the dark without caffeine or sweets to tide us over. Seems a shame we can't have a damned carb now and then."

"It's like being put on a permanent diet of tomato juice," I agreed. "I still miss Betty's gingerbread roll. Too bad she wouldn't leave the recipe when she closed up shop and moved to Florida."

For a moment, the air seemed weighted with our grievances. Or maybe it was just the humidity.

"I guess we could sit all night and list the things we'll miss," said Linda. "But I don't want to jaw about what's gone."

Her tone had gone soft, wary. I felt tension emanate from her. I said nothing, waiting for her to talk. A light wind rustled the leaves of the weeping willow in my front yard. And as always, the gorgeous scent of honeysuckle filtered in with the welcome breeze.

"You know that binding thing?" Linda asked. "If you have sex and share blood and magic . . . well, you're hitched for a hundred years."

"Yeah," I said. "I know. And I'm trying to avoid that particular state with Patrick." I looked at her profile and saw that she was gnawing on her bottom lip. "What are you saying, Linda? Are you binding with someone?"

"Ivan," she admitted.

Shock chilled me to the bone. I couldn't speak for a full minute. Then I said, *"What?"*

"Lookie here, girl, I know you don't like him. And he sure don't like you. And I'm sorry for that, but he's really just a big ol' teddy bear. And . . . he wants me."

"Okay. Well . . . okay. Do you want him?"

"Of course I want him!" Linda fluffed her hair then tapped her nails against her neon-pink capris. Her anger was palpable, but I wasn't sure if she was mad at me or the world. "Ivan's rich. He's an older vamp, too, so he's got some status, some power. And he'll claim Marybeth and protect us both forever. A hundred years seems a long time to me, but it's really just a blink of the eye for vampires."

I mentally chewed on her words, trying to come up with a response that wouldn't piss her off. But hell, everything I wanted to say would spin her into anger, so I figured I should say what I meant. "I hear you, Linda. I hear you talk about money and status and protection."

"I never had your kind of life," said Linda. "You had a man with a steady job. He made a good wage and kept you in a pretty house. Bought you a car. Paid for your kids' summer camps and karate and ballet lessons."

"Every rose has thorns," I said. I had forgiven Rich. It seemed wrong to keep bellyaching about his mistakes. While the truth was that he'd slept with Charlene and gotten her pregnant, that shouldn't be his defining moment in our lives. I didn't hate him anymore. And because I didn't, I was free.

"Rich screwed up at the end. But for nearly sixteen years, he stood with you. That's saying something." Her long nails drummed the wood seat. "I worked all kinds of shitty jobs because I don't have skills or smarts. I ended up as Patsy's nail girl because I got steady hands and an extensive collection of polish. Now, I got a chance to live like a queen. Why shouldn't I?"

From Linda's perspective, I supposed that Ivan seemed like an ice cream cone on a hot, summer day. But, still, it didn't seem right, this union between my friend and that big-mouthed crazy Russian.

"What about love?" I asked.

"What about love?" Linda bristled. "I loved Earl and he was a cheating piece of shit. You loved Rich and same goes. Think about it, Jessie. Think about being with a man who will always be faithful and who will always protect you." She looked at me, a fever in her gaze, a brightness that reflected manic hope. It scared me, that look. "You love Patrick. And you're not binding with him," she pointed out, as if my decision not to bind for love justified her decision to bind for security.

"It's more complicated," I said. "He wants more of

a soul mate forever thing. Besides, I don't think it's fair to him, me having kids and all."

"Jessie, honey, that doesn't make any sense."

"When Patrick was human, he had a family. But his wife and children were murdered—the same night he was Turned."

"Oh. Oh, honey. That's terrible." Linda patted my shoulder and I accepted the comfort, even though it was really Patrick who warranted the empathy. "Tell me, Jess. How do you feel about losing Jenny and Bryan?"

"Like my soul would be ripped out. That my life would be empty and hollow and meaningless."

Linda nodded. "Sure enough. Patrick's managed to live a thousand lifetimes feeling the same way. Seems to me that you're the one scared. And you're using Jenny and Bryan to push away Patrick. He needs time is all. So do you. Both of you've got enough baggage to put Paris Hilton to shame."

"Ha ha." Was Linda right? Was I protecting my kids? Or using them as the buffer from making a decision that scared the hell out of me?

"You should ask 'em."

"Ask Patrick? Ask him what?"

"Not Patrick. Your kids. Sit 'em down and lay it out. Get their feelings about what's going on."

"They don't get to decide who I date," I said.

"Yes, they do. If you're using 'em as an excuse to not be with Patrick, then they are deciding who you date."

"Quit making sense," I groused. I launched the swing a little harder than necessary and Linda's head snapped back. She glanced at me with a little grin. And I grinned sheepishly back.

"Tell you what. I'll think about what you said. But . . . oh Linda, I don't know about Ivan," I said, hoping she had softened enough to really listen to me.

"Don't start, Jessie. Like I said, he's got treasures stashed all over the world and a palace in Russia."

"La-de-freaking-*da*!"

Linda stood up, so agitated that she started pacing the length of the porch. "Ivan's my Master. I may not love him, but he's better than Earl."

"Oh Linda! Every man is better than Earl."

"Shut your mouth. He's still Marybeth's daddy."

I jumped off the swing and turned to face Linda. "I'm not the one who shot at Marybeth's *daddy* with a .38 Special!"

Her mouth dropped open and she stared at me. The fury in her eyes died, replaced by merriment. She cackled and slapped her thigh. "I sure as shit did and I'd do it again. Damned near winged him."

I laughed with her. "Yeah. That was some shooting, Calamity Jane." I leaned against the porch railing, arms crossed, and met Linda's gaze. "You really want to marry Ivan?"

"Guess so."

"What about Stan?"

Surprise etched her face. "Stan?" She shook her head, bemused. "He's a sweet guy, Jessie. I like him. But he's not for me. He's too smart. I can't understand half of what he says when he's talking. And he's not . . . well, he just doesn't have a spine. Hell, I've fought off gnats that were more vicious than him."

"Sounds like you've been thinking enough about him to come up with all those qualities." My gaze flicked to the front door where Stan stood, his hand still on the handle.

"Don't forget he's a human," said Linda. "And there's no way I'd Turn anyone. No way would I condemn someone to this kind of life."

"I see your point."

Stan reversed direction, his expression full of hurt and heartache, and pulled shut the door. Linda, for all her vamp senses, didn't notice the man had heard all the things she'd said about him. Poor Stan.

"So, look. I'm gonna bind to Ivan. And there's a ceremony and stuff. I want you to be there. I've been making arrangements. So, everything's set for tomorrow."

"Okay," I said. "Have you done the deed yet?"

"No." She cleared her throat. "Ivan wants to make it all official after the wedding." Her hands fluttered like escaped birds. "I'm kinda nervous about that part."

"It's like riding a bicycle," I said with a straight face. "Or so I've heard."

She cackled again. "I think my parts have gone rusty." She paused. "You gonna be there, Jessie?"

"No offense, babe, but I'm not watching you have sex with Ivan."

"Smart ass. You know what I meant."

"If Ivan is who you want . . . if marrying him is what you want . . . then I'll be there to toast to your happiness."

Linda nodded her thanks. "It's a double celebration," she said. "Our wedding and Marybeth's eighteenth birthday."

"Wow. Good thing you died at the very youthful age of twenty-nine."

"Damn right." She grinned at my joke, then rounded the swing and plopped onto it. I joined her and once again, we rocked. Comfortable silence weaved around us, interrupted only by the swing's creaking chains and the clicking songs of crickets. It was enjoyable to swing and stare at the lush foliage of my yard, at the weeping willow and bright colors of summer roses mixed with the hedges. All that green growth . . . beautiful and temporary. In no time at all, summer would end. Then winter would arrive, and all that I saw here would die, only to revive again when spring appeared. I swear to God that "Circle of Life" song from *The Lion King* revved in my head. *Gak.*

"I can't stand knowing I'll outlive my children." My confession was surprising and painful. I wasn't sure I'd meant to vomit that information, but there it was, out in the open and stinking up the air.

"Sucks a big ol' sour tit!" exclaimed Linda. "But think about it, Jessie. You'll know your kin for generations. The children of your children's children and on down the line. You'll be your family's guardian angel for damned near ever. Isn't that a wonderful gift?"

I glanced at Linda with raised brows. "Have you been talking to Brigid? Because that hogwash sounds like something she'd say."

"What? I can't have maternal insight and Earth Mother qualities?"

She didn't sound too offended, though, so I knew I'd been right. I laughed. "Yeah, that's you, all right. Miss Mary Sunshine."

"You're such a bitch."

"Aw. You say the sweetest things."

Chapter 25

In honor of weddings and birthdays, we decorated the high school gym with yellow and white crepe paper, balloons, and roses plucked from the abandoned yards of the houses on my block.

While the bride-to-be enjoyed an impromptu bridal shower hosted by her daughter in a corner of the gym, I directed a very sullen Stan in the placement of the cake, which I had baked and frosted.

"Vampire wedding cake," I said, smiling, as Stan put the three-tiered chocolate and raspberry delight in the middle of the table. On either side were the two vanilla cakes I'd baked for Marybeth's birthday.

"I'm sure it's delicious," said Stan. "But I'm not staying for the wedding."

"Stan," I said. "If you want her, fight for her."

His lovesick gaze meandered to where Linda was squealing over a filmy white negligee, which she held up to show the giggling women around her. The naked longing in Stan's face darn near broke my heart. "I'm a human," he said. "Just a drone. She needs a vampire. Ivan's . . . well, he's Ivan. And I'll be dead of old age before their binding ends."

"Oh, hon! Isn't love worth fighting for?" I asked.

His hound-dog gaze riveted to mine. "You ever ask yourself the same question?"

With that stupid PDA quivering in his hand, Stan walked away, muttering as he tapped on its screen. I stood there watching him go like a lightning victim who'd been melded to the floor. *It's different for me*, I wanted to rail at him.

Patrick had kissed me good-bye last night, er, this morning. He arrived a few minutes after I awoke to let me feed. Then he disappeared. Literally.

Occasionally I'd feel him brush at my mind. And I'd brush back. I had fiddled with the idea of crawling around in his thoughts the way he did mine. But I knew I didn't have the finesse to extract what I wanted to know without Patrick figuring out what I was doing. I was probably better off trying to figure out things the old-fashioned way.

"Ah, *ma chérie*, you set a lovely table." François leaned forward and sniffed the wedding cake. "It has been a long time since I yearned for dessert."

I laughed and smacked his shoulder. "You are so full of crap. But thanks for the compliment."

"Hey," said Johnny as he sidled next to us. "Nice cake."

"Thanks. It's a shame neither one of you can taste it."

Both of them grimaced and I grinned. They'd been on a blood diet too long to miss human food anymore.

I wondered if I'd ever get to the point where I didn't miss chocolate. Hah. Never.

With a wave, Johnny sauntered off. I saw Lucifer wend through the chairs we'd set up for the guests. As Johnny passed by her, she trotted after him. Then he stopped to chat with Ivan. The big, brash Russian looked less like a rampaging giant and more like a guy about to get married. He actually wore a black tuxedo with a red rose tucked in its lapel. His riot of hair was slicked back into a ponytail. Now, if he'd only get rid of that awful beard . . .

"Alas, I must also leave your radiant presence," said François. He lifted my hand and kissed my knuckles. Then, he, too, strode across the gym to join Ivan and Johnny. What could those three men possibly have in common to merit a casual conversation?

The setup for wedding and birthday party complete, I crossed the room to join Linda's bridal shower. As I passed the three men, I got a whiff of the same garbage scent I'd noticed before in the gym. The door to the locker room was open. Huh. Maybe the lockers needed to be emptied. I bet they were full of moldy socks and half-eaten sandwiches. Blech.

I wiggled myself a spot among the ladies and watched Linda open gifts. As more lingerie was taken from glittery-wrapped packages, my mind wandered.

Nearly all of Broken Heart's human citizens had packed up and moved. We were like a ghost town . . . if not with spirits at least with a few of the undead. The Consortium had knocked down the Barley & Boob Barn and had poured foundations for at least two buildings. Slowly, but surely, changes were taking place. Guess that was the best and the worst aspect about life, how it was fluid and malleable. Some days, the changes were big, and some days, they were itty bitty. But nothing or no one ever stayed the same.

"Thanks, Jessie!" said Linda, pleased as she held up the pair of ruby earrings I had given her. "They're gorgeous!" I'd bought the jewelry on a day-trip to Tulsa. I'd stashed them away thinking I'd give 'em to my mother for Christmas. I could see now that they were better suited for Linda. She liked sparkly and dangly things.

An hour later, with guests milling about, and a nervous Linda talking to a nervous Ivan, I went in search of Patrick. I had seen him a few times in the gym, but he hadn't sought me out. I was miffed, though I shouldn't have been. I went outside and prodded our mental connection. Nothing. He hadn't taken the phone off the hook. He just wasn't answering. Okay, but we *had* claimed each other. Technically, he was mine for a while even without the binding.

That was my last thought just as I spotted Patrick. He stood, his back to me, at the corner of the building. But I knew who was wrapped in his arms, because she chose to pry her foul mouth away from his neck and look at me over his shoulder. Her mouth bloodied, her gaze wide, Charlene's expression was one of panic as I marched toward them. I was going to kill her dead, this time permanently. Fury roared through me. Oh no. Not again. Not fucking again.

"Get away from him!" I put out my palms and pushed the air in front of me. I was still five feet away, but that bitch sailed away from Patrick's embrace.

Holy shit. I watched her fly through the air, screaming, until she hit the thick branches of an oak tree and fell to the ground.

Patrick turned to face me, his gaze shuttered. "She's feeding, love. That's all."

"What, a donor isn't good enough for her?" I bared my fangs at him. "But don't fucking talk to me."

"I'm her Master and must provide for her."

"Are you deaf? Don't. Talk. To. Me."

I flew to where Charlene had landed. She got to her feet, shame blazing in her eyes. "He's my Master, too."

"I don't give a shit."

She shook her head, looking too much like a lost little girl. "Why do you care so much, Jessica? You don't want him."

"Yes, I do!" I shouted. "The thing is, I can't always have what I want, especially if getting what I want hurts someone else. But that's a concept you just don't get, is it?"

Poor Charlene. Did she think that Patrick would give what Rich would not? Maybe her goal was the same as Linda's—protection, security, faithfulness. At any cost. I got pissed off all over again.

"Rich was coming home to me. Why do you think that is?" I asked softly.

Oh, that got her back up, all right. "Rich wasn't thinking straight. He was . . . confused." She licked her lips, her eyes dulling as she tried to piece together what she wanted to say. "Rich. Oh, hell. Just a warning. A warning, that was all."

She stepped back, entranced in her memories. "He . . . he didn't want me. I was carrying his child.

Trying to make a home for us. I . . . needed him. Wanted him. Wasn't I enough? Wasn't my love enough?" Her fingers plunged into her hair. Her lips peeled back and she mocked in a deep voice, *"I want to go home, Charlene. I love my wife, my children. I'm sorry, honey. I'm sorry. I'll see that you get settled, that you have money."*

Patrick chose that moment to join us, standing behind me. I don't know if he meant to let me handle Charlene or meant to grab me if I attempted to wring her neck. Either way, his presence was a comfort.

Charlene's whole body quaked like she was getting electric shock therapy. When she pulled her hands away from her head, clumps of blond hair fluttered to the ground. She didn't seem to notice. "My father owned a garage in Tulsa. Other little girls had tea parties and played dolls. I had tools and played cars."

My stomach twisted as I watched her fall apart. It was terrible to witness, but I couldn't look away. Patrick's hands clutched my shoulders and he steadied me. But my emotions were still on a roller coaster ride. Hadn't I wanted Charlene to hurt, too? Oh God. Not like this. The poor soul was losing her mind.

"You ever take apart the engine of a sixty-four Mustang?" she asked.

"No," I said. "I was more the tea-party type."

She nodded. "Yeah. Most girls are the tea-party type." She paced a square. "Don't make me tell. Don't. I don't want to. Don't make me tell."

"Go on, Charlene," said Patrick in a soothing tone. I realized he was using glamour on her. "It's okay. You'll feel better. Don't you want to feel better?"

"Yes. Of course. This is the only way to feel better. To explain."

She walked the square, staring at nothing. Watching her made me dizzy, sick. I swallowed the knot of dread clogging my throat.

"That night, when Rich said he was leaving me, I decided he wasn't going to go. So I fixed his car something good. Sure did. I was having contractions. The stress of arguing, probably. So . . . Rich went off in his car thinking he was going home. And I went off in mine to the hospital knowing he wasn't going anywhere."

She stopped pacing, and looked at me, tears streaking her face. "It was an accident. I don't know what happened. I just wanted him to stay. But I must've . . . it was just supposed to stop. Get a few miles down the road and stop."

"You . . . killed Rich." Shock chilled me until my teeth chattered. Patrick's arms wrapped fully around me and he pulled me against his chest.

"That's not what I meant to do," she pleaded. "He wasn't supposed to die." Her eyes blazed in anger. "It's your fault," she wailed. "If he hadn't wanted you, I wouldn't have fixed the engine. I wouldn't have . . . it's your fault! Yours!"

What the hell was wrong with her? One minute she was pathetic innocent and the next she was calculating nymph. Had she always been crazy? Had she teetered on the edge of sanity only to go over it when she'd been Turned?

"Charlene," said Patrick. "Wouldn't you like to lie down?"

"Yes," she said, her rage suddenly and abruptly doused. "I'm very tired."

"Drake and Darrius are waiting for you. Do you see them?"

"They're behind you. I'll go now."

She trudged around us and joined the twins. They nodded good-bye and they took Charlene and headed toward the fleet of RVs in the parking lot. I hoped one had a padded room with quadruple locks. I stepped out of Patrick's embrace and turned to face him. "Does she have the Taint?"

"No," said Patrick. "What she has is a guilty conscience and a fragile psyche."

"How did you know that she . . . that she killed Rich?"

"I didn't. I realized she was trying to work up the nerve to tell you something important. So I helped a little."

"Could you make her use a donor from now on? I can't stand the thought of her fangs in your neck."

"I'm sorry, Jessica. I won't allow her to feed from me if it soothes your mind."

"Or touch you."

"Or touch me." He smiled. "Are you okay?"

I knew he was asking about how I felt now that I knew Charlene had, accidentally or purposely, caused Rich's death. It was shocking. Horrible. And something I would never tell my children. But knowing why he'd died wouldn't change the fact that he was gone. "I made my peace with Rich and the life we had together. Knowing the truth won't bring him back. And there's something else you should know . . ."

He waited and I couldn't get my tongue to work. Then he prodded, "What?"

"I've been thinking on it. What happened between me and Rich. Truth is, Patrick, even if he had come home and begged for another chance . . . it was too late. I was mad and grieving, but I'd already changed inside. Already made room for something different. Something new. What I'm trying to say is that . . . okay, what happened sucked. It was painful. And I didn't want to go through it. But no matter how it happened, it was meant to be so."

"You believe that, Jessica?"

"Yes. Because I was meant . . ." I licked my dry lips, my nerves jumping. "I was meant for you."

He pulled me into his arms and kissed me until I damned near melted. I wished I could give him more than my words. But, for now, we had this moment. And damn, that man could kiss!

When I could think again, I said, "Isn't it interesting that Drake and Darrius were just moseying on by?"

Patrick smiled sheepishly. "Uh . . . they were following you."

"What?"

"I asked them to watch out for you. Every time you go somewhere by yourself, you get into trouble."

"I don't need baby-sitters!"

"Yes, you do." He kissed me again, and this assault was far more brutal than the last. Heat licked through me until I felt completely ablaze. I clung to him, meeting his lips, thrusting my tongue against his, and wanting . . . oh God, did I ever want.

The thing is, I can't always have what I want, especially if getting what I want hurts someone else.

My words to Charlene. My mind wasn't going to

give me a break no matter how much my heart wanted
Patrick. Damn it. Reluctantly, I broke the kiss.

"I love you, Patrick."

In his silver gaze, I saw truth. Love. Devotion. And I
didn't really deserve those emotions. Or Patrick. Yet, he
drew me into his embrace and said, "I love you, too."

"I'm glad," I said, my heartache giving way to dry
sobs. "I know it's wrong and unfair to say the
words . . . because . . . because . . ."

"I know, *céadsearc.* I already know."

The ceremony for Ivan and Linda was short and
sweet. Then the party swung into full gear and for two
solid hours we danced and laughed and remembered
what it was like to enjoy life.

We took a short break to see Marybeth blow out the
candles on her cake and open her presents. After the
last gift was unwrapped, the illusive Damian and his
security team shepherded all the kids to my house for
the ultimate sleepover, which included junk food, bad
movies, and loud music. I suspected there might also
be water-balloon wars and food fights, but I was having too good a time to lecture Jenny and Bryan on appropriate behavior.

Until Charlene came to her senses, Patrick and I
agreed that Rich, Jr. would stay with me. It was time
Bryan and Jenny got to know their little brother. If
Charlene would allow it, maybe we could arrange vis-
its for the siblings. I don't know how Jenny and Bryan
would see Richie without extensive contact with his
nutso mother, but we'd work it out.

For now, my only worry was getting through this

slow dance with Patrick. It was killing us to touch each other, to feel so intensely tender about one another, and yet know, in our heart of hearts, that we had no future. Then again, I was the one who believed we had no future. I tell you, I was tired of pondering it. So, I gave myself up to the moment, to Patrick, and soaked in every glorious second.

Brigid's sudden appearance put a real crimp in my enjoyment. Patrick and I stopped dancing and leaned in to hear what she wanted.

"Have you seen Drake or Darrius?" she asked. "Damian has lost contact with his brothers."

"First, I am not the D-men's secretary," I said. "Second, who the hell is Damian?"

"I am."

Next to Brigid was the spitting image of Drake and Darrius. I squinted at him and noticed his hair was a touch shorter and lighter than either of his . . . *brothers*? "No way. There are three of you? You're triplets?"

Damian's brows rose and his lips thinned. Humor flashed in his eyes, but it dissipated like mist exposed to sunlight. I realized this guy wasn't as soft as his brothers. He was different. Hard-hearted. More controlled. But man-oh-man, he was just as beautiful and buff as Drake and Darrius.

Jessica, I don't wish to tolerate your lustful mental descriptions of other men.

Then quit poking in my head.

You're broadcasting it.

I don't lust after them. They're cute, sure. But you're the one I want to fuck.

I felt his hands squeeze my waist so I looked into his

eyes. It was painful to watch, that thick desire swirling in his gaze. Then he brought the emotion to me, infused my body with it so that I knew how he felt.

Oh God. It was . . . beyond lust. Beyond love. So intense. So beautiful. So sad. I almost couldn't stand the roiling emotion, but it was familiar, his need. So, I gathered my own and pushed the energy into him. And we stood there, oblivious to everyone, and created unquenchable fires that consumed us, ravaged us, but denied us even the smallest pleasure.

"We're . . . uh, just gonna go," said Damian. "Obviously, you two are busy. Or will be."

Vaguely, I realized Damian had taken Brigid's arm and led her away from us, but I couldn't break away from Patrick.

Patrick's fingers wove into my hair and he tugged my head back. "I want to be inside you so badly right now, I can think of nothing else."

He bit me.

Right there, in the middle of the gym with vampires and humans bebopping around us, and our lust already raging out of control, Patrick sank his fangs into my neck.

It was like having sex in public.

He wrapped me in his arms, and pressed me close. His hard-on slid in the vee of my thighs and pushed against my clit.

My world spun.

I grabbed onto Patrick as he drank from me and tried to find purchase. But I had stepped off the cliff. The air rushed around me, my stomach dipped and crumpled as I fell. Lights exploded in my head.

Trembling in his arms, silently giving my submission to him, the orgasm detonated. I went limp, my moan drowned out by the music.

He wrenched away from my neck, his gaze silver fire, and scooped me up.

Within the blink of an eye, he'd taken us outside. In another, he'd flown us to the roof.

Before I realized what was happening, Patrick had taken off my dress, panties, and swords, then pressed his mouth against my vulva. "Jessica," he whispered, his lips erotically moving against my flesh. "Just this once, I want the privilege of a mate."

"Please," I murmured.

His fangs pierced me, his tongue flicking my clit as he siphoned blood from the most intimate part of me. If his hands hadn't steadied my thighs, I would've fallen to my knees. As it was, I held on to his skull with quivering hands and tried to keep upright.

Sensation wasn't a big enough word to describe what I felt. *Pleasure* nowhere near covered the phenomenon, either. Erotic energy pulsated, heated, plunged me into pure bliss. It was endless, this indescribable feeling. Good thing I was already dead because I don't think anyone alive could handle this kind of excruciating joy.

The orgasm imploded. I shattered into a million pieces, unable to collect the splinters of the person I'd been.

Then there was Patrick, my beloved mate, picking up the shards, fitting them back together so that once again, I existed.

When I came to, I was fully clothed, sitting in

Patrick's lap, his arms wrapped around me, his face buried in my hair.

I loved Patrick. I lusted for him and no other. I would walk the rest of my days alone because I wouldn't choose him over my children and I would never choose another man over him. Though I knew all these things. . . .

Only now, only after this . . . did I finally understand the concept of soul mate.

"Céadsearc," he whispered, "thank you."

"I should be thanking you," I said, trying to find my footing on old ground. There'd been an earthquake in my very soul. I don't think I'd ever feel whole again. Not without Patrick. "That was . . ." I hesitated. "I don't think there's a word for it."

"There's one," he said, his head lifting. *"Sonuachar."*

Tears shone in his eyes. Diamonds scattered on silver. I gasped, my hands cupping his jaw. "Oh, Patrick."

"Tá mo chroí istigh ionat," he whispered, smiling. "My heart is within you."

How lovely it might've been if the evening had concluded with those words. That was the kind of lovelorn phrase a girl could turn over in her mind as she fell asleep and dreamed about happy endings.

But nope—I didn't get a romance book.

I got a horror novel.

The building shook. Then a whooshing roar busted off the metal doors and shattered all the windows.

And before I could scream, "Oh shit!" the roof gave way beneath our feet.

Chapter 26

Patrick whisked us off the roof and away from the crumbling building.

"Oh my God." I couldn't get my bearings. "What is it? What's going on?"

"Wraiths," said Patrick. "They've bombed the gymnasium."

"Bombed? *Bombed!*" Comprehension rushed through me. Jesus, God. The children. My house. No. No! "We've gotta get to the kids. Oh my God. My babies."

He settled us in a copse of trees several hundred yards away from the gym. He grabbed my shoulders and shook me. "Jessica! Stop, love. Damian knows what to do. The children are fine. Okay?"

"You've got to let me check the house."

"Use your connection to the kids. You'll see."

I couldn't calm down long enough to do such a simple thing. Patrick rubbed my shoulders until the fear receded.

Finally, I connected with Bryan and Jenny. They were fine. Really excited about a road trip and wreaking serious havoc on Patrick's bus.

"They're all in your RV. Where the hell are they going?"

"A contingency location. We've been prepared for the possibility of a Wraith attack."

"Hel-*lo*. They just fucking blew up the high school gymnasium and everyone in it!" I tried to calm myself. "So does this mean the Wraiths survived the cave-in? Or are these guys like . . . I don't know, back-up Wraiths?"

"I don't know." His eyes went dark, lethal. Any Wraith who ventured into his path wouldn't live long.

I unsheathed my swords, then together we rose into the air and flew toward the smoking ruins of Broken Heart High School.

Chaos reigned in the parking lot. People ran to and fro, shouting, and after a minute of watching, I realized it was organized chaos. Apparently, any fighting that had occurred was over.

Good Lord. The gymnasium was a smoldering pile of rubble. The flames had been put out, but smoke still filled the air—a silent ghost wailing the loss of its body.

"Where are the Wraiths?" I asked Patrick.

"Gone," said Damian as he joined us. "A hit and run, mostly. Looks like you missed a few when you destroyed their hideout." Damian's eyes flashed and I damned near swallowed my tongue in fright. Thank goodness I wasn't a Wraith. I sure as hell wouldn't want to be on Damian's bad side.

Patrick grimaced. "They are cockroaches—it isn't surprising a few squirmed away."

"They're not as sneaky as they think. We had enough warning to get everyone out, but we couldn't find you two." He looked at the swords I still held, his gaze curious. Oh, right. I slipped them into my hip holster.

"Everyone's accounted for?" asked Patrick. We'd reached the only RV left in the parking lot. I assumed that all the rest had hauled ass, going who knew where.

"There's a human missing . . . Marybeth Beauchamp. Right before the blast, I found Drake and Darrius—unconscious and locked in a security RV. It looks like Charlene escaped."

My stomach dipped. "Shit. You're just full of good news, aren't you?" I chewed my lower lip. "Who's searching for Marybeth?"

"We have several security teams sweeping the area, but they've come up empty," said Damian. "It'll take a while to get through the debris, but everyone who mentally probed the building agrees there is no one trapped in it." He nodded to the RV. "Stan got hurt. He looks bad."

I looked at Patrick. His jaw clenched. Stan had called himself a drone, but I know Patrick thought of him as a friend. And you know what? So did I.

As we entered the RV, I realized it was a medical facility. A human female in a white uniform sat at a minidesk, tapping the keys of a laptop. "Go on," she said. "They're in there."

We entered the room. On the left side, hooked up to wires and tubes, lay Stan, the one human casualty. Beside the bed stood Linda, looking like her whole world had been ripped in half.

"Did you find Marybeth?" she asked, anxious.

"No," I said gently. "But we will, hon."

She gazed bleakly at us. "She turned eighteen tonight. Helluva birthday party." She leaned down and stroked Stan's forehead. "Look at him. He's so pale. God. Poor Stan."

"How bad is he?" I asked.

"Real bad." Her voice broke, but she stuffed a fist to her mouth and tried get ahold of herself.

I exchanged a glance with Patrick. He nodded then put his hands on her shoulders. "Don't you feel tired, Linda?"

"Don't try to glamour me." She shrugged off his hands and stooped to drag the thin white blanket up to Stan's chin. "I'll stay here with him. You go find my Marybeth."

Feeling dismissed, we trooped off the bus and stood in the parking lot looking helplessly at each other. The acrid smell of smoke clung to the air. People milled around the parking lot, some looking through the debris, others picking up pieces, and a few with big, black guns ringed the perimeter.

The cell phone on Damian's hip beeped. He picked it up and flipped it open. "Damian."

"We found Marybeth. She's been injured, sir," said the disembodied male voice.

"Damn it! Was it the blast?"

"No, sir. She's been clawed by some kind of animal. Her torso looks like spaghetti. She's alive, but I don't think she'll make it."

Oh my God! Clawed? That meant Georgie the insane lycan had escaped the cave-in. Was he attacking humans for the hell of it? Or because Ron had also escaped and told his pet to hurt Marybeth?

"Give me your location," said Damian.

"The edge of the soccer field," said the voice. "We've been through this area twice already. We found her on the third sweep."

"So, she was attacked then dumped. Stay there. We're on our way."

We hurried across the parking lot and the soccer field. A group of men who looked like the vampire SWAT ringed the still, pale body of Marybeth. I noted that the only one not in uniform had blond hair and silver eyes.

Lorćan.

The men parted, fanning out to give us room and protection. Glittering green orbs floated around her. I poked at one. My finger went right through it and tingled from its pulsating energy.

"Fairy lights," said Lor. "A specialty of mine."

We kneeled around Marybeth. She'd been covered with a blanket that looked like a big sheet of aluminum foil. I'd seen those before on a show about avalanches. Thermal blankets. As he lifted it away, the material crankled noisily. I had to swallow down my gorge, but at least the wounds didn't look as bad as those on Emily or Sharon. Marybeth might have a chance.

"We need to get her back to the medical bus," I said.

"Céadsearc," said Patrick, and his hand clasped mine. "She's not going to make it."

"She's still breathing. The gashes aren't as bad as the others who were attacked. If we get her some help—"

He shook his head.

"Brigid. You said she was the greatest healer in the world."

"And she told you she had limitations. I'm afraid this is one of them." He took my hand and rubbed it between his palms. "The claws of the creature that did this are poisonous. Even now, the toxin is moving through her system, shutting down her organs."

"Toxin?" Realization dawned. "You tested Emily and Sharon."

"Full autopsies on both," he admitted. "If the victims don't bleed to death from the wounds, they'll die from the venom."

"But . . . what about me? I lived."

"You're a vampire with *sidhe* blood," said Lor. "The poison didn't react the same way. Even so, Patrick had to travel beyond the veil to retrieve you."

I felt jittery, like I'd consumed too many mocha lattes. Once again, I felt a shift in my emotional landscape. Patrick had risked his own life and soul for mine. It was a burdensome thing to know a person loved you more than his own self.

Sitting back on my heels, I looked at the ashen complexion of Marybeth Beauchamp. Sleeping Beauty. She'd never wake. Never find her prince. I brushed away a loose red curl from her face and sighed. "Poor, sweet baby."

"I'll get Linda," said Patrick. He kissed me . . . then misted away.

I cried because, well, it's all I could really do.

When Patrick led Linda to her dying daughter, she fell to her knees and keened. We moved back and

allowed her to grieve. She prayed to God, she begged
the devil, and she sent her sorrow into the Universe,
asking for a miracle.

Marybeth's breath shallowed.

Her skin grayed.

Little by little, her soul seeped away.

Lor watched Linda and I could see that he longed to
sit with her and offer solace. Anguish filled up the
space, damned near suffocating all of us.

I thought about Brigid saving Ruadan. And Ruadan
saving Patrick. Parents who loved their children so
much they made difficult choices. What was worse?
Letting your child die? Or damning him?

What would I do to save Bryan and Jenny?

Anything. Anything at all.

Patrick.

Yes, love?

Can Marybeth be Turned?

*It's possible, but I told you, most humans don't make
the transition. And watching it fail would be much
worse than watching her pass now.*

Lorćan can Turn her.

*I'm sorry, love. But Lor won't do it. He's never
Turned anyone.*

Well, I'm gonna ask anyway.

I aimed my mental radar at Lor. *Will you Turn Marybeth? You can save her.*

*Condemning her to the existence of a vampire isn't
saving her.*

*Marybeth's life was stolen from her. And you can give
it back. Linda's already buried her only sister because of
this creature. Don't make her bury her only child, too.*

She is not the first mother to lose a daughter. And she won't be the last. I'm sorry, Jessica.

You selfish, pigheaded coward!

Lorćan turned to look at me, his expression stunned.

That's right, I shot into his mind along with a big dose of fury, *you're a coward. You killed Linda. Remember? Sucked her dry and left her for dead. You owe her. Give her this. Give her back Marybeth.*

You don't know what you're asking of me. I vowed I wouldn't ever Turn a human.

I was breaking his heart, I knew it. Reminding him of his own sins and his own sorrow to get what I wanted. It was cruel of me. But I wasn't going to stand here and let Linda lose Marybeth. Not if there was a slim chance we could save that precious girl.

Patrick could try to Turn her, but you're the key, Lor. The key to why we all lived. I know that if you change her, she'll live. Please, Lor. Please! I'm begging you!

Damn you. All right. Only if Linda agrees. And only if you promise to never ask me to do such a thing again.

I promise. Thank you.

"Linda . . ." I closed the distance between us and sat next to her. I wrapped my arms around her shoulders. She looked at me, her eyes glassy, her face swollen from dry-weeping.

"Patrick told me she couldn't be saved," she said. "Your Irish cutie wouldn't lie to me. Jessie, I'm going to lose my baby."

"There's one option." Oh God. Was this the right thing to do? Should I even offer her the possibility? "We can try to Turn her."

"Patrick?" she said. Hope blazed in her eyes. "Why didn't I think of it? Yes. Let Patrick Turn her."

"If you want Marybeth to have a fighting chance, Lorćan needs to do it."

Her jaw went slack. "He's the reason we're vampires. No!" She leaned over her daughter and stroked her hair. "I won't let him get near her."

"If you want Marybeth to have a fighting chance, he's got to be the one," I said with enough steel to snap her attention to me.

Silence settled between us as Linda fought an internal battle. I didn't envy her decision. It was a horrible choice to make, and I hoped to God that I'd never be forced to make a similar one.

"I don't want her to die," she said finally. "Is that selfish of me, Jessie? I love her more than my next breath. I'm not ready for her to go." She laughed, the hysteria of grief. "There I was just yesterday going on about how we'd be guardian angels to our children's children. I'm such a fool."

"She doesn't have much time," said Patrick, his voice soft with empathy. "What do you want to do, Linda?"

"I want you to save her."

Chapter 27

We moved Marybeth to the medical RV. The doctor and Lor got Marybeth settled into the bed opposite from Stan.

Linda insisted that Patrick stay through the process. Why she trusted him and not his twin . . . well, I guess it made sense. Patrick was the buffer between her and Lor. Having faith in your own murderer to save your child would be a big leap for anyone.

While Patrick agreed that he would stay, he vehemently denied me the same privilege. Honestly, I didn't want to watch Marybeth's Turning, but I wasn't going to abandon Linda.

"It's okay, Jessie," said Linda. "Now, don't fuss. I need Patrick's help and he can't focus when you're around."

Put that way, I really had no choice but to go. Patrick didn't like my idea of going home and waiting for him, but I told him "tough noogies" and flew to my house, anyway.

I checked the house. Doors and windows were locked and the security system engaged. Security teams milled around the area so it wasn't likely Wraiths were hanging around. I should've felt safe, but I didn't.

I don't know if it was the constant admonitions of Mr. Paranoia or just walking around in a place where I knew I was utterly alone, but suddenly my little Victorian two-story had a high creep factor. I would rather listen to the sounds of Bryan and Jenny fighting than the silence of an empty house. I hurried into my bedroom, which had been cleaned and fixed by Drake and Darrius and Johnny. I locked the door and leaned against it, suddenly relieved.

I checked on my kids. They still partied down in Patrick's RV, safe and sound. Grateful that they were okay, and missing them like crazy, I wondered if I should track them down and stay in the bus. But, I didn't know where they were . . . and if someone was watching me and followed me, say the creature or a Wraith . . . no, it was better to stay here and wait for Patrick.

I decided to indulge in a rare treat: a long, hot, uninterrupted bath. With lots of bubbles, expensive soaps, and soft music. Even without the requisite glass of wine, the bath was pure heaven.

Afterward, I slipped into a red lace gown that had crisscrossed ribbons across the top and two long slits up the sides. I felt like a very sexy vampiress in the getup and grinned to think about what Patrick might think of it.

And thinking about Patrick reminded me where he was and what he was doing. Then I felt really selfish for enjoying myself with something as silly as a bubble bath. Marybeth fought for her life, Linda for her sanity, and Lor . . . well, he had more demons to wrestle with, thanks to me. I sat on the edge of the bed, a mire of guilt and worry. Only one way to know . . .

Patrick? Everything okay?

The exchange's been made. Lor is tired. Linda is . . . upset. A Turning isn't pleasant to watch. After we wake from the day's rest, we'll know if Marybeth made the Turn.

Just a bit longer, love. Then I'll be with you.

See you soon.

I picked up the latest MaryJanice Davidson novel that had gathered dust on my nightstand. I'd been dying (har) to read it, and I figured it would pass the time as I waited for Patrick to return. As I reached to pick up the hardcover, I notice a metal cylinder. Okay. Another interesting object left mysteriously in my house. Was this left by Brigid, too?

I picked up the cylinder and examined it. It was about six inches long and heavy. I couldn't pry it open, not even with my vamp strength. I looked at it more closely and discovered that embedded in the middle was a familiar circle.

Dairine's coin.

I had put the necklace in my jewelry box for safe-keeping. My plan was to present it to Patrick tonight . . . hopefully before we did some more dream noogie.

After I retrieved the coin, I placed it in the "lock." The cylinder clicked open. With trembling fingers, I withdrew the parchment from inside.

I unrolled the scroll. It was about six inches wide and about the same in length. It felt like a particularly tough onion skin, holding together now but if I pinched in the wrong place, it could crumble.

Written in black ink, the words in a bold, sweeping cursive, I couldn't quite make sense of it. The document shimmered and shifted. Suddenly, I could read sentences. More magical protections, I supposed. Either that or I needed vampire eyeglasses.

These words are bespelled so that only the one who is destined to read them can decipher what I, Ruadan the First, have written.

If you are reading this scroll it means that the fede *ring created by Brigid and blessed by the* sidhe *has found Patrick's true love.*

To know the value of the ring, you must know its story . . .

Upon the death of his beloved wife, Patrick begged his grandmother to melt Dairine's fede ring into a coin so that he might wear it as a token. He wished for no other to ever wear the ring of the one he'd loved so well.

As for his own ring, he honored his wife, who had loved the sea, by tossing his fede *ring into the ocean. His father's grandmother, the Crow Queen, prophesied that Patrick would once again find true love . . . and he would know his own heart again. He would know his mate for only she could wear the ring that had once been his.*

Nearly four millennia passed. In 1887 CE, an Irish fisherman named Sean McCree cut open a fish caught and found the ring. He gave it to his new bride, Mary. Though she could not wear it on her finger, for she said the metal made her finger itch and swell, she placed it on a chain around her neck.

A year later, the couple arrived in America.

A year after that, they traveled to Oklahoma to compete in the land run.

The McCrees were happy for a while. As the years passed and the farm prospered, they had two children, a boy and a girl. Despite the hardships that came with starting anew, Mary thrived in the Oklahoma territory. But Sean became dissatisfied with everything in his life, including the one to whom he'd pledged his love.

One night Mary McCree found Sean making love to another woman, the grown daughter of friends who owned a neighboring farm. Unable to bear the pain of his betrayal, Mary put the chained ring around her daughter's neck, telling the five-year-old lass that a broken heart was worse than death. Then Mary McCree walked into the creek and drowned herself.

When her daughter, Lorna, grew up and the five original farms eventually formed a township, she requested that it be named Broken Heart, to honor her mother—and to forever remind her father and all husbands the price of infidelity.

No one in the McCree family knew the truth about the fede *ring. But no female could wear the ring.*

None but the one meant to wear it.

And that, dear reader . . . is you.

"Hi there!" said a cheerful male voice.

I screamed and threw the scroll, rolling off the bed in a disgraceful display of fear. As I struggled to my feet, the gentleman seated so calmly on the other side of my bed looked at me as if I'd lost my mind. He wore a black T-shirt, jeans with holes in the knees, and a pair of scuffed Nikes. He had black hair and silver eyes and the face of Remington Steele. His gaze meandered along my chest.

"Hey!" I crossed my arms over my breasts. "Those are . . ."

"Patrick's?"

"Well, his name isn't tattooed on them, but yeah, currently they are reserved for him." I peered at him and noted the similarities between him and his sons. "Ruadan, I presume?"

"Got it in one," he said, silver eyes twinkling.

"You scared the shit out of me."

One corner of his mouth lifted into a grin. He picked up the parchment and tapped on it. "So, you're Patrick's soul mate."

"No."

"But you read the scroll. Only his *sonuachar* can do that."

"Let me explain." I paused. "No, there is too much. Let me sum up."

"*The Princess Bride!*" Ruadan exclaimed in happy surprise. "I love that movie. 'Hello, my name is Inigo Montoya. You killed my father. Prepare to die!' " He leapt off the bed and made fencing motions.

"Ruadan, we're in a bit of crisis around here."

"Hey! My swords." He practically skipped to the

dresser where I had left them when I got ready for my bath. He whirled the half-swords like a master swordsman, which, of course, he was. "My mother really knows how to smith a weapon, doesn't she? Real fairy gold." He stabbed an invisible foe's chest with one and his stomach with the other. "Die, evil one! Die!"

He jumped up and down, the swords held above his head, and did a victory dance.

"You're like a big puppy!" I exclaimed. "A big, dumb puppy."

"I'm potty trained," he said, unaffected by my ire. "And I won't hump the legs of your guests." He put the swords on the dresser. "If you're not Patrick's soul mate, who are you?"

"Well, okay . . . see, he says I am. And honestly, I love him a lot. So I guess, technically, I—"

"Terrific! Have you done Step Three?" He waggled his brows as he opened up the top left drawer of my dresser.

"No. Hey! Do you mind, Nosy Newton?"

"Are these panties?" he asked, holding up two of my thongs. "Because they look like dental floss to me."

Oh my God. My almost father-in-law was digging around in my lingerie. Embarrassment bloomed in my face. "Ruadan, get out of my underwear!"

"Fine," he said, closing the left drawer and opening the right one. "Oh! Lookie here!"

"If you touch that box," I said menacingly, "I will cut off your head with your own swords. And I'm not talking about the one on your shoulders."

He laughed, shutting the drawer. "You won't need a vibrator anymore. You've got Patrick." His gaze slid toward the dresser. "Unless you have different toys in there. Nipple clamps?"

"I . . . what . . . oh God." I fell onto the bed, curled into the fetal position, and covered my face. "I'm soooo not talking to you about my sex life. Is that why you wrote that story? So you could embarrass to the death the person who read it?"

"No," said Ruadan. "That's just a bonus."

I felt the bed dip as he settled against the pillows piled along the headboard. I rolled onto my back and scooted up into a sitting position. "Give me the four-one-one, Ruadan."

"I sorta helped Sean McCree find the ring," said Ruadan. "One of the perks of having my grandmother's dark blood is that it gave me second sight. I knew a female of the McCree line would be the one meant for my son. I have to say, when I arrived in Oklahoma in the 1920s, I was damned sad about Mary's death. I liked that girl."

"You knew her?" Duh, Jessica. Dumb question.

"Yeah. I'd show up every generation or so." Ruadan glanced at me. "I was here about six months ago . . . I saw you wearing the ring. I knew Morrigu's prophecy had finally come to pass."

"So you're the one who suggested that the Consortium come take a look at Broken Heart."

"Guilty." He looked at the lockbox on the nightstand. He wiggled a finger at it, and it floated toward him. "When my mother smelted the coin for Padraig, I had her make the box, too."

"And made it so that only Dairine's coin opened it."

"Yeah. Too bad Nara traded my swords for it." He grinned. "But apparently you got it back from her."

"I ripped it off her neck," I said proudly. "You don't have to worry about her anymore. Patrick banned her."

"Woo-hoo!" Ruadan pumped his fist in the air. "After the binding ended, Nara sought the protection of her Family and stayed out of Patrick's sight for several centuries. Never would give him the coin, no matter what he offered. She would settle for nothing less than another binding.

"I heard she joined the Consortium. And Patrick probably let her so that he could figure out how to retrieve the necklace. Then again, Lor's been working on him to learn forgiveness and all that jazz."

"She was trying to cut off my head with your swords," I said. "That's when he banned her."

"'Atta boy! That woman's soul is black as sin and always will be. All Nara will ever care about is herself."

I glanced at him, at the handsome, silly vampire who'd created a master freaking race. *Big dumb puppy*. But handsome. I was beginning to think *GQ* looks were a requisite for male vampires.

"So, what's your name, lass?"

"Jessica Matthews."

"Jessica. Good name. Yeah, I like it." He waved a hand around in approval or dismissal. "So when's the binding?"

"Well, you see . . . I have two kids and I'm not—"

His eyes widened and a smile split his lips. "Hot damn! I've got grandkids! What are their names? Do they like Disney World? Do they like Paris? Do they like Porsches?"

I stared at him, at his elated expression, and realized that the first freaking vampire ever made was the almost-grandfather of my kids. It completely blew my mind. I mean . . . *whoa.* "Ruadan . . . my children are mortal. And Patrick and I are practically immortal."

"So what?"

"They're going to *die.*"

"Everyone dies," said Ruadan.

"You haven't!"

"I imagine I will eventually." He shifted, making himself more comfortable. "This is a nice bed."

Was he really thickheaded? Or did he have an undiagnosed case of attention deficit disorder?

"If I do the binding with Patrick, we'll be hitched forever. I'll watch my kids grow up and . . . pass away."

"Or not."

"Huh?"

"Jessica." He turned onto his side and looked at me. The wisdom of ancients sparkled in a gaze that had looked at the world for more than four thousand years. "You don't know what life will bring you. And you only live one moment at a time. What if Jenny and Bryan wish to attempt a Turning? What if they get married and have families and grow old and die? What if you and Patrick decide to greet the dawn when their time has passed? Or live on to guard the children of your children's children?"

"I . . . don't know."

"Exactly." He smiled. And in that smile, I saw the joy of a man who'd learned a thing or three about living. "Life is change. So what if you don't know what's going to happen next week or next century? You only have to live now, right now. And you can find happiness today, with Patrick.

"I like you, Jessica." He leaned over and kissed my forehead. "You're cute and tough and sexy." He rolled off the bed and jumped to his feet. "Gotta go. Got a hot date in Malaysia."

"Wait a minute. You're leaving?"

"Well, yeah. But I'll be back for the ceremony and to meet my grandkids."

"Ruadan," I said, "maybe you could stick around and help us out. The Wraiths are causing all sorts of problems. We're trying to build a whole new kind of town."

"Don't worry so much, Jessica. Everything will be fine."

"Is that a prophecy?"

He shrugged. *"Is fear rith maith ná drochseasamh."*

As Ruadan sparkled out of sight, I remembered that Patrick had said the same thing to me. *A good run is better than a bad stand.*

"Fine!" I yelled to the disappearing ancient. "I'll fix things myself. But you are so buying us a Porsche . . . in Paris!"

I rolled up the scroll, tucked it into its box, and put it away, along with the coin, in the nightstand drawer. I checked on my kids . . . asleep, finally. Good. I was feeling the pull of the sunrise. *Patrick, are you coming home?*

I climbed into bed and fluffed the pillow under my head. Exhaustion sat on me like a row of anvils. *Patrick?*

Céadsearc. *Lock your bedroom door. Keep it locked. Don't open it for anyone.*

Yeah. Okay.

Sheesh. I'd locked everything and checked it twice.

Jessica . . . I love you.

Love you, too.

I succumbed to the darkness, falling into dreamless sleep.

Chapter 28

"Jessica!"

I nearly leapt out of my skin. As it was, I went on full alert and scrambled out of my bedcovers. I truly missed coffee. I could use a pot about now. The digital clock on the nightstand blinked 7:11 P.M. in big, annoying red numerals.

"Jessica!" A fist pounded on the door. Wait. I'd fallen asleep. Patrick never arrived. But the last thing I remembered was that he told me to keep my bedroom door locked.

"Jessica? Are you awake?"

The voice had a French accent and an urgent tone. I crossed the room and put my hand on the knob. "François? How the hell did you get into my house?"

"I am a vampire," he said. "It is nothing to circumvent locks and alarms. We must go, *chérie*. The Wraiths followed the RVs. They have taken Patrick's bus and hold the children hostage!"

I immediately tried to connect with my kids. They

were still asleep. So . . . were they asleep because they were safe and sound with Damian? Or were they knocked out by gas or glamour by the Wraiths? My entire body tingled with apprehension. I wanted to trust François, but right now, the pope could be on the other side of that door and I wouldn't open it.

"If you got through the other security," I asked, "why can't you get in here?"

"Patrick has spelled it. Only he can go in."

"Why would he put spells on my bedroom?"

"To protect you, of course. Come, *chérie*. We need your help. Are you not worried about Bryan and Jenny?"

Yes. But I was also worried about why François needed me out of this room so urgently. I quickly changed clothes and retrieved the swords from the dresser. I wasn't sure what I was going to do.

Patrick?

He didn't respond. Foreboding wrapped cold fingers around me. Something was wrong. *Patrick? Hey, sleepyhead, are you there?*

There was complete silence in my mind. This was bad. Patrick had been living inside my head with me and he wasn't there. Which meant he had blocked me (and he'd sworn never to do that again) or he was incapable of thought. As in still unconscious or . . . my stomach squeezed. Okay. I wasn't going to think that. Patrick was fine. He was just . . . well, I didn't know. I reached out to the only other person with whom I had a mind connection. *Lorćan?*

Jessica? What do you want?

He sounded pissy and I figured I deserved whatever anger he harbored. But he was going to have to rake me over the coals later. *Are you still with Marybeth and Linda?*

They are still at rest. Patrick and I both gave Linda a strong suggestion for sleep, which will keep her out for a little longer. Marybeth hasn't stirred, but she survived the Turn . . . she is a vampire, just as you wanted.

Give me the guilt trip later, okay? I asked you to do something difficult and it sucked for you and I'm sorry. François is here and he really wants me to leave the room. He really wants me outta here. He says the kids are in trouble, but they're asleep, and as far as I can tell, safe. Worst of all, I can't reach Patrick. It's like he's . . . well, he's not there. And he told me to keep the bedroom door locked.

Something must be wrong if you're actually doing as my brother asks.

Hel-lo. Hysterical woman here. Make fun of me later. I'm scared.

All right, bean-shithe. *Give me a moment.*

"Jessica?"

"Oh, uh . . . sorry, François. I had to go to the bathroom."

"What? Why?"

Crud. Vampires didn't have to potty. "To get my . . . lotion. I have dry hands."

"You wait to rescue the children because you wish to put lotion on your hands?" He pounded on the door. "Come out, Jessica! I cannot help you as long as you remain in there."

Was François really trying to help me? I didn't believe my kids were in trouble. But I knew Patrick was. Maybe François had been told that the RVs had been attacked and was relaying that information to me. Or maybe François had hoped I would panic and open the door to him so he could harm me.

Jessica?

Lor! Thank God. Can you reach Patrick?

No. Patrick left here just before sunrise to go to you.

Oh my God. You don't think he got caught in the sunlight, do you?

No. I think he was captured.

The Wraiths? Shit, shit, shit! Okay. Look. You have to protect Linda and Marybeth and Stan. I'll figure out what François really wants and if he acts like a dickhead, I'll use my swords on his sorry ass. I'll meet you at the RV and we'll figure out how to rescue Patrick and save the day and all that.

Jessica . . . that's the dumbest idea I've ever heard.

You got a better one?

Jessica—

I'll see you in a few minutes.

Oh for . . . fine! But don't die.

"Jessica? This is getting tiresome, *mon chérie.* Please open the door."

François was a nice guy. A really nice guy. He had a groovy accent and buff bod and mischievous sense of humor. I liked him. All the same, I got on my knees, head low, and opened the door.

As it creaked open, François slashed out with a long, silver sword, probably hoping to gut me by surprise.

He missed me.

But I didn't miss him.

"Hi Frankie." I shoved the first sword into his stomach. The second plunged into his chest. I whipped them out and danced backward. He followed, looking more annoyed than injured.

The garbage stench that I had whiffed in the gym so often nearly knocked me over. Whatever he'd done to suppress whatever was causing that rank scent wasn't working anymore. It was like diving headfirst into a septic tank.

He swiped at me, but I salsa'd out of the way. He swung again and again, in a clumsy way, and I had to wonder if he was inept with the weapon or trying to fool me enough that I would lower my guard. The swords clanged against each other, and slowly, I maneuvered so that his back was to the bed and mine was to the door.

Then I knocked aside his sword and plunged my blades into his stomach. I shouted, *"Fulaing!"*

For once I knew what a Gaelic word meant: Suffer. The *sidhe* magic in the swords blazed, and for a moment, François glowed gold. He jolted as if shocked and, howling in agony, fell to his knees and swayed.

Body quaking, he dropped the sword. *"Ma chérie,* you are always surprising."

I felt sick. François might deserve the pain he was enduring, but it still made me nauseous to be the one inflicting it. "Why are you trying to kill me?"

His lips curved into a self-deprecating smile. "Ah. Time for the confession of the villain?"

"Something like that."

He shrugged then grimaced. I held my swords at the ready even though he wasn't going to attack me. At least, not yet. That *fulaing* move must've really fried him.

"You are Patrick's *sonuachar*. If we kill Ruadan's son, we start a war of the ancients. If we kill Patrick's true love . . . he walks into the dawn and saves us the trouble. And we frame his brother, eh? Two birds, one stone."

"And you decided to up the ante by killing Emily and Sharon and Marybeth?" Heck, no reason to tell him that Marybeth was one of the newly undead. What if he was somehow transmitting to someone?

"No," said François. "To Ron, the deaths of the humans were merely entertainment. Georgie was his cousin—the one who Turned Ron. The poor soul was going mad from the Taint. So, Ron attempted the same cure that Stan had concocted."

"You told Ron about the transfusion."

"*Oui.* But he killed a lycan to do it whereas Lor's transplant was given from blood collected by live lycans. You saw the results Ron got."

François looked down at the blood spurting from his wounds. "These cuts will not kill me."

"I know." I lifted the swords and held them up crossed, just the way I'd learned from my "download." All I had to do was swing down and . . . God. I stared at François, who looked amazed that I would even consider removing his head. Stabbing a guy was one thing, particularly one who had wanted to stab me back. But *this* . . .

Was I really going to cut off François' head? I wasn't sure it was the right thing to do. Then again . . . he didn't have a soul. *"Droch fhola."*

François looked at me, his blue eyes mad, and grinned. Then I knew. "Oh my God. You have the Taint."

"*Oui, chérie.* To die will be a great relief."

"But the cure . . ."

"Too late for me." The manic look in his eyes blazed as he shook his head and tried to step back from the edge of his own insanity.

"What did you do to Patrick?"

"Ah. He has not been so lucky."

"Where is he? What did you do to him?"

"I'm afraid that I'm through with my little confession." He weaved to his feet, his body trembling, and tried to lunge at me. "Kill me," he taunted, lumbering at me like a drunken fool. "Kill me!"

It was neither fear nor anger that made my decision. It was pity.

I swung both swords at his neck. They sliced through his skin smoothly, one from the left, the other from the right. They met in the middle with a wet metallic snick.

His eyes went wide, then blank.

I watched as the handsome head of François tipped forward and as it fell, both body and head exploded into ash.

As worried as I was about Patrick, he had survived almost four thousand years without my help. If I even allowed myself a second to think about what had just happened, I might lose it. I took a shower to get the blood and ash off my body. Then I dressed in new clothes: jeans, a T-shirt, and sneakers. I avoided the gray pile and red splatter as much as was possible. I was starving, but at the same time, my stomach roiled with nausea.

With my swords in hand, I left the house. I wasn't ready for . . . well, whatever. So, I gravitated to the swing and sat on it, rocking slowly. One thing I knew for sure, I would never step foot in my bedroom again. In fact, we'd have to move to another house. One that didn't have the stench of death or the taint of old lives or the echoes of pain.

I didn't realize I was dry-crying until Lorćan sat next to me and put an arm around my shoulders.

"François was a bad guy. He had the Taint and I . . . well, I killed him." I showed Lor the swords, clutching the handles and raising them up to glitter in the moonlight. "They're pretty. I wonder how many they've murdered."

"I wonder how many they've saved."

I looked at Lor and offered a tentative smile. "That's a better way to think of it. Thanks."

"I still haven't been able to connect with Patrick," said Lor. "The RVs are still at the contingency location—and everyone there is safe."

"Jessica," said a deep Russian-accented voice. Ivan Taganov climbed onto the porch and stood there, looked at me doubtfully.

"What?" I asked irritably.

Ivan crossed his massive arms and stared down at me. But there was no rancor in his eyes, only confusion. "I go to find my Linda," he said. "She's nursing Stan back to health. I see them together, and I think, 'Ivan, she is not for you.' And so, I call off the binding."

"How did Linda take it?"

He shrugged his massive shoulders. "It does not

matter. Right is right. Damian tells me that Patrick is missing."

I nodded. "Did Charlene ever turn up?"

Lor grimaced. "We found her . . . ashes on Rich's grave."

Horror scrabbled in my belly. "What?" I swallowed the gorge knotting my throat. "She committed suicide?"

"We think she laid down in front of his tombstone and waited for the dawn."

"Oh Charlene." I closed my eyes, absorbing this news. Despite everything that had gone on between us, I didn't want such a bad end for her.

"It is sad, Jessica. I am sorry," said Ivan. "But it is time to find Patrick."

"Yes," said another male voice, this one tinted with German. I saw Damian lounging against a tree in my front yard. "I see that you don't follow orders."

"What did you expect me to do? Cower in my bedroom and wait for you to rescue Patrick?"

"Yes." He straightened and sauntered toward us. "Patrick would rip my head off my shoulders if anything happened to you."

"Goddamn it. You're my new babysitter?"

He grinned. "If you would bind with the man, he wouldn't have to send people chasing after you all the time. Me? I think you'll be too troublesome a mate."

"Huh. Well, good thing I'm not marrying *you*."

"Indeed."

"Children," said Lor drolly. Everyone turned to look at him. "We need to track down Patrick and the Wraiths. It's been sundown for almost an hour. If Patrick still lives . . . it won't be for much longer."

"How can you say that so calmly?" I asked as panic washed over me. "He's not dead. He's not!" I tried to calm myself. I wouldn't believe that Patrick had been killed. We had unfinished business.

"Our security teams are waiting for me to report," said Damian. "We believe we're dealing with a small contingent of Wraiths, and we're not sure if Ron is among them."

"Georgie is certainly alive," I said, thinking of Marybeth.

"Not anymore," said Damian. "Drake and Darrius took care of him."

I flinched. It wouldn't be too big of a leap to think that a showdown between lycans would be fierce and bloody. I tried to get a grip on my yo-yoing emotions. "Where can they hide? It's freaking Broken Heart. We're a small town in the middle of nowhere." I stood up and leapt over the railing to the front yard. I started pacing and swinging the swords in the patterns I'd learned. "Where? Where are they?"

The men stayed on the porch. In fact, they crowded into a little circle and conversed in low voices. Making plans without me. But I didn't care. I wanted to get to Patrick. My heart keened for him. *Patrick, baby! Tell me where you are!*

You are safe, love?

Yes! What about you?

I've been better. I just wanted to say . . . I love you.

Oh no you are not! You are not talking to me like it's the last time. Where are you?

I don't know. I'm facing a wall and I'm . . . restrained. If I look left, I see crates of 2-liter soda bottles. On my right, there's a stack of empty boxes. And this sounds weird, but I smell nacho cheese.

Nacho cheese? Soda bottles? Empty boxes? Broken Heart had one convenience store/gas station. He was at the Thrifty Sip. In the storage room. Yes! I lifted into the air, swords at my sides, and aimed myself toward the edge of town.

The kids, céadsearc. *I heard them talking about taking the children hostage. You must go to Bryan and Jenny. Protect them.*

They are protected. They have the guardians and a fleet of men with machine guns.

I'd been periodically poking at their minds. At last check-in, Jenny and Bryan, along with the other kids, had awakened. They were eating cereal and watching cartoons. Whatever the Consortium had done to hide the RVs and protect the location of the kids had worked.

They're safe, Patrick. And they are safe because you made sure they would be. You're a wonderful father.

Jessica . . . that is the second best thing you've ever said to me.

What's the first?

That you love me.

Silence descended. Thick, heavy, sudden. Either he had blocked me or someone had blocked him.

"Jessica! Where the hell are you going?" I blinked at the voice so near me and turned my head. Lorćan soared next to me and he looked pissed off.

"Sorry," I said. "Patrick's at the Thrifty Sip."

"You go tell the others," he demanded. "And I'll meet you there."

"No."

"Jessica, this isn't a game. Or a television show. Or a romance novel. You could get hurt. And Patrick—"

"May already be hurt. I'm going to him."

To my amazement, Lor pulled a cell phone out of his pocket and punched a number. "Damian? She says Patrick's at the Thrifty Sip. Yeah. Okay."

"You're stubborn," said Lor as he shut the phone and shoved it into his pocket. "And you better hope you know what you're doing."

Yeah, I knew what I was doing all right. I was going to save the man I loved. At the Thrifty Sip.

Chapter 29

For the second time tonight, I stabbed someone in the gut. Granted, the skinny, foul-breathed fool tried to claw out my eyes, but still, it was icky and nauseating to render him painfully unconscious with the *fulaing* move. Lor didn't need weapons to punch out the other guard.

"They both have the Taint, Jessica," he said, quietly.

I handed him one sword. After we cut off their heads and they blew into dust, we entered the dark and empty Thrifty Sip. Lor returned the sword to me and I held them at the ready.

"Two guards," I said. "That's all they put on this place?"

"Two of their sickest people. Most didn't escape the cave-in. The guardians went to the location and threw flash bombs in every nook and cranny."

"But a few must've escaped."

"Enough to retaliate by bombing the gym."

"And to kidnap Patrick." Panic burbled through me

again, but I quelled the clawing fear. He wasn't dead. I would *know* if Patrick was dead.

I also knew that the Wraiths would return to Broken Heart. If Ron had escaped the destruction of the caves, he would come back with a lot more bad guys. Not only to get the cure for the disease he'd probably put out into the vampire world, but also for revenge. He seemed like the kind of guy who relished punishing people.

While Lor checked out the front, I hurried toward the back. On my right was the tiny hallway that led to the restrooms. At the end of it was the opened door leading to the storage room. In less than a minute, I'd found the entrance to the basement.

A bare bulb hung from the ceiling, its paltry light barely illuminating the space.

"Patrick!" The swords clattered to the concrete and I rushed to him, kneeling on his left side. "Lorćan! He's down here!"

Within a second, Lor was kneeling on the other side of his brother.

Patrick's shirt was missing. And his shoes and socks. All he wore was the pair of black Dockers I'd last seen him in. He looked paler than usual, but other than the big gaping hole in the middle of his chest . . . God oh God. Who was I kidding? I tried not to give way to panic.

"It'll heal," I said, hearing the desperation in my voice. "He's a vampire. An ancient one. He has more power in his little pinky than most vampires have in their whole bodies. This is nothing. It's . . . a . . . a scratch."

"Jessica. They took his heart."

I looked at him, not understanding. Vampires were dead. We didn't need things like hearts and lungs and bladders. So, Patrick wouldn't have a heart. He'd live. That was the important thing. He'd live.

"When a human is Turned, certain organs are no longer needed and they shut down," explained Lor in a quiet voice. "However, we need our hearts. After we feed, we require the heart to pump the blood through us. Once it does, it shuts down."

"But I thought a vampire could only be killed if his head was cut off or he walked into the dawn. I mean . . . a stake to the heart won't kill us, right? He's alive right now."

"Because he's ancient and stubborn." Lor looked at me, and I saw the truth in his gaze.

"You can't expect me to say good-bye to him. He's my soul mate. I love him."

"I'm so sorry, Jessica," said Lor. "But a vampire can't live without a heart." He paused, obviously gauging how to comfort me. "If it's any consolation, you're lucky you are not bound to him. Otherwise—"

"I know. I would be dying, too. Except Lor . . . I am dying." I waved him away. "Go away. Just . . . please. I'll call you in a minute."

Lor turned into mist and slipped away, leaving me alone with Patrick. I leaned down and kissed his forehead. "I understand now. At least . . . I think I do." I took a precious second to steady myself then hollered, "Ruadan, you get your ass here now!"

He appeared instantly, kneeling on the opposite side of his son, where Lor had been moments ago. He looked down at his dying boy, for the second time in four millennia, and smiled sadly.

"You could've mentioned this part," I said.

"Well . . . that's the problem with seeing into the future. Too many variables." He brushed a lock of hair away from Patrick's forehead. "It's easy to sacrifice for a child."

That was the last thing I expected him to say. "What the hell are you talking about?"

"A child earns sacrifice just by being beloved of his parents. For a woman, born of her body. For a man, created by his seed. Is it a difficult choice . . . your life for the lives of your children?"

"No. Of course not. My kids are important. More important than anything. Even me."

"Yeah. I know. And I think it's easier to give up your life for your kids than to risk your heart for the love of a soul mate."

What a stupid thing to say. I looked at Patrick. He was leaving the world before I could right the wrongs between us. I loved him . . . and Ruadan was sitting here asking me how much I loved him. If I loved him more than my children. Damnation. Love wasn't a strong enough word for how I felt about Patrick. "He said something to me once. Something important. And beautiful. *Tá mo . . .*"

"*Tá mo chroí istigh ionat,*" said Ruadan. "My heart is within you."

I nodded. I got it. I finally freaking got it. And it was okay. Patrick had gone beyond the veil to find me, to return me to the earthly plane. He'd given me back my life twice and never asked for one thing in return. How was that for love? For sacrifice? "You'll make sure Jenny and Bryan go to Paris? And if you do get them Porsches, you make sure they go to driving school. Or rocket school. I'm not sure what the classification of a Porsche is."

"What are you saying, Jessica?"

"His heart," I said softly, "is within me." I looked at Ruadan, resolved. "What are you waiting for? Give it to him already!"

"You would give your heart to him so that he would live? What about Jenny and Bryan?"

"I'm their mother. My only wish is for them to be protected, happy, and loved. They have all of those things because of Patrick. And so do I." I waved my hands at him. I was terrified to do this. To make this offer. My mind flew to my kids who seemed content enough in the RV. Jenny played with her Bratz dolls. Bryan had discovered an Xbox and a stash of Pepsis. *I love you,* I sent into their minds. *I love you, my babies.*

I looked at Ruadan. "Well? Go on. Give my heart to your son."

Ruadan grinned. "You already have." He looked down at Patrick. "Is she always so melodramatic?"

"Sometimes," croaked Patrick, his eyes opening. "But she's so cute, I put up with it."

"Patrick!" I leaned down and peppered kisses on his face. "I'm here. Oh honey, I'm here. I love you. Don't forget that, okay? I love you a lot."

"I know, *mo ghrá.*"

"Are you ready, Jessica?"

"Yes." I held Patrick's hand, staring into his gorgeous silver eyes. "I love you," I said again. "I don't

think that can be overstated." Then, taking a deep
breath, I looked at Ruadan and waited.

He put out his hand, palm side up, and aimed it at
my chest. In amazement, I watched gold glittering
swirls form. With his other hand, he pointed at his own
chest. Red magic seeped out, whirling to join the gold.
They bound together, a circle of pulsating light, and
drifted like a big snowflake into Patrick's chest wound.
"I call upon the *deamhan* and the *sidhe*," Ruadan
prayed. "To heal their son, flesh of their flesh, magic
of their magic. So do I will it, so mote it be."

I watched in terrified amazement as the whirling
lights weaved into a heart. A real heart. The pulsating
organ connected to the veins. Then the flesh sealed itself and within seconds, no wound existed at all. I
stared at Patrick then looked at Ruadan, mouth gaping.

"Neat, huh?" he said. "I like the sparkling lights the
best."

"That's *it*?" I asked.

"Yep. Need a hand up, son?" He grasped his son's
shoulder and hauled him to a sitting position.

"Thanks, Dad."

"You kids have fun!" He disappeared. Just *pop* . . .
and he was gone.

Patrick pulled me into his lap and kissed me until I
was a puddle of goo. I wrenched my mouth from his
and stared at him. "I don't understand."

"My father's a show-off, love."

"But the whole heart business . . ."

"The important thing, Jessica, is that you were willing to give your heart for mine. You love me that
much?"

"Duh." I traced his face from temples to jaw. Happiness trilled through me. I loved this man. And he was mine oh mine. Woo-hoo! "Wanna go have hot all-the-way monkey sex?" I waggled my brows.

"So, you want to bind? You're sure?"

"Oh yeah. But I don't just want a hundred years." I cupped his face and looked at him, my beautiful vampire, and said, "I want you forever."

"It just so happens," said Patrick, "I have forever free."

My New Family

by Jennifer Matthews O'Halloran

My name is Jennifer. I am almost ten years old. I am *not* a vampire. Sometimes I wish I was a vampire so that I could bite my dumb big brother Bryan. He is a butthead.

I have a new daddy. His name is Patrick. He says I should always remember my real daddy. And just 'cause he died doesn't mean I have to stop loving him. I like Patrick.

When my new daddy and my mommy got married, Patrick gave her the same ring she always wears. I watched him put the heart on the outside of Mommy's finger. He says that means her heart is occupied. Then Mommy put a chain with this pretty silver coin on it around his neck. Then they kissed and it was all gross. Marybeth said it was "romantic." Yuck.

Anyway, Patrick bought me a tiara. He also bought me a pony. My mommy wasn't happy about the pony, even though we have lots of space in the backyard of our new house.

I have a new grandpa, too. We call him Ru because it's easier to say than his real name. He promised to take us to Paris on Christmas break. He also bought me a tiara.

My uncle Lor spends a lot of time in the library bus. He tells me all the time why it's important to write stuff down. So I am. He also bought me a tiara, and Mommy said, "Enough already." (So I didn't tell her that Drake and Darrius gave me one, too.)

Finally, I have a new baby brother. His name is Richie. He's really cute and sweet. He is not a butthead. Or a vampire. Mommy says he's ours forever because his mother went away.

Well, I guess that's it.

For now.

GLOSSARY

Celtic Irish Words/Terms

A ghrá mo chroí: Love of my heart

A thaisce: My dear/darling/treasure

Bard: Poet-Druid (see *Filí*). Storyteller and singer of Celtic tribes.

Céadsearc: First love/beloved one

Droch fhola: Bad or evil blood

Druid: The philosopher, teacher, and judge of Celtic tribes

Filí: (Old Irish) Poet-Druid (see *Bard*)

Go dtachta an diabhal thú: May the devil choke you (Irish curse)

Leamhán sléibhe: A Wych Elm (the only species of Elm native to Ireland)

Mo chroí: My heart

Ovate: Healer-Druid. Healer and seers of Celtic tribes.

German Words/ Terms

Liebling: Darling

Mein freund: My friend

Other Words/Terms

Ankh: Ancient Egyptian symbol that means "life"

JESSICA'S GLOSSARY

Stuff No One Told Me So I Figured It Out On My Own, Damn You All

Ancient: Refers to one of the original seven vampires. The very first vampire was Ruadan, who is the father of Patrick, my husband. Ruadan is supposed to be this awesome and terrifying creature. But he's really like a kid who thinks the world is a candy store. Some people fear him. Me? I have to keep telling him to stop sliding on the tile in his socks.

Banning: If you piss off an Ancient, they shoot your ass into limbo and you have to stay there (see *World Between Worlds*) until you meet the conditions of the spell. It's not too often that someone gets released from banning because they're usually loser assholes who deserve to spend their lives in limbo.

The Binding: When vampires have consummation sex, they're hitched for a hundred freaking years. This was Ruadan the First's brilliant idea to keep horny vamps from screwing while blood-taking. In other words, if a penis meets a vagina (or other orifice) for a little fun-fun, they better really like each other. No one's ever broken a binding.

The Consortium: About five hundred years ago, Patrick and Lor created the Consortium to figure out ways that paranormal folks could make the world a better place for everyone (this is the opposite goal from other vamps—see *Wraiths*). A lot of the sudden leaps in human medicine and technology are because of the Consortium's work. And so I blame them for PDAs, which I hate and still haven't figured out how to use.

Drone: Mortals who do the bidding of their vampire Masters. The most famous was Igor—drone to Dracula. The Consortium's Code of Ethics forbids the use of drones, but plenty of vampires still use drones.

Family: Every vampire can be traced to one of the seven ancients. The ancients are divided into the Seven Sacred Sects (it still cracks me up to say it out loud), otherwise known as the Families.

Lycan or Lycanthrope: A shape-shifter who turns into a wolf. Lycans have been around a long time (originally from Germany) and are, in fact, the basis for humans' myths about werewolves. They worship the lunar goddess (thus the whole full moon thing), but they can change anytime they want. They're in big-time trouble because they don't have a lot of females and only one out of three children born live past their first year.

Master: The vampire who successfully Turns a human is the new vamp's protector. Basically, a Master is supposed to show the Turn-blood how to survive as a vampire. A Turn-blood has the protection of the Family (see *Family* or *Seven Sacred Sects*) to which their Master belongs.

Seven Sacred Sects: The vampire tree has seven branches. Each branch is called a Family and each Family is directly traced to one of the seven ancients. The older you are, the more mojo you get. A vampire's powers are related to his Family. For instance, only the vampires from the Family Ruadan can fly (because Ruadan is *sidhe* or fae or fairy).

Taint: This is the Black Plague for vampires. We're close to a real cure, but our brilliant scientist Stan is still creating formulas.

Turn-blood: A human who's been recently Turned into a vampire. If you're less than a century old, you're a Turn-blood.

Turning: Vampires can't have babies. They perpetuate their bad selves by Turning humans. Unfortunately, only one in about ten humans actually makes the transition. I haven't seen anyone Turned, but my friend Linda assures me it's gross and not to be attempted. Ever.

World Between Worlds: It's like limbo. According to Ruadan, there's a place between this plane and the next where there is a void. Some people can slip back and forth between this "veil," but it's a sucky place to take a permanent vacation.

Wraiths: Vampires with a crazy idea about world order. They're run by Ron, who's been running around for three thousand years doing all kinds of evil and stuff. I heard he has the Taint. I don't know if he does, but his minions keep getting in our hair. I'm getting really annoyed with them.

AUTHOR'S NOTE

In creating the story about Ruadan in the *Legends of the Seven Ancients*, I researched Celtic myths and Irish lore. In particular, I read up on the Fomhoire and the Tuatha de Danann. I narrowed my focus on Bres and Brigid, who were the parents of Ruadan, and his part in a tale called *The Second Battle of Magh Tuiredh*.

Research is both a boon and a burden. No one tells the stories with the same details. No one agrees on the parentage of anyone. And *no one* spells the names just one way. Irish myths and folklore were oral traditions passed along for centuries. It seems that around the seventh century, a Christian monk finally said, "Wait. I gotta write this down. Do you have some cowhide and a quill pen?"

The stories we know today as Irish mythology are probably not the stories that grandparents told their grandchildren thousands of years ago. When we pass along heritage and history to the next generation, it's only natural that we shine it up, embellish it, and make it worthy—from our own perspective—for passing along.

In other words, my dear and darling readers, I

picked out bits and pieces of Irish lore, chose my favorite spelling of names, and fabricated my own myth. So, yeah. I'm probably wrong about places, times, people, and intent. The reason I write novels instead of nonfiction books is because I can fictionalize historical accounts and rewrite mythology to suit my own purposes.

If one day, hundreds of years from now, an archaeologist dusts off the yellowed, crumbling pages of *I'm the Vampire, That's Why*, and discovers the story of Ruadan from *Legends of the Seven Ancients*, and gets a big, fat commission for discovering an important lost work . . . well, then . . . that would be really freaking cool.

But for now, you and I know the real story.
Don't we?

ABOUT THE AUTHOR

In junior high school, Michele Bardsley desecrated paper daily with angst-filled poetry, angst-filled journals, and angst-filled short stories. Eventually she wandered off to college to get a journalism degree, but she ended up majoring in marriage and motherhood. She promptly failed housework, plant care, and staying calm in the face of big owies.

Born and raised in Oklahoma, Michele now lives in Florida, where she is held hostage by her two children, her husband, and three cats. Occasionally they remember to feed her, but mostly she's forced to nibble on copy paper while eking out her next story. The manacles make it difficult to type, but she manages.

E-mail her at michelebardsley@yahoo.com or visit her Web site at www.MicheleBardsley.com.

Read on for a preview of the next exciting book
by Michele Bardsley

Don't Talk Back to
Your Vampire

Coming in July 2007 from Signet Eclipse

"Mom, this is the dumbest idea *ever*," said my daughter as she watched me pull on the hiking boots.

I would've reprimanded Tamara, who was fifteen going on fifty, if she hadn't been right. This *was* the dumbest idea ever. But once I determined the path to take, it took serious road construction to make me change course.

I stopped messing with my shoes, then put my hands on my hips and struck a pose. "Evangeline Louise LeRoy, librarian to the rescue!" I winked at her. "But you, little lady, can call me Eva."

"Oh my *gawd*." Tamara slapped a hand to her forehead and shut her eyes. "Swear on your undead soul to never do that again."

"Eva the Librarian makes no promises she can't keep." I grinned at her, then bent to lace up the hiking boots.

We sat on the rickety front-porch stairs of our three-story house. The place was in major disrepair, but I couldn't afford to fix it. The smells of dust and mold were still prevalent despite a hefty investment in Glade candles and two Ionic Breeze machines.

I really was the town librarian, a job my paternal grandmother had held until her death a year before. My father died when I was two years old; my mother had lost touch with the LeRoys long ago. Inheriting the job and the mansion/library had been a lucky break for Tamara and me. We needed a fresh start. And believe me, I was ready for a different kind of life.

Admittedly, becoming a vampire wasn't what I'd had in mind.

The light of the full moon shone down on us. It was nearing the end of August, but summer still clutched Oklahoma in a lover's embrace. The air was humid and hot, even now, when the sun had been down for hours. A breeze offered some respite and brought with it the sweet scent of honeysuckle, a flower that bloomed in bunches nearly everywhere in town.

I was dressed in a green T-shirt and khaki shorts, my dishwater blond hair pulled into a ponytail. Tamara, as usual, was dressed in unrelenting black. She eschewed the term "Goth," though she kohled her eyes in black, wore bloodred lipstick, and brought the word "sullen" to a whole new level of meaning. Her hair, which used to be the same color as mine, was cut chin-length and colored raven black except for the two cherry red stripes on either side of her face. She also had both of her eyebrows and her belly button pierced with silver rings—and that was the *compromise*. My darling daughter had wanted her tongue pierced and a coiling snake tattooed on her ankle. I called for the smelling salts any time I thought about it.

"Mom . . . you should tell him."

"No."

"You're being stubborn."

I pressed my lips together. Right again, darn her. Just who was the adult in this relationship?

"If you're not going to tell him, then you should tell Jessica."

"She's got her own problems." My friend Jessica's mother had unexpectedly arrived in town the previous evening and discovered that her daughter had been turned into a vampire. Not only that, Jessica had also gotten remarried—to one of the most gorgeous vampires on the planet, Patrick O'Halloran.

Patrick had an equally gorgeous twin brother, Lorćan O'Halloran, but we avoided him—and he avoided us. After all, he was the rampaging beast who'd attacked eleven of us single parents, draining us of all blood and unintentionally killing us. If the Consortium—a sort of vampire Peace Corps—hadn't rolled into town and brought several vampire Masters willing to Turn us, none of us would be alive. Well, *undead.*

"Did you feed?" Tamara asked.

"Yes, mo-*ther.*" I finished tying the laces, then stood up and stomped my feet on the old wooden porch. *Thud. Thud. Thud.* Sturdy. That was good, considering the terrain I was headed for. "Where's the flashlight?"

"In here," she said, handing me a black backpack. "I would've packed a snack, but y'know . . . *ew.*"

Yeah. *Ew* was right. I hadn't quite gotten used to my

new diet, either. It had been three months since Lorćan yanked me out of my car and noshed on my neck. I'd just been returning from an ice cream run.

I never did get to eat that pint of Ben & Jerry's Chunky Monkey.

If you've ever read those romance novels where the soul-tortured vampire hero reluctantly brings his mortal woman to the Other Side—well, my experience was the exact opposite of that. There wasn't anything sexy about big, furry paws grabbing my hips and or sharp, yucky teeth digging into my neck. The scariest thing about what happened was that I couldn't see my attacker. I just *felt* him—he'd been huge, hairy, snarling. When he was finished, he'd tossed me into the driveway and loped away.

Than I died.

When I woke up, I was latched to the neck of a vampire named Mortimer. (Yeah, I know . . . someone named *Mortie* saved my life.) He was cute, too, but he was also married, and soon after Turning me, he returned to London.

Lorćan had been suffering from the Taint, a terrible disease that only affected vampires. Everyone, including the Consortium, was scrambling for a cure. They'd managed to rid Lorćan of it, but whatever they'd done seemed to work only for him.

After we got all the vampire stuff straightened out, the Consortium revealed that it had been buying out residences and businesses in Broken Heart. They wanted to build the first-ever paranormal community in the States. I guess there were a few already established in Europe. Over the summer, nearly all the human residents had moved out. The town was practically empty, its buildings under constant demolition and construction.

"The cell phone is in there, too, and it's turned on," said Tamara sternly. "Call me and check in, okay? Sunrise is in two hours. *Two.*"

"I know how to tell time."

"I wasn't sure," she said drolly, "since you don't have a watch."

"I have acute vampire senses, thank you very much." I slung the backpack over my shoulder and saluted my worried progeny. "I'll report in later, sir. Carry on!"

Tamara gave me a quick hug, which was thoroughly unlike her. Showing affection to the parental unit was strictly verboten. Since she was in a mood to accept a hug, I risked kissing her forehead. She said nothing, but grimaced in a manner that suggested acid had been applied to her skin.

Chuckling, I jogged down the steps to the cracked sidewalk that meandered through the huge, weed-filled front yard. I waved to her, she waved back, and then *vroom* . . . I was outta there.

Before I was—as my daughter put it—"vampified," I used to run to keep in shape. As a vampire, I didn't need exercise. In fact, getting killed had rid me of cellulite, acne scars, and crow's-feet—the ultimate makeover. But I still liked to run, and using my new powers to put on the speed always gave me a thrill.

Within minutes, I reached the area Tamara and I had named Ooky Spooky Woods. Broken Heart was surrounded by pockets of thick, tangled brush and densely packed trees. This particular forest hid a secret. It wasn't mine per se, but I had agreed to keep it. For now.

You'd think a vampire with the ability to run fast, jump high, and hit hard wouldn't be afraid of walking into a little ol' forest at three A.M. Still, my nonbeating heart gave a little squeeze as I entered the woods. Leaves crunched and twigs snapped under my boots. I was tempted to get out the flashlight, but truthfully I could see perfectly well. It didn't take me long to reach the meet spot—a rotted, fallen tree trunk stuck between an oak tree and a weeping willow.

"Nefertiti?" I whispered. "Here kitty, kitty, kitty . . ."

A gold-furred cat wearing an ankh around its neck leapt onto the trunk and sauntered toward me. She stopped about a half foot away and shimmered gold. Within three blinks of an eye, the cat turned into a caramel-skinned woman with obsidian eyes and long black hair. She was beautiful. And naked.

"If you can keep the necklace on during the change," I said, digging in the backpack for a nightgown, "why can't you figure out how to wear clothes?"

"I told you, the spell for my transformation relies on the ankh. I must wear it at all times," said Nefertiti, her voice edged with a light, exotic accent. "Besides, Johnny would wonder why his pet cat needed to wear a dress." She slipped on the nightgown, then stared at me expectantly.

I rolled my eyes, then sat on the log and offered my wrist. She held my hand between delicate fingers, then sank her fangs into the pulse point. It stung a little, but vampire teeth released an anesthetic and soon all I felt was the pressure of her sucking mouth.

The night before, I found Nefertiti sneaking into my house. She had been "checking out" books and returning them on the sly. No one knew that the cat everyone called Lucifer was really a vampire named Nefertiti. Not even Johnny Angelo, her so-called owner, knew. Yeah, he was a vampire, too. Nearly everyone around these parts was a bloodsucker.

Three months of sneaking around town, trying to avoid detection, had broken the poor woman. She'd been living off animal blood, not exactly a prime meal for a vamp, and occasionally sneaking blood from sleeping donors. Donors were humans the Consortium paid to hang out and be our nightly snacks. Think of them as a really, really skewed version of fast food.

"You should tell him," I said, echoing my daughter's words. "It's been fifty years."

She released my wrist. The wounds sealed almost immediately (helped along by vampire saliva), and she delicately wiped away the spots of blood. "After another fifty, he will be free, as he deserves."

I sighed. After she'd scared the crap out of me—and I put down the hardcover of *War and Peace* I'd been about to bash her with—she'd laid out the whole story for me and begged for my help.

You see, half a century before, Nefertiti had seduced the 1950s movie star Johnny Angelo. Because she'd fed on him and had sex with him, she'd bound them together for the next hundred years. Then she Turned him, kind of without him realizing it.

Having sexual relations is a serious business for us

vampires. If we feed *and* do the mattress mambo, we are linked to the person of our affection for the next century. Needless to say, most of us were real discriminating about our love lives.

"I need to return to my owner," she said softly. Her sad gaze met mine. "He says that he does not like Lucifer, but if I am not there when it is time to rest, he worries about me."

"Nefertiti, he's not your owner. He's your husband."

"Not by choice." She took off the gown and handed it to me. Oh, man. I looked at the ground, not really wanting to get another eyeful of ancient Egyptian nudity. She said she'd been Turned during the reign of Cleopatra, the last pharaoh to ever rule Egypt. "Thank you, Evangeline."

Still looking at the ground—wow, wasn't that an interesting stick right there?—I said, "What're we going to do? You can't feed from me exclusively. Or hide from the Consortium forever. We need to tell somebody, even if it's not Johnny."

She didn't respond, so I dared a peek. The woman was gone, but the cat trotted out into the darkness, her golden tail waving like a flag as she disappeared under some shrubs. Oh, well, *fine*.

Grabbing the backpack, I held it in one hand as I leisurely strolled in the opposite direction. I had plenty of time before sunrise. I sighed. Poor Nefertiti. I really didn't know the solution for her mondo problem. Did she realize she was in love with Johnny? Then again, what did I know about love?

Diddly-do-dah, that's what. I had been a starry-eyed seventeen-year-old the summer Michael Hudsen noticed me. Typical story of a crush gone awry, so key up the violins and hand out the Kleenex. Title it: *Shy Geek Meets Handsome Jock.* Michael had just graduated from our high school and broken up with his cheerleader girlfriend. I couldn't believe he remembered my name, much less that I liked the color blue. (I don't like it anymore. Green is my favorite color. Blue sucks.)

Michael spent two months seducing me with words, flowers, and romantic gestures. The week before he left for an out-of-state college, I gave him my virginity.

He gave me Tamara.

Branches crackled and leaves fluttered around me. What the heck? I looked up, fear tingling up my spine. Even with vamp vision, I couldn't see anything—or anyone—above me. Only the full moon peeked through the canopy of trees, looking like the round eye of God.

"Big squirrels," I muttered. "Or raccoons. Mutant ones."

The brush was too dense and the ground too pockmarked with holes for me to use vamp power to run. I hurried up, suddenly nervous. The backpack slapped my thigh as I quickened my pace, dodging low limbs and jumping over forest debris.

Then I heard it. Something loped behind me, growling softly. *Don't panic.* Could be anything: wild dog, coyote, mutant raccoon. I dared a peek over my shoulder.

And screamed.

The creature was huge and fast, coming at me like a lion after an antelope. Good God! It smelled like it had taken a bath in the sewer. Oh, no. No! *What if it's Lorćan?* Supposedly the slobbering, murdering beast he'd become was a temporary side effect of the wacko cure. What if the Consortium had been lying about Lorćan? Maybe he could still turn into the thing that had killed me.

Terror skittered through me, ravaging my ability to think. *Run, Eva, you idiot!* I dropped the backpack, running faster, but not yet using my vampire speed. I had to wait until I cleared the forest—otherwise I might trip and fall. Then I'd be monster chow for sure.

It howled, an unearthly cry that vibrated my bones. I swear to heaven, I felt its fetid breath on my neck, its claws scraping at my back. I looked over my shoulder again. The thing had gotten closer, but not near enough to grab me. I could see its eyes glittering with malice and hunger.

My death was in that gaze.

My foot connected with a fallen branch. Damn it! I couldn't stop the tumble. I went down hard, skidding face first into a knotty bush. By the time I'd extracted myself and gotten to my feet, it was too late.

The monster of Ooky Spooky Woods had caught up to me.

And he'd brought friends.

Four sexy stories of a very unusual dating service,
where the Gods fulfill every mortal desire.

CUPID, INC.

An Erotic Romance Novel

by Michele Bardsley

0-451-21757-8

It's not easy to fall in love—especially in Sin City. Nobody
knows this better than Greek deities Psyche and Eros, who
keep a watchful eye on the mortals in Las Vegas. With a little
divine intervention from Aphrodite and the rest of the gods
and goddesses, Psyche and Eros set out to fulfill the sexual
fantasies of their clients, hoping to turn lust into love.

**Available wherever books are sold or
at penguin.com**

All your favorite romance writers are
coming together.

SIGNET ECLIPSE